The story so far . . .

Fourteen oy by day, a d n date Half-Pint Houdini.

Two years ago Max's father, Alexander – also an escapologist – disappeared mysteriously in the Central American country of Santo Domingo. Although Alexander's body was never found, Max's mother, Helen, was convicted of his murder and sentenced to twenty years in prison.

Convinced that his father was still alive, Max and his guardian, Consuela, travelled to Santo Domingo to try to track Alexander down. But while they were there, they were captured and taken to a fortress on the sinister Shadow Island, where billionaire tycoon Julius Clark was conducting horrific scientific experiments on prisoners, using a drug called Episuderon.

Max found the names of other prisoners who'd been held captive on the island, including his father, who had apparently managed to escape and then vanished. Using his escapology skills, and helped by another prisoner, Chris Moncrieffe, Max and Consuela got away from Shadow Island and destroyed the fortress. They then found a letter from Max's father proving conclusively that he was still alive and referring to a mysterious organization named the Cedar Alliance. But what was this Alliance and what was its connection to Alexander Cassidy?

Max has now returned to Britain, where he is determined to continue the search for his dad and prove that his mum is innocent. But his enemies are right behind him – and they will stop at nothing to make sure he does not succeed.

MAX CASSIDY's mission does not end here,
read the whole trilogy

Escape from Shadow Island

Jaws of Death

And coming soon:

Attack at Dead Man's Bay

jaws
of death

PAUL ADAM

CORGI BOOKS

JAWS OF DEATH
A CORGI BOOK 978 0 552 560337

First published in Great Britain by Corgi,
an imprint of Random House Children's Publishers UK
A Random House Group Company

This edition published 2011

3 5 7 9 10 8 6 4 2

Set in Lomba

Corgi Books are published by Random House Children's Publishers UK,
61–63 Uxbridge Road, London W5 5SA

www.**randomhousechildrens**.co.uk
www.randomhouse.co.uk

Addresses for companies within The Random House Group Limited can be found at:
www.randomhouse.co.uk/offices.htm

THE RANDOM HOUSE GROUP Limited Reg. No. 954009

A CIP catalogue record for this book is available from the British Library.

The Random House Group Limited supports The Forest Stewardship
Council (FSC®), the leading international forest certification organisation.
Our books carrying the FSC label are printed on FSC® certified paper.
FSC is the only forest certification scheme endorsed by the leading
environmental organisations, including Greenpeace. Our
paper procurement policy can be found at
www.randomhouse.co.uk/environment

Printed and bound in Great Britain by Clays Ltd, St Ives PLC

For R and J

Escapologists like Max undergo years of training before they can try the dangerous stunts like the ones in this book. Random House Children's Books would like to make it clear that we do not recommend you try any of these stunts yourself.

ONE

Max Cassidy was back in his element, doing what he enjoyed most. He was up on stage, a spotlight illuminating his face, a crowd of spectators watching intently to see what astonishing trick he was going to perform.

Only this time there was one important difference. He wasn't in a theatre, as he usually was for his shows: he was outside in London's Hyde Park, standing on a stage that had been erected on the north bank of the Serpentine, the long, snake-like lake that curves across the centre of the park. The audience was in the open air too, sitting on camping chairs or picnic rugs, or sprawled on the grass immediately in front of the stage, the adults drinking wine and beer, the kids eating hot dogs or licking ice creams bought from the bustling food stalls.

It was almost dark – a clear, warm night, the sky speckled with stars. Behind the stage, the waters of the Serpentine were smooth and black, lights glimmering across the surface in silvery streaks.

Max gazed out at the audience, trying to estimate

how big it was. One or two thousand, certainly – maybe more. He felt a flutter of butterflies in his stomach. He'd never performed in front of so many people before.

The presenter – a Capital Radio DJ named Jonny Sinclair – was at the microphone, reminding everyone that this was a charity show to raise money for children with leukaemia and that all the artists taking part were giving their services for free. There'd already been a girl band on stage, then two dance groups, a stand-up comedian and a twelve-year-old singer who'd shot to fame on a television talent show. Now it was Max's turn. He was the last act, the finale of the whole evening's entertainment.

'He's well known to audiences at the London Cabaret Club,' Jonny Sinclair was saying. 'If you haven't seen him before, believe me, you're in for a treat. Ladies and gentlemen, please welcome fourteen-year-old escapologist Max Cassidy, the Half-Pint Houdini.'

A huge cheer went up across the park as Max stepped over to the microphone. His mouth was dry, his heart pounding. He licked his lips, trying to steady his nerves.

'Thank you, Jonny,' he said, and was surprised at how self-assured he sounded over the loudspeakers. 'It's great to be here, and to be able to help such a worthwhile cause.'

He could see the eager faces stretching away into the darkness: couples, families, parents with children, teenagers – many of them about his age. Every pair of eyes was fixed on him, a tall, muscular, fair-haired boy who was already establishing a reputation as one of Britain's most exciting performers. *Show us, Max*, they seemed to be urging him fervently. *Show us what you can do. And whatever it is, make it spectacular.*

And spectacular it was going to be.

'As always,' Max went on, 'I can't do this alone. I need the help of my brilliant Spanish assistant, Consuela.'

He waved his arm, and from the wings of the stage came a slim, dark young woman wearing tight gold trousers and a crimson top, her thick black hair curling over her shoulders. She was pushing a low, wheeled metal platform bearing a wooden trunk big enough to hold a man – or, in Max's case, a boy. Another cheer went up from the crowd, punctuated by appreciative wolf whistles from some of the more raucous young men. Consuela smiled warmly, unfazed by all the attention, and came to a halt beside Max.

'A few months ago,' Max said into the microphone, 'the Metropolitan Police asked me if I would check out some new handcuffs for them, to see whether they're completely escape-proof. Well, tonight I'm going to put those handcuffs to the test.' He looked towards the side of the stage. 'Would my special guest come out now, please?'

From the shadows in the curtained-off wings, a tall, heavily built man emerged. He was in his fifties, with a balding head and grizzled toothbrush moustache. The crowd applauded politely. No one wolf-whistled this time.

Max shook hands with the man, then said, 'Will you tell the audience who you are, please?'

'I am Detective Chief Superintendent John Richardson, of Scotland Yard,' the man said. 'I have been a police officer for thirty-five years, the last ten as head of the Criminal Investigation Department of the Metropolitan Police.'

'So you've seen a few villains in your time?' Max said.

'More than a few.'

'Have you something to show us?'

Chief Superintendent Richardson reached into the pocket of his tweed jacket and pulled out a gleaming pair of metal handcuffs.

'Would you tell the audience what you're holding?' Max said.

'This is a pair of Conqueror handcuffs, made of titanium steel by Hamshaw and Verney of Sheffield, who claim that they are the toughest, strongest hand-cuffs ever manufactured. They say that no one could possibly escape from them' – Richardson's mouth twitched slyly beneath his moustache – 'even you.'

Max smiled with quiet confidence. 'We'll see about that.' He held out his hands. 'Chief Superintendent, would you put the handcuffs on me, please?'

The detective clipped the cuffs around Max's wrists and made sure they were securely fastened.

'And the key?'

Richardson held up the key to the handcuffs, then slipped it away into his pocket.

Consuela came forward, lifted up the lid of the wooden trunk and removed a heavy canvas sack.

'Chief Superintendent,' Max said, 'would you take a good look at the trunk? Check that the sides are solid, that there's nothing hidden inside it.'

The detective examined the trunk, peering closely at the wood, hammering the sides and bottom with his fists, inspecting the hinges and the lock. 'It seems a good strong wooden box,' he said. 'Nothing funny about it.'

'And will you check this sack too, please? Make sure there are no holes in it, no secret escape slits, no loose stitching.'

Richardson gave the sack a thorough examination. 'It all seems to be in order,' he said.

'Thank you, Chief Superintendent.'

Consuela placed the sack in the bottom of the wooden trunk and spread open the mouth for Max to climb inside.

'There is a leather drawstring around the top of the sack and a padlock,' Max said to the detective. 'When I duck down, I'd like you to pull the drawstring tight above me and secure it with the padlock.'

Max crouched down inside the sack so he was hidden from sight. Chief Superintendent Richardson tightened the drawstring and fastened it with the padlock, then Consuela pushed the loose folds of the sack down into the trunk, closed the lid and locked it.

Two more assistants came out from the wings. They picked up the trunk between them, carried it down the steps at the side of the stage and walked twenty metres along the Serpentine to an open space where the audience had an uninterrupted view of the water. Everyone watched in fascinated silence, intrigued by what was going to happen next.

At the edge of the lake was moored a floating wooden platform, about two metres square. In the centre stood a large black cabinet, about the size of a bedroom wardrobe. The assistants placed the trunk inside the cabinet and closed the doors. Then they retreated and Consuela took over the next part of the act.

She was standing by a console, hidden in the wings of the stage, with the side curtain pulled open a little so that she could see the floating platform. She checked her wristwatch, which had a special dial calibrated in tenths of a second, like an athlete's stopwatch. Timing was crucial here. She had to get it just right. Wait too long and the stunt would have less of an impact; go too soon and she might put Max in jeopardy. She let the second hand tick round to twelve, then pressed a green button on the control panel in front of her.

Down on the lake, the floating platform began to glide slowly out onto the water, drawn across by an electric motor and a simple arrangement of pulleys and steel wires that had been strung from one side of the Serpentine to the other.

Inside the trunk, Max felt the platform start to move and knew that the clock was ticking; knew that he had twenty-five seconds to free himself before the climax of the act. He was already out of the sack. That bit had been easy: he'd just taken the razor blade that was secreted in the sole of his trainer and sliced through the canvas. Now he was working on the handcuffs, and that was much trickier.

The Conqueror manacles were good, probably the best he'd ever encountered. He very much doubted that any ordinary person, criminal or otherwise, would be able to escape from them. But Max wasn't an ordinary person and he also had the advantage of having seen a pair of the handcuffs before. Unbeknown to Chief Superintendent Richardson, Max had obtained his own set direct from the manufacturers several weeks earlier, taken them apart to study how the locks worked, then practised incessantly until he could pick them blindfold in under fifteen seconds. This charity show had been organized months ago and he left nothing to chance. Every stage of his stunts was always meticulously planned and executed. It had to be. Escapology was an inherently dangerous business. It was rarely possible to eliminate the risks altogether, but Max always did his utmost to minimize them. Some stunts were relatively safe, but not the one he was performing tonight. If this went wrong, he knew he would be lucky to escape with his life.

How many seconds had passed since the platform had moved away from the shore? Five? Six? Max was still tackling the lock on the left-hand cuff, using a couple of tiny picks he'd concealed in a special slot in the end of his jacket sleeve – where he could always be sure of reaching them. Some manacles only required one pick to crack them, but the Conquerors were so complex they needed two – one to hold open the keyhole, the other to manipulate the tumblers inside.

Max twisted the angled point of the pick deeper into the lock. It was pitch black in the trunk, but that wasn't a problem. He was used to working blind. The mechanisms of most locks weren't visible – they were hidden away behind a metal plate – and Max always went by touch and instinct, feeling his way through the process.

How many seconds had elapsed now? Ten, probably more. This was taking longer than it should have done, certainly longer than it had in his practice sessions. Stage nerves – that had to be part of the explanation. Performing outdoors for the first time and in front of such a big audience. His hands were less steady than usual; he was trying to go too fast. But that wasn't the only reason. It was the cuffs themselves. They were slightly different from the ones on which he'd practised. The lock was stiffer, the tumblers sticky, as if the cuffs had been stored in a damp environment – something that he couldn't possibly have foreseen. He could crack them, he was sure of that. It was just taking a few seconds too long. *Take it easy*, he told himself. *You've plenty of time*. Yet he knew he *didn't* have plenty of time. He had only another fifteen seconds before— He tried not to think about what was going to happen in fifteen seconds' time.

Up on the stage, Consuela was looking continually

from her watch to the cabinet on the floating platform, which was now ten metres out from the shore. One of the show technicians had a powerful spotlight trained on it, following its progress across the water, illuminating the cabinet so the crowd could see it clearly. Consuela gauged the distance to the middle of the lake – just another few seconds. She glanced at her watch again. Max would be out of the cuffs by now, waiting to make his next move. Wouldn't he? Consuela felt a sudden flicker of doubt. She had moments like that – strange intuitive moments when she could sense that something was wrong; when Max was in trouble. Her stomach tightened. *Are you there, Max?* she asked silently inside her head. *Talk to me. Just let me know you're all right.*

Click! The last of the tiny tumblers inside the lock snapped back and the cuff came loose. Max tore it off his left wrist and turned his attention to the right-hand cuff. This one would be easier, quicker to tackle now he had one hand free. He eased the first pick into the key-hole, then slid the second one in underneath, probing into the heart of the mechanism. He wasn't sure how much time he had left. Eight, nine seconds, he thought. That should be enough, provided he was slick and stayed calm. Then he heard the electric motor cut out, felt the float come to a stop. A sudden shiver of fear pulsed through him. He'd run out of time.

Consuela looked out across the lake at the cabinet, lit up in the beam of the spotlight. An eerie silence had descended over the crowd. They were waiting, watching, their gazes locked on the cabinet.

Max knew he had to change his plan. And quickly. The second cuff could wait. Right now, he had to get out of the trunk. Get out fast. He thrust the lock picks into his pocket and groped along the side of the trunk, feeling for the concealed catch that opened the sliding panel in the base.

Consuela couldn't take her eyes off the cabinet. Her pulse was hammering furiously, nausea rising in her throat. What was going on out of sight in the trunk? Was Max OK? The spectators were still waiting patiently, but they wouldn't wait for ever. She couldn't delay any longer. She just had to have faith in Max, trust him to get it right. Taking a deep breath, she pressed a red button on the console.

Out on the platform, the shallow, petrol-filled metal troughs that surrounded the cabinet suddenly ignited, sending a wall of fire shooting up into the air. A gasp of surprise reverberated around the crowd, the people recoiling at the explosion. Max was inside the cabinet, in a trunk, handcuffed, locked in a thick sack. He had a reputation for pulling off the impossible, but surely this time he had overstretched himself. No one, not even the Half-Pint Houdini, could possibly survive the inferno that was raging in the middle of the lake.

The cabinet was a roaring ball of fire, almost invisible behind the searing red and yellow flames that hissed and crackled and leaped upwards in smoking tongues, the heat and light reflecting off the surface of the lake so fiercely that some of the audience had to turn their heads away. Other spectators had their eyes tightly shut, a few with their hands over their faces – not just because of the glare, but because they simply couldn't bear to watch.

Max heard the petrol erupt around him, felt the force of the explosion through the thin sides of the trunk. It was as if he'd been punched in the head. For an instant he was stunned by the shock, unable to move; then he recovered his senses and forced himself into action. The base panel had already slid back, leaving an opening big enough for him to get through. He could feel the rough boards of the platform beneath his hands. In the centre was a small trapdoor on a spring. Max pushed down on it and felt it give way a little. The flames were licking around him now. The trunk was on fire. The acrid stench of petrol stung his nostrils; smoke poured in, scorching his lungs. He felt a sharp pain in his feet and realized his trainers were alight. He took one last breath and hurled himself at the trapdoor, plunging down through the platform and out into the cool embrace of the lake.

Never had it felt so good to be in water. Max kicked out hard, propelling himself diagonally away from the blazing platform, the handcuffs dangling from his right wrist. It was only forty metres to the shore, a distance that he could normally swim underwater with ease. But he hadn't had time to take in much air inside the trunk and knew that he would struggle to get that far. His chest was already tight, his body running out of oxygen. He pulled back with his arms, taking it one stroke at a time, trying to ignore the pain. He couldn't afford to surface, even for a second. The crowd would surely see him and the stunt would be ruined.

Just a few more metres . . . He could do it. He *had* to. He saw bright lights shining down through the lake ahead of him that could only be coming from the stage. That gave him a target to aim for. He stared at the lights through the cloudy water, watching them get closer with every stroke. *Five metres . . . four . . . three . . .* He gave one final almighty kick and his outstretched arms touched the concrete wall. His head broke the surface and he sucked in the air gratefully, taking care to make as little noise as possible.

He was immediately behind the stage, out of sight of

the audience. He hauled himself out of the water and crouched down to remove the handcuff from his wrist.

Out on the Serpentine, the fire was beginning to die down. A thick cloud of smoke was still billowing up into the air, but the flames had largely subsided. The cabinet had gone completely, and the trunk was nothing but a smouldering heap of ash and charcoal.

There were murmurs of concern in the crowd, whimpers of distress from some of the younger children. What had happened to Max? Was he lying there dead in the embers, or had he escaped from the trunk before it went up in smoke? If so, how? How had he done it?

Max heard a noise above him and looked up. Consuela was peering out behind the curtain at the back of the wings, her eyes scouring the lake. Then she saw Max down below and her face lit up with joy and relief. She reached down with a hand and helped him up onto the platform.

'Thank God, Max,' she whispered. 'I thought . . . I thought . . .'

'Relax,' Max said coolly. 'It all went according to plan.'

He hoped that she wouldn't notice that his clothes were slightly singed, the soles of his trainers half melted. She'd find out later, of course, but he didn't want to worry her right now.

'You ready?' he asked.

Consuela nodded and combed his wet hair with her fingers. He let her do it with good-humoured resignation. He was dripping with water, his clothes were charred around the edges, but at least his hair was neat and tidy now.

'Get in position,' Consuela said. 'I'll tell the technicians.'

Max slipped behind the curtains at the back of the stage. The lights went out suddenly. A buzz of anticipation swept through the audience. Then a spotlight zeroed in on the backdrop. The curtains parted and Max stepped out, holding up the handcuffs for all to see.

For a moment there was a stunned silence, then a deafening roar as two thousand spectators let out cries of astonishment, then cheers of delight.

Max gestured to Consuela and she joined him on stage, bowing with him as an ear-splitting burst of applause boomed out across Hyde Park like a thunderclap. Then, as one, everyone got to their feet and gave them a standing ovation. Five times Max and Consuela left the stage, and five times they were called back by wild cheering and more applause until, finally, they were allowed to slip away.

Chief Superintendent Richardson was waiting for them by the mobile dressing rooms next to the stage. He shook Max's hand vigorously. 'That was incredible, Max. One hell of a stunt. Congratulations.'

'Thank you,' Max replied. He held out the handcuffs. 'I believe these are yours.'

'So what's your verdict on them? Should we buy them for the Met, issue them to our officers?'

'I'd say yes. They're good.'

'Even though you managed to get out of them?'

'No handcuffs are one hundred per cent escape-proof. I used a few tricks that most criminals won't know.'

'Tricks? What kind of tricks?'

Max grinned at him. 'Now, that would be telling.'

TWO

In the car driving home, Max closed his eyes and slumped back in his seat. As usual after a show, he was both exhilarated and exhausted. That had been a close thing. He could still smell the petrol fumes, taste the smoke in his mouth, feel the burning sensation in his feet. A few more seconds and he wouldn't have been going home in Consuela's Nissan, he'd have been in an ambulance or, worse, a body bag.

But he didn't want to think about that – it unsettled him too much. He let his body relax, taking long, deep breaths, allowing his mind to slip into a trance so that he was no longer aware of the world around him – a meditation technique that his father had taught him years earlier. It was as if he were floating deep in the ocean, complete darkness, complete silence enveloping him.

He stayed like that for a few minutes, but found he couldn't maintain the trance any longer; he had too much on his mind. Opening his eyes, he gazed out through the windscreen at the cluttered city landscape

– the buildings passing by, the streetlamps and neon signs, the red glow of the tail-lights on the vehicles in front. During the stunt in Hyde Park – his first public performance since he got back from Central America – he'd been concentrating so hard that he'd managed to shut out all distractions, clear his mind of everything except the immediate needs of the act. But now he was off stage, those other parts of his life came flooding back in.

Since his return to England, he had thought about little except his traumatic experiences in Santo Domingo. About his search for his missing father, his search for proof that his mother hadn't murdered him, his escape from Shadow Island with Consuela and Chris Moncrieffe. All these things had obsessed him during his every waking hour and even while he was asleep, when nightmares about Shadow Island would torment him until he jolted awake, trembling and clammy with sweat.

But what worried him most wasn't the events of the past, but what was to come in the future. He had made an enemy of the ruthless tycoon Julius Clark, and Clark wasn't the kind of man to let his foes escape. Max knew that he would come after him, and come after him soon. The thought was terrifying. What would Clark do? When would he strike? And what, if anything, could Max do to protect himself?

Consuela turned off into their street, coming to a stop outside their house. She reversed the car into the drive in front of the garage and they got out. Max unlocked the front door. As he stepped inside the house, he felt a tingle on the back of his neck, some sixth sense telling him that something was wrong.

Consuela saw him hesitate, saw the frown on his face. 'What's the matter?' she asked.

'I don't know,' Max replied softly.

He moved cautiously across the hall, listening hard, his eyes alert, flicking from side to side. The house felt different – he couldn't work out why.

Then he went into the kitchen and saw the piece of paper on the table, the words written on it in bold capital letters:

I'M IN THE BASEMENT
ACT NORMALLY
DON'T MENTION MY NAME
THE HOUSE IS BUGGED
CHRIS

Max stared at the message, feeling his stomach lurch. Consuela came up beside him and read the note too. She let out a low, barely audible gasp of surprise and looked at Max. He pointed to the instruction 'Act normally', and Consuela nodded.

'I need a coffee,' she said, heading for the kitchen sink. 'You want anything? A biscuit? Toast?'

'Toast would be good, thanks,' Max said, trying to keep his voice as natural as possible.

He went to the basement door, turned on the light and padded quietly down the stairs. Chris Moncrieffe, wearing jeans and a black leather jacket, was sitting on the floor, his back propped against the wall. His deep blue eyes were tired and there was a thick growth of stubble on his rugged face. He smiled warmly at Max, then put his finger to his lips and stood up.

Consuela? he mouthed silently.

Max pointed to the ceiling.

Get her.

Max crept back upstairs. Consuela was spooning coffee into a silver espresso pot, two pieces of bread sliced on the wooden board beside her, ready to be popped into the toaster. Max performed an exaggerated mime, gesturing towards the basement door. Consuela nodded to show she'd understood, then turned on the radio on the worktop, the channel tuned to Max's favourite pop music station. Max watched her admiringly. She caught on quickly. That was a clever move, providing background noise to cover their absence from the kitchen.

Chris had the door to the garden open when they went downstairs. He beckoned them out, then headed across the lawn. Max and Consuela followed him, stopping when they all reached the small patio near the rear boundary wall. A trellis covered with wisteria and climbing roses shielded them from the house, turning the patio into a private little enclave where they could talk without being observed.

'We're safe here,' Chris said, keeping his voice low.

'What do you mean, "safe"?' Consuela asked. 'What's going on?'

Chris pulled out one of the plastic chairs from under the garden table and sat down. Max and Consuela took the other chairs. It was late. The darkness closed in around them. An earthy dampness drifted up from the flowerbeds.

'What's this about the house being bugged?' Max said. 'How do you know?'

'Because I looked,' Chris replied. 'There's a tiny eavesdropping device in one of the sockets on the kitchen wall, and another in a socket in the sitting room. They're no bigger than a thumbnail, but powerful enough to pick up every sound in the house.'

Max gaped at him in alarm. 'Someone's listening in to us?'

Chris nodded. 'They'll be tapping your phone too, monitoring your computer, your emails. There's a car parked up your street, sixty, seventy metres from your front door. A dark blue Toyota Avensis. There are two men inside it, watching your house.'

Consuela leaned urgently over the table, her eyes wide with shock. 'Julius Clark's men?'

'That would be my guess,' Chris said. 'His kind of money can buy a lot of manpower, a lot of expertise.'

There was a silence while Max and Consuela took in what Chris had told them. Max's stomach was knotted with anxiety. He had no doubt that Chris was right. They were being watched; their phone calls, their Internet searches, their conversations were being monitored. Their entire lives were under surveillance, and that was horrifying.

'What can we do about it?' Max asked.

'I know some people, guys I used to work with,' Chris replied. 'I'll go and see them tomorrow, borrow the equipment to do a proper sweep of the house. I found two bugs just by guesswork, but there'll be more. They'll be all over the place.'

Consuela looked at him shrewdly. 'There's something you're not telling us, isn't there?' she said, her voice unsteady. 'What made you check for bugs in the first place? What made you suspicious?'

Chris hesitated, as if thinking over his response.

'You *have* to tell us,' Max said quickly. 'Has something happened?'

'When I flew in this evening, they were waiting for me at Heathrow. I was followed all the way into central London by a young guy in a suit. I lost him at King's Cross. Got off the tube, then doubled back again to Leicester Square.'

'You're sure he was tailing you?' Consuela said.

'I was in the security business long enough to spot a tail.'

'They knew the flight you were on? How?'

'They must have had access to the airline passenger lists. They were watching out for my name.'

'The passenger lists? How could they get hold of those?' Max said.

'Because they have friends in the right places,' Chris replied.

He glanced away towards the house. Light from the kitchen window was radiating out across the garden, glowing on the lawn with a golden lustre, then seeping through the trellis, casting fragmented shadows over their faces. Max could see Chris's mouth pulled tight, his expression calm but serious.

'The tail put me on my guard,' Chris continued. 'Made me wonder what else was going on. So I checked out the area around the house as soon as I got here, spotted the guys in the car immediately.'

'Did they see you come into the house?' Consuela asked.

Chris shook his head. 'I was careful. I came over the garden wall from the next street, picked up the key you left me and found a toolbox in the garage. These people are professionals. I knew that if they were watching the house, they'd also plant bugs inside if they could, to keep tabs on you. So I checked a few obvious places, and there they were.'

He smiled wryly, looking from Max to Consuela, then back to Max. 'But we haven't said hello yet. It's good to see you both again. How are you?'

'We're OK,' Max replied. 'It's good to see you too. How was your journey?'

They'd split up after their escape from Shadow Island, agreeing to travel back to the UK separately. It seemed safer that way.

'Pretty easy – until I got to Heathrow,' Chris said. 'So what's the situation? You found out much since you got back?'

'Let me get my file,' Max said.

He went back into the house and returned with a

thin cardboard folder he'd taken from one of the kitchen drawers. Now that Chris was back with them, Max felt an immense sense of relief. Without the soldier turned environmental activist, Max and Consuela would never have got away from Shadow Island. It was reassuring to have him by their side again. He knew all about fighting dangerous enemies. And Max had no illusions. They had very dangerous enemies – some out in the open like Julius Clark, others hidden and waiting to strike.

Max opened the folder and pulled out a sheet of paper. 'I did some research on the Net,' he said. 'Looked into the drug they were using on Shadow Island – Episuderon. The drug they gave my dad when he was a prisoner there. It was developed here in Britain after the Second World War. At a place called Porton Down. Have you heard of it?'

'It's the government biological and chemical warfare establishment in Wiltshire,' Chris told him. 'Nasty place. It's where they developed and tested all sorts of diseases and gases that could be used to attack an enemy – anthrax, mustard gas, nerve gases like sarin that kill people in particularly horrible ways. They tested some of them on young volunteer soldiers in the nineteen fifties, killing at least one of them in the process.'

'I couldn't find out much about Porton Down itself.'

'You wouldn't. It's a top-secret place. Everything's classified.'

'But I found stuff about Episuderon on some other websites. I didn't understand it all – some of it was very complicated – but it seems it was originally invented in Nazi Germany, under Hitler, as a drug for brainwashing people – making them do as they were told. After the war the British got hold of the Nazis' research material and developed the drug further before abandoning it because it was too unreliable. It worked well on some people, apparently, but made others mentally ill and affected their memories. That fits with what we know about my dad.'

'A brainwashing drug?' Chris said. 'Why would anyone want to brainwash your dad?'

'Or us.' Consuela shuddered slightly. 'They were going to give the drug to us too, remember.'

'They gave it to a lot of people,' Max said. 'Those files I found in Julius Clark's office . . . I remembered some of the names in them – other Shadow Island prisoners they experimented on. I've been trying to trace them, find out who they were.'

He took more sheets of paper from his folder and spread them out on the garden table. It was too dark to read the words on the sheets, but he didn't need to. He knew what they were without looking.

'There were five names – all men, some of them foreign-sounding. James Abbott, Sergei Alekseev, Narang Anwar, Redmond Ashworth-Ames, Erik Blomkvist. I wrote them down just after we left the island. Then there was the other prisoner, the one who was shot as we escaped – Arhat Zebari. I haven't got very far. All I have is their names and the dates they were taken to Shadow Island. No addresses or dates of birth or other details. I found an Erik Blomkvist in a newspaper database. He was a Swedish man who went on holiday last autumn and disappeared. His clothes were found on a beach, but there was no sign of Erik. There was an air and sea search for him, but his body was never found. The police concluded that he had been washed out to sea and drowned.'

'What makes you think he was the Erik Blomkvist on Shadow Island?' Chris said.

'The date he disappeared ties in closely with the date on the file I saw. And there's something else. He had something in common with you.'

'With *me*?'

Max nodded. 'You were working for an environmental charity in the Amazon, watching out for illegal logging, when you were kidnapped and taken to Shadow Island. Erik Blomkvist also worked for an environmental charity – Grön Värld, in Stockholm.'

'What about the other names on your list?' Chris asked.

'James Abbott, Narang Anwar and Sergei Alekseev – I can't find out anything about them. The fifth man, Redmond Ashworth-Ames, sounds English. That's a pretty unusual name. I've found a few R. Ashworth-Ameses on the Internet, got their phone numbers, but I haven't made the calls yet. I've been too busy with school and my shows.'

'Two environmentalists, and then your dad, a professional escapologist,' Consuela said. 'That doesn't make any sense.'

'Not if a professional escapologist was all Dad was,' Max pointed out.

Consuela looked at him sceptically. 'You mean this "secret life" you think he had?'

'Julius Clark said he did. He said Dad's shows were just a cover for his other activities. But *what* other activities?'

Max took another sheet of paper from his folder. It was the letter his father had written to him and left behind in Santo Domingo; the letter that proved beyond all doubt that he was still alive. Max looked at it again, though he knew every word of it by heart.

. . . I am a hunted man and I fear that if I surface too soon, I will be killed. Or worse, that you and your mother will be harmed. I cannot let that happen, you are both too precious to me. I cannot risk putting either of you in danger. I have work to do that means I must go away for a time – I do not dare say too much here in case this letter falls into the wrong hands. You must be careful, Max. You are a clever, resourceful boy, but the forces ranged against us are powerful and ruthless. They will try to destroy you, as they are trying to destroy me, and as they are trying to destroy the earth with their greed. But the Cedar Alliance is strong. It has the conscience of the world on its side and I truly believe that good will triumph over evil . . .

Max must have read the letter a hundred times, but it still made him emotional. It still brought tears to his eyes. This was a message from his father – the father whom, for two long, unbearable years, he had thought was dead. But what did the message mean? What 'work' did his dad have to go away and do? What powerful and ruthless forces was he talking about? And what was the Cedar Alliance?

That was the part that intrigued Max the most. *The Cedar Alliance is strong. It has the conscience of the world on its side and I truly believe that good will triumph over evil . . .*

Max lifted his eyes and gazed at Consuela and Chris. 'I've spent hours on the Net, trying to find out what the Cedar Alliance is, but there's no mention of it anywhere. Whatever it is, it's important, I'm sure of that. We find the Cedar Alliance, and we find the key to everything.'

THREE

Max didn't want to go to school the next day. He wanted to skive off and spend the day following up the leads he'd found, trying to track down Redmond Ashworth-Ames. But Consuela insisted, and Max knew better than to disobey her. On stage she was his assistant, but at home she was very much in charge. Since Max's father had disappeared and his mother been imprisoned, Consuela had become Max's legal guardian and she took her responsibilities very seriously. With Max's escapology act taking up large amounts of his spare time, it would have been easy for Consuela to indulge him, to let him have occasional days off school to train or rest. But she never did. His studies always came first. No matter how busy he was, she always made him go to school, always made him do his homework.

And this morning there was another factor to take into consideration: they were under surveillance. Everything they did was being monitored. Chris had experience of that kind of situation from the other side, from the watchers' point of view, and he knew that it was vital for Max and Consuela to act normally, to stick to their daily routines. At the moment they had an advantage. They knew where the bugs were, knew where the watchers outside were, and could make sure they didn't do or say anything that would give away what they were up to. But if the watchers got any hint that their surveillance had been detected, they would change tack and find some new way of spying on their lives that Max and Consuela might not be aware of.

So Max had to go to school as usual. He left the house at the normal time, walked off up the street, just as he always did. Everything about him was the same – his school sweatshirt and trousers, the rucksack over his shoulder. On the outside he appeared no different from any other school day, but inside he was on maximum alert, his mind, his senses finely tuned to his surroundings. He saw the car immediately. It took just a single, casual glance to absorb the details: dark blue Toyota Avensis on the far side of the street, seventy metres from the house, just as Chris had said; two men inside, the driver reading a newspaper, the passenger drinking coffee from a paper cup. Neither man looked at Max as he went past; neither noticed his fleeting glance. Max stayed calm, but he had butterflies in his stomach. This surveillance unnerved him, made him wonder what else was going to happen.

The morning's lessons were deadly dull. Max had to endure three interminable hours of English, history and biology before he could get a moment to himself at lunch time. He bought a sandwich and a drink from the canteen, then asked his best mate, Andy, if he could borrow his mobile phone.

'What happened to yours?' Andy wanted to know. 'You lost it?'

'I don't want to use it,' Max replied.

'Why not?'

Max hesitated. He and Andy were close. They'd known each other since infant school, shared all their secrets. When Max's dad had first disappeared and his mum had stayed on in Central America to help the local police, it was Andy and his parents who had taken Max in and looked after him for a few days. Andy knew all about Max's unusual family circumstances and had always been a loyal, supportive friend. Max had told him a bit about his own recent trip to Santo Domingo, but he'd kept some things back – the dangerous things. He didn't want to put Andy at risk. But he couldn't keep him completely in the dark; he deserved better than that.

'I don't think my phone's safe,' Max said. 'Someone may be tapping it.'

Andy stared at him. '*Tapping* it? Who?'

'I'm not sure. I'll pay you for my calls.'

'Don't be stupid. I don't want any money.' Andy pulled his phone from his pocket and handed it over.

'Thanks,' Max said. 'I'll give it back at the end of lunch break.' He saw the puzzled, uncertain look in Andy's eyes. 'I'm sorry. I'd tell you more, only I don't know what's going on myself.'

'This to do with your mum and dad?'

Max nodded.

'That's OK,' Andy said. 'I understand.'

Max went up to a quiet corner of the school playing fields and sat down on the grassy bank overlooking the football pitches. He'd brought with him the list of phone numbers he'd got off the Internet – twenty-five people named Ashworth-Ames with the first initial R. He knew from the different dialling codes that they were scattered across the country. He punched in the first number on the list. A man answered.

Max put on his most polite voice. 'Hello, I'm sorry to trouble you, but I'm looking for a Redmond Ashworth-Ames.'

'There's no one of that name here,' the man replied.

'You don't know a Redmond Ashworth-Ames, do you? He's not a relative of yours?'

'No, there's no one called Redmond in the family.'

'Thank you. I'm sorry to have bothered you.'

The second and third numbers on the list produced the same result. There was no answer from the fourth number, and the fifth and sixth were also dead ends. Max ate some of his ham salad sandwich, then tried a few more numbers without success. He found three Richard Ashworth-Ameses, one in Cornwall, one in Birmingham and one in Newcastle. There was a Rupert Ashworth-Ames, a Rebecca Ashworth-Ames and a Roland Ashworth-Ames, but no Redmond. It was such an uncommon name that he thought one of these people must be related to Redmond Ashworth-Ames; but no, none of them had ever heard of him.

Max crossed fifteen numbers off his list, then the bell rang and he had to go back into school. It was a frustrating afternoon. Never had lessons seemed so boring, so irrelevant to Max's life. What did he care about algebra or the periodic table when he had more important work to do? His father was missing, presumed dead by just about everyone except Max and his mother was in prison, serving a twenty-year sentence for his supposed murder. Max was desperate to continue his enquiries, to get on with his phone calls, but he was trapped in a classroom having to listen to teachers droning on and on about nothing.

At the final bell he threw all his books into his rucksack and borrowed Andy's phone again, promising he'd return it later, and forcing a fiver on his friend to cover the cost of the calls. Then he sprinted for the exit – along the corridor, down the stairs and out into the rear yard of the school, which was enclosed by a high wire-mesh fence and was known to the pupils as the Prison Yard. Max hurried across it, searching in his bag for his list of phone numbers. Perhaps it was his location that made him suddenly think of his mother. Where she was, the prison yard wasn't a joke name, it was the real thing. It was the only place where she ever saw the sky above her, ever felt the fresh air on her face. The rest of the time she was locked up in a cell just a few metres square, with only a tiny barred window to look out of. And she would be a prisoner in that cell for many years to come if someone didn't get her out. *No*, Max corrected himself. *Not someone.* Me. *There is no one else. If I don't get her out, she will probably die in prison.*

Max went up the path onto the playing fields and sat down on the grassy bank again. He put his list of phone numbers on the ground beside him and resumed where he had left off at lunch time.

The first few calls produced nothing. Max was disappointed, but he kept going. Someone somewhere must have heard of Redmond Ashworth-Ames. On his seventh attempt he struck lucky. It was a woman who answered.

'Yes, Redmond is here,' she said after Max had explained who he was and what he wanted.

'He *is*?' Max said.

He couldn't believe it. Finally he had tracked down the elusive Mr Ashworth-Ames. But was it the right one?

'May I speak to him?'

The woman gave a faint, hesitant murmur. 'Well, no ... I don't think that would be possible. Redmond isn't very well, I'm afraid.'

'Oh, I'm sorry to hear that, Mrs Ashworth-Ames.'

'It's Miss. I'm Redmond's sister, not his wife.'

'Perhaps I could call back at another time?'

'Look, I don't want to be rude, but why do you want to speak to my brother?'

'It's complicated,' Max said. 'It's all to do with my father, who went missing in Central America two years ago.'

There was a short silence on the line, then Miss Ashworth-Ames came back on, sounding less hostile now.

'You said your name was Max Cassidy?'

'That's right.'

'The son of Alexander Cassidy, the escapologist?'

'Yes.'

'I remember the story in the paper. But what on

earth has Redmond got to do with your father's disappearance?'

'I'm not sure,' Max replied. 'Would you mind if I asked you some questions about your brother? You said he's unwell. Could I ask you what's wrong with him?'

'I don't think that's—'

'Please, Miss Ashworth-Ames. This is important.'

'Well, Redmond is . . .' She paused, trying to find the right words. 'He has a condition, a long-term illness. His speech, his mobility, his memory – everything has been affected. Some days he can talk, other days he can't.'

Max's heart skipped a beat. Those were the classic side-effects of Episuderon, the same side-effects from which his dad had suffered after his escape from Shadow Island.

'I think my dad may have had the same illness,' he said. 'Has your brother been to Central America recently?'

'Not Central America – but South America, yes. He went to Peru a year ago. He fell ill just after he came back. No one seems to know what it is. The doctors are baffled.'

Max felt a tingle of excitement. This had to be the right man. 'Can I ask what his job was?'

PAUL ADAM

'Redmond was an ecologist. He worked for an environmental charity in London.'

Max clenched his fist. *Yes*, he exclaimed silently. 'I think I may know what's wrong with your brother, Miss Ashworth-Ames,' he said.

'You're just a boy. What can you possibly know about it?'

'Please trust me. I can help you. But I'd rather not talk about it on the phone. Can I come and see you? Where do you live?'

'In Oxfordshire. Near Henley-on-Thames. But—'

'As soon as possible,' Max broke in. 'Please, Miss Ashworth-Ames. This is vital. For both your brother and my dad. What's your address?'

FOUR

The two men in the dark blue Avensis were still there when Max walked past on his way home. He was careful not to look at them, to behave exactly as he normally would. He opened the front door and went into the house, dumping his rucksack in the hall as usual and going through into the kitchen, where Consuela was chopping vegetables for their evening meal.

'Hi,' Max said.

'Hello,' Consuela replied. 'Good day?'

'Yeah, fine.'

Max helped himself to a couple of biscuits from the jar in the cupboard, then opened the fridge and poured a glass of fruit juice.

'What did you have today?' Consuela said.

She was doing her best to act naturally too, to have the same conversation they had every day when Max came in from school, but Max could detect an underlying note of strain in her voice. He told her about his day, part of his brain remembering what lessons he'd had and finding the words to describe them, another part thinking, *This is really weird. We're putting on a performance here, like actors reading from a script, and someone is listening to everything we're saying.*

After a few minutes their conversation began to peter out. Consuela mouthed the word *Chris* and pointed towards the basement door.

Max nodded, then went quietly across to the door and down the stairs into the basement. Max's father had set up a small gymnasium down there, a training area where he could practise his escapology techniques. Max had used the equipment alongside his dad in the past, but for two years now he'd had the gym to himself, working out on the exercise machines or honing his lock-picking skills on some of the dozens of pairs of handcuffs and manacles that hung from the walls.

Chris Moncrieffe was sitting on the exercise bike, pedalling at a steady rhythm, a thin sheen of sweat on his forehead. As Max came in he looked up and stopped pedalling. Then he slid off the saddle and closed the door behind Max.

'It's OK, we can talk in here,' he said softly. 'But keep your voice down. We don't want any sound drifting up into the rest of the house.'

'It's not bugged?' Max said.

Chris shook his head. 'I went out this morning – over the garden wall into the next street to avoid the guys in the car at the front – and saw those old friends I mentioned. They lent me an electronic sweeping kit that can pick up the tiniest listening device. I've been over the whole house. The kitchen and sitting room we already knew about, but I've discovered bugs in your bedrooms too. Only the garage and this basement are clean.'

'You're sure?'

'Positive. I bought you a new mobile phone too. It's in the kitchen. A pay-as-you-go they can't trace. Best not to use your old phone again.'

'I haven't been using it,' Max said. 'I made some calls today, but I borrowed a mate's phone.'

'Smart boy,' Chris said. 'You get anywhere?'

Max told him about tracking down Redmond Ashworth-Ames. 'I think he's our man,' he said. 'His job, his holiday in South America, his illness since he came back. Everything points to him having been a prisoner on Shadow Island.'

'You speak to him?'

'His sister said he was too ill. But I've arranged to go out there tomorrow evening to see them. Henley-on-Thames – that's not far. I thought maybe you or Consuela could drive me.'

'No problem.'

Chris wiped his gleaming forehead with the back of his hand. 'I'm knackered,' he said. 'You've some gear down here, haven't you? Not just the exercise machines, but all this other stuff . . .' He pointed at the handcuffs and ropes and chains on the walls and laughed. 'If you weren't a professional escapologist, you could get arrested for this lot, you know. And what about this?' He indicated a black wooden coffin that was propped up in a corner. 'You're seriously strange, Max, keeping a coffin in your house.'

'That was my dad's. It was sort of a speciality of his, escaping from coffins, being buried alive. I never use it in my act – it doesn't feel right.'

'Don't want to tread on his toes, copy what he used to do?'

'Something like that.'

Chris fingered the wood of the coffin, inspecting the joints and the screws that held it together. 'Your dad used to be buried alive in this?'

'Yes.'

'Really?'

'He used it when he was performing outdoors. He'd get in the coffin and it would be lowered into a hole in the ground and covered over with soil. An hour later, the coffin would be dug up and my dad would emerge alive and smiling. I saw him do it a few times. It was hell.'

'Hell? Why?'

'There was no trick involved. He used a coffin on stage sometimes, but that had a false bottom that he could remove from the inside. The coffin he used outdoors was the real thing. He really was buried alive in it. It was a very dangerous stunt. Every time he did it he risked his life.'

'How did he survive?'

'Controlled breathing. There's a certain amount of air inside the coffin. If you breathe normally, you'll use it up very quickly. My dad, through years of practice, could take very shallow breaths, slow his whole metabolism down. But it wasn't easy. He used to come out smiling, but I could always see the strain on his face. He pushed himself to the limit.'

'Can you control your breathing too?'

'A bit. I'm not as good as my dad. I could last maybe half an hour in a coffin.'

Chris gave a shudder. 'The thought of it makes me go cold. I'm not bothered by many things, but being shut up in a box . . . that would terrify me.'

'You finished on the bike?' Max said. 'I usually do my training about now.'

'Go ahead. Don't let me get in your way.'

Max went upstairs to his bedroom and changed into T-shirt, shorts and trainers, then returned to the basement and went through his usual routine on the exercise machines. Chris joined him for part of the workout, lifting some weights while Max rowed and cycled.

'You train like this every evening?' Chris asked when they paused to rest.

'Not every evening. Sometimes I have a night off, go out with my mates, or just chill out in front of the TV.' Max rubbed the sweat off his face with a towel. 'I'm going out for a jog now.'

'You want me to come with you?'

'No, thanks. I'm meeting a friend in the park.'

Chris grinned at him. 'Oh, yeah? A girl?'

Max didn't rise. 'See you later,' he said.

He went upstairs and let himself out of the front door. It was a warm evening, the sky grey and overcast. Max jogged down the street, noticing the Avensis out of the corner of his eye as he ran past. It was too brief a glimpse for him to see what the two men were doing, or even whether they were the same ones as earlier. *They must have a change of shift at some point*, he thought. *Bring in the night-watch team.*

In the park, he met up with Andy and gave him back his phone. Andy was in the school football team and played in the local Sunday league too. He came out jogging with Max a few times a week to keep up his fitness. They did three circuits of the park, a total of about three miles, then sat on a bench for a while chatting before heading back to their homes. The two men in the parked car were still there.

Max paused outside his front door and looked back up the street. The men were staring straight at him now. One of them leaned forward, lifted something off the dashboard and put it to his mouth. He was talking into a radio. Seconds later, Max heard the roar of an engine. A dark blue police van slewed round the corner and came racing down the street.

For a moment Max was paralysed. The van was getting nearer. He could see another vehicle behind it, a sleek black Mercedes that looked somehow familiar, though he couldn't place it. Were they coming for *him*? A vanload of police officers for one teenage boy? Surely not. Who then? Consuela? That was just as unlikely. Chris? Were they after Chris? He had been followed from Heathrow when he arrived back in the country, but had shaken off the tail. Did the police suspect that he was holed up in Max's house? Were they coming to arrest him? Max had a sudden inkling that they were.

He broke out of his trance, threw open the front door and dashed inside the house, locking the door behind him. He ran down the hall to the kitchen. Consuela was measuring out rice with a cup, pouring it into a saucepan. Chris was sitting at the table, drinking a cup of coffee.

'The police are here,' Max whispered breathlessly into his ear. 'I think they're looking for you.'

Chris stiffened. He glanced at Max in alarm and stood up quickly. There was a loud hammering on the front door. A voice shouted, 'Police! Open up!'

Max grabbed Chris's arm and gestured towards the basement door. They crossed the room and hurtled down the stairs. Max pulled open the door of the large metal cabinet that he used in his act and felt along the inside edge for the hidden catch. A panel in the base slid open, revealing a shallow compartment.

'There are air holes. You'll be able to breathe. Above all, don't panic. Get in.'

'Look, I'm not sure—' Chris broke off as an almighty crash reverberated through the house. The police had smashed open the front door. 'I could hide in the garden,' he went on.

'There's no time,' Max hissed urgently. '*Get in.*'

There were heavy footsteps on the floor above them, then on the basement stairs. Chris scrambled into the compartment and curled up on his side, his knees tucked up against his chest. Max slid the base panel back into place and closed the cabinet door, then dashed over to the cycling machine. He was in the saddle, just starting to pedal, when the basement door slammed open. Two policemen burst in. One of the officers turned the key in the door that led to the garden and went outside. The other one started searching the room, checking the cupboards and the cubby hole that contained the central-heating boiler.

'What's going on?' Max said.

The officer ignored him. Max got off the exercise bike and went upstairs. There were more police officers in the kitchen, and a man in a dark suit who had his back turned so Max couldn't see his face. The man swung round. Max froze, staring in astonishment at him, realizing now why the black Mercedes had looked familiar.

'Hello, Max,' Rupert Penhall said smoothly. 'Surprised to see me?'

Max took a moment to respond. His heart was racing, his mouth dry as sandpaper. 'What . . . what're you doing here?' was all he could mumble.

'You're in trouble,' Penhall said.

'Trouble?'

'Ask your lovely lady assistant over there.'

Consuela was standing by the oven, looking pale and shaken. She handed Max a piece of paper. 'They have a search warrant,' she told him.

Max peered at the piece of paper. He'd never seen a search warrant before, didn't know what he was supposed to be looking for. He skimmed over a lot of legal jargon about statutory powers until he got to a paragraph explaining what the police were searching for: *Any equipment or other materials that might be used in the furtherance of any offence under the Prevention of Terrorism Act.*

Max read the words three times, wondering whether he'd understood them correctly. '*Terrorism?*' he said incredulously. 'You think we're *terrorists*?'

'I don't know what you are, Max. Or what you're mixed up in. That's why we're here. You ever come across a man called Chris Moncrieffe?'

Max kept his face expressionless. 'No,' he said.

Penhall took a step towards him, his manner turning aggressive. 'You're lying, Max. I know you are. Where is he?'

'I don't know who you're talking about,' Max said.

'Don't play games with me. Is he here? If he is, we'll find him.'

'There's only me and Consuela here, no one else. You can look around, if you like.'

'That's what we intend to do,' Penhall said.

He leaned in closer, so his face was only inches away from Max's. Max could smell the cloying scent of his aftershave.

'You should have listened to me last time. I told you not to meddle in things that didn't concern you.'

'You think my dad disappearing doesn't concern me?' Max said defiantly. 'You think my mum being in prison for a murder she didn't commit doesn't concern me?'

'What do you mean, "last time"?' Consuela asked. 'Have you met this man before, Max?'

Max didn't reply.

Penhall gave a thin, humourless smile. 'Didn't he tell you? Naughty boy, Max, keeping things from your guardian.'

'Max?' Consuela said. 'Have you been in trouble with the police?'

'No,' Max said. 'You're not the police anyway, are you, Mr Penhall? But what exactly are you? That's what I'd like to know. Maybe you should tell us.'

'Not the police?' Consuela frowned. 'Then who are all these men?'

'These men are police officers, as you can clearly see,' Penhall said. 'They have a legal right to search your house.'

'And you?' Consuela stared at him. 'Who are you? How do you know Max? I want some answers.'

'He's "connected to the government",' Max said. 'Isn't that what you told me when we met before, Mr Penhall? When you threatened me.'

'He *threatened* you?' Consuela stepped forward to

confront Penhall. She was a couple of inches taller than he was. She looked down at him, her eyes burning with anger. 'I want to know what's going on,' she said. 'Show me some identification.'

Penhall shook his head contemptuously and started to turn away. Consuela grabbed hold of his arm. 'I want to see some ID.'

'Let go of my arm, Miss Navarra,' Penhall said calmly. He held her gaze, a smug half-smile on his pink, fleshy face. 'My arm, Miss Navarra.'

Consuela glared at him for a moment, then released his arm.

'Sir, I think you should see this.' One of the police officers had been searching the kitchen drawers. He held out a cardboard folder.

'Hey, you can't take that!' Max yelled. 'Give it here.'

He tried to snatch the folder away from the officer, but he was too slow. The officer pushed him back with a hand the size of a shovel and passed the folder to Penhall.

'That's got nothing to do with terrorism!' Max shouted.

He tried to reach Penhall, to retrieve the folder, but the police officer held him back. He was a big man, well over six foot tall and packed with muscle. Max was powerless against him.

'Those are personal papers,' he said angrily. 'You can't take them.'

'Calm down, Max,' Penhall said soothingly. 'We can take whatever we like.'

He put the folder down on the kitchen table and looked through the papers inside it – Max's notes on Episuderon and the men who'd been held on Shadow Island, his father's medical file from the island and the letter he'd left for Max. Penhall took the letter out and studied it carefully.

'Well, well,' he murmured. 'Now that *is* interesting.'

'It's mine,' Max said. 'You can't have it.'

Penhall slipped the letter back into the folder. Max lunged forward, trying to grab it, but the police officer restrained him, holding him at bay with an arm that was as strong and unyielding as a steel girder.

'This is outrageous!' Consuela snapped. 'You can't do this. Let him go, you brutes.' She pulled Max away from the policeman and stepped protectively in front of him. 'Leave him alone – he's just a boy. And those are his papers. Give them back.'

'Get in the way, Miss Navarra, and I'll have you arrested. Max too,' Penhall said curtly. He tucked the folder under his arm. 'You should have listened to me before, Max. I'll tell you again now. You're out of your depth, meddling in things you know nothing about. You carry on and you'll get hurt. Badly hurt. You understand me?'

He looked at Max, then at Consuela, his small, piggy eyes glinting with malice. Then he turned to the police officer. 'Call me if you find anything else.'

He spun round and left the room. Max watched him go, the anger like a furnace inside him. Never in his life had he felt so helpless. The police could break into his house on some fabricated excuse about terrorism; they could search everywhere, remove his private papers and he could do nothing about it. Nothing.

He went out into the hall. The front door was wide open, the wood around the lock crushed and splintered where it had been forced open with some heavy instrument. Rupert Penhall was outside in the street, climbing into the back of his chauffeur-driven Mercedes. He paused, half in and half out of the car, and looked across at Max, who was watching him from the house. For a few seconds the two of them locked eyes. Then Penhall slid inside the Mercedes and closed the door, the tinted glass hiding him from Max's furious gaze. The car pulled away and purred off up the street.

Max retreated into the hall. There were police officers searching the sitting and dining rooms and, when Max went upstairs, more officers in the bedrooms, checking the wardrobes, the drawers, the bookshelves. They'd even climbed up into the loft to explore the roof space and eaves. Max stood on the landing and watched them searching his desk, his cupboards, snooping through his clothes and other possessions. He was outraged that they could do this. Worried too. And, if he was honest with himself, scared.

He went back downstairs. Consuela was still in the kitchen, sitting at the table while the policemen went through the cupboards and drawers, taking down her cookery books one by one and flicking through the pages. Max sat down opposite her. They didn't speak to each other, not with a room full of coppers and bugs in the wall. They would talk later, when it was safe to do so.

The two officers who'd been in the basement came up the stairs with empty hands. Max felt a surge of relief. At least they hadn't found Chris. Max wasn't surprised. His father had built that trick cabinet himself. The secret compartment in the base was cunningly constructed so that it was very difficult to detect, and the catch that opened the access panel was even harder to find. Max had used the cabinet several times on stage and it had never let him down yet. Thank goodness for Alexander Cassidy's incomparable craftsmanship.

It was another hour before the police finally left, leaving behind them the messy evidence of their search – cupboard doors hanging open, clothes tossed on beds, duvets and cushions strewn around the floors.

Max watched the blue van depart, then ran down into the basement to release Chris, Consuela following behind. Chris was red-faced and sweating, his whole body stiff and aching from being confined in such a small space.

'That was the worst experience of my entire life,' he said with feeling. 'I've been in a few tight corners, but nothing like that.' He stretched his arms and rubbed the back of his neck. 'What happened?'

'They were looking for you,' Consuela said. 'And for anything else they could find. They had a warrant that mentioned terrorism.'

Chris froze, his hand still on his neck. '*Terrorism?* That's ridiculous. Me, a terrorist?' He thought about it for a few seconds, then gave a nod of understanding. 'It's good, though. You want someone out of the way, a trumped-up charge of terrorism is a pretty failsafe method of doing it. I knew we couldn't trust the police.'

'It wasn't just the police,' Max said. 'The man in charge claimed he was connected to the government in some way. I met him once before, after Luis Lopez-Vega was killed in that hotel near King's Cross. He warned me off, told me to mind my own business.'

'"Connected to the government"?' Chris said. 'The Security Service – MI5?'

'I don't know. He took away my folder. My research, my dad's medical file, his letter to me. I should've hidden them, but I didn't have time. I *need* that letter. It's the only proof I have that Dad is still alive. The only proof that Mum couldn't have killed him. Without it, I can't get her case reopened, can't get her out of prison.'

Chris put a reassuring arm around Max's shoulders. 'Hey, we're going to crack this. You've got me and Consuela with you. We're in this together.'

'But in *what* together?' Consuela said, her voice unsteady with anxiety. 'What's going on? Terrorism? The police involved, maybe the Security Service too . . . ? This isn't just Julius Clark we're up against. It goes further than that. But how much further? Who else are we fighting?'

Max had no answer to that. The police search had frightened him. So had Rupert Penhall. Who was he? Why had he taken Max's file? What was he going to do with it? Max felt as if he were stumbling around in the dark, unable to see where he was going, to see what hazards lay ahead. Santo Domingo and Shadow Island had been dangerous places, but Max had got away from them. He had thought he would be safer back in England, on his home territory. Now he was beginning to realize how wrong he'd been.

FIVE

Max didn't sleep that night. He was too wound up, too worried. He lay awake into the small hours, thinking back over the evening's events: the police search, his conversation with Rupert Penhall, the loss of his folder. It was the folder that bothered him most. He was furious with himself for being so careless, for not hiding it somewhere more secure, for not taking photocopies of all the documents and depositing them in a safe place. But how was he to have known that the police would come and search the house? That possibility had never crossed his mind. In the days since his return from Central America he had been preoccupied with Julius Clark. It was he who seemed to be the threat. It was Clark, after all, who had imprisoned Max, Consuela and Chris on Shadow Island, just as he had imprisoned Max's father there two years earlier. It was Clark who had intended to inject them with the brain-washing drug Episuderon, and it was Clark's armed guards who had tried to kill them as they escaped from the island.

The intervention of the British police was something Max had not expected. It put a different perspective on everything. Did Clark have the kind of influence that could prompt the police to carry out a search of Max's home? Maybe he did. He was a very rich man, and rich men had powerful friends.

But his influence went further than just a simple search. The police had been looking for Chris too; they'd been looking for materials relating to some kind of terrorism. That scared Max. He wasn't a terrorist; nor were Chris or Consuela. Did the police genuinely think they were, or was the whole terrorism thing a big excuse to search Max's house looking for something else – for papers connected to Max's father and Shadow Island, for instance? If that was the case, then the plan had been unquestionably successful. Rupert Penhall had all Max's papers now. Without them, Max couldn't prove that his father had been a prisoner on Shadow Island, or indeed that he was alive at all. It would just be Max's word against Julius Clark's. And who would be believed – a fourteen-year-old schoolboy or an influential business tycoon?

Max knew he had to get the papers back. That was absolutely vital. But how? He didn't know who Penhall was. He didn't know where the papers had been taken.

He thought about it through the night, and by

morning had come to the conclusion that he needed help from someone who knew how the legal system operated. An insider, an expert. He considered going to a lawyer. His mother had a solicitor, Malcolm Fielding, who had offices near the Royal Courts of Justice. Max had met him a few times and didn't think much of his abilities. Fielding was supposed to be trying to get Max's mum out of prison, but in the eighteen months he'd been on the case he'd charged a massive amount in fees but achieved precisely nothing.

There was somebody else, however, to whom Max could turn for help and advice – Detective Chief Superintendent Richardson. Max wondered about him over breakfast and then during the morning at school. He liked Richardson. The detective had known Max's father, both professionally and socially: Alexander Cassidy had worked with the Metropolitan Police on several occasions, advising them about locks and security, and Richardson had been to the Cassidy house for dinner a few times. Max had had a couple of meetings with him before the detective took part in his stage show and they'd got along well. The chief superintendent had seemed a straight, honest police officer, a man who couldn't be bought or corrupted. Max had good instincts about people, and he had a feeling that Richardson could be trusted. At lunch time he went up onto the field with his new mobile phone and called Scotland Yard.

The chief superintendent seemed pleased to hear from him. 'Max, hello. How are you?' he said warmly.

'I'm OK,' Max replied.

'I didn't get much of a chance to talk to you after the show the other night, but I thought it was absolutely brilliant. I was really impressed.'

'Thanks. And thanks again for taking part.'

'It was nothing – I enjoyed it. Thank *you* for testing those cuffs for us. So what can I do for you?'

'I want to ask you a favour,' Max said.

'A favour? Of course. What?'

'Can I meet you? It will only take a few minutes.'

'Meet me? Why, yes. When?'

'As soon as possible.' Max calculated how much time he had – when he'd need to leave for Henley. 'Is there any chance today? I could come and see you after I finish school.'

'Let me check my diary. I have a meeting at three, but that shouldn't last more than an hour. What about four thirty? Would that suit you?'

'Yes, that would be great.'

'You know where I am, don't you? Come to the main desk and ask for me.'

'Thanks – that's really good of you.'

'What's this all about, Max?'

'I'll tell you when I see you.'

Max had often seen the outside of New Scotland Yard on TV crime reports – the mirror-glass windows to stop people seeing in, the distinctive triangular revolving sign by the main entrance – but he'd never been inside the building. The reception area didn't feel like a police station; it was more like the headquarters of a large international corporation – except that the two men and a woman behind the long counter were in uniform.

He asked for Detective Chief Superintendent Richardson, said he was expected, and was told to wait in the area to one side where there were chairs for visitors. He didn't sit down. The building made him nervous. The search of his house was still very fresh in his memory. He had visions of police officers swooping down on him and dragging him away to the cells.

The chief superintendent took only a few minutes to appear. He shook hands with Max and gave him a welcoming smile. 'You want to come upstairs to my office, or do you fancy a bit of refreshment? There's a café just round the corner that does a nice range of cakes.'

'The café,' Max said without hesitation. He didn't want to linger any longer than necessary in police headquarters.

The café was perfect for their meeting – small enough to feel comfortable, but with plenty of space between tables so that no one could overhear their conversation. Chief Superintendent Richardson bought himself a cup of tea, a Coke for Max and two chocolate brownies.

'So what's this favour you want to ask?' he said, adding sugar to his tea and stirring it.

Max studied him for a moment, thinking again about his reasons for asking the detective for help and deciding that he was doing the right thing. His instincts hadn't let him down – Richardson was definitely a man who could be trusted.

'Do you think I'm a terrorist?' Max said.

Richardson stopped stirring his tea and eyed him narrowly, his expression puzzled. 'Is that a joke?'

'No, I'm serious.'

Max had brought with him the copy of the search warrant that the police had given Consuela. He took it out of his rucksack and put it on the table between them. 'The police came to our house yesterday evening. They searched it from top to bottom.'

'*Searched* it?' Richardson was incredulous. 'Your *house*?'

'This is the warrant they had.'

The detective read the sheet of paper, his eyes

opening wide when he reached the section giving the purpose of the search. Max watched him carefully. Richardson seemed genuinely shocked.

'I don't understand,' the detective said. 'This doesn't make sense. Who were the officers? They must have given you their names.'

'I don't know who the police were,' Max replied. 'They didn't show any ID. But the man in charge was called Rupert Penhall.'

'Penhall?' Richardson frowned. 'I don't know the name, and that's odd because I thought I knew pretty much every senior officer in the Met.'

'He wasn't a policeman.'

'How do you know?'

Max hesitated. *Don't complicate things,* he told himself. *Richardson doesn't need to know you've met Penhall before.*

'He said he wasn't.'

'And you say he was in charge? What did he look like?'

'Short and plump. A fat face with red cheeks.'

Richardson fixed Max with a penetrating stare. 'I have to ask you this, Max . . . are you mixed up in anything illegal?'

'No.'

'You're sure about that? This warrant was provided

63

by a magistrate. They would have needed a good reason to issue it.'

Max had thought long and hard about how much he should tell the chief superintendent and had decided to keep things simple, to be selective about the inform-ation he gave him. It was safer that way. He had confidence in the detective as an individual, but he wasn't so sure of the Met as a whole. It was a big police force and there might be other officers who were not so trustworthy.

'All I've been doing is looking into my mum's case. You know about my mum, of course. There's no way she killed my dad. I went to Santo Domingo at half-term to see if I could find evidence to prove her innocence.'

'And did you?'

'Yes. None of the facts added up. The Santo Domingo police, their judges, are all crooked. But nothing I've done has anything to do with terrorism. That search warrant is rubbish. I think someone in Britain is trying to stop me investigating my dad's disappearance.'

'Why would they want to do that?'

'I don't know. But this man Penhall took a folder of mine. Stuff about my dad. I want to get it back from him. It's really important. I thought you might be able to help me.'

Chief Superintendent Richardson took a notebook

from his jacket pocket and wrote down Penhall's name. Then he picked up the search warrant. 'Can I hang on to this? I'll make a few enquiries, see what I can find out. I can't make any promises, Max, but there does seem to be something strange going on here. I'll give you a call when I've something to tell you.'

'Thanks. I really appreciate that. I've got a new mobile phone.'

Max gave him the number. Richardson scribbled it in his notebook, then took a bite of his brownie.

'Are you sure there isn't more to this, Max?'

Max didn't want to lie to him. 'Yes, there is,' he admitted. 'I can't tell you the rest at the moment. I need to find out what's going on first.'

'Are you sure that's wise? This warrant – anything to do with terrorism – those are very serious matters. Why don't you tell me the whole story now?'

'Because I don't *know* the whole story. I'm sorry,' Max replied. 'But I *do* need your help.'

The chief superintendent regarded him intently for a long moment. Then he gave a nod of understanding. 'OK, have it your own way, Max. I'll do what I can and be in touch.'

Max noticed that the front door had been repaired when he got home forty minutes later. A new lock had been fitted to replace the one the police had broken and two extra bolts added, one at the top and one at the bottom of the door. Consuela was alone in the kitchen, sorting out some household bills. They had another choreographed conversation about Max's day at school for the benefit of the bug in the wall and whoever was listening in. They were both less stilted, less awkward than they'd been the day before. They knew that this little charade had to be as convincing as possible.

Then Max mouthed the question, *Chris?* and Consuela pointed to the basement door.

They went downstairs together. Chris was sitting on the floor, reading a biography of the legendary escapologist, Harry Houdini, who was one of Max's all-time heroes and the inspiration behind many of his stage tricks. Max waited for Consuela to close the door before he spoke.

'Our visit to Redmond Ashworth-Ames this evening – we need to discuss how we're going to do it. The surveillance car is still outside, I noticed it on my way home. What if they try to follow us?'

'You think they will?' Chris said.

'I don't know. But I think I might have been followed to school this morning by another car. I've been working out how we might shake them off . . .'

Max outlined his plan. Consuela and Chris listened,

then asked a few questions, looking for flaws in the plan, but Max had thought it all through thoroughly.

'That's pretty good,' Chris said approvingly. 'It's certainly worth a try. When do we go?'

'As soon as we can,' Max replied.

Max and Consuela went back up to the kitchen. Consuela made a quick dinner of pasta and pepperoni, Max taking a plate down into the basement for Chris; then they were ready to leave.

Chris came upstairs quietly and went through into the garage with Max. Max removed a fifteen-centimetre nail from a drawer and slipped it into the pocket of his jacket. Then he unlocked the main garage doors. There were two of them, big, old-fashioned wooden doors that opened outwards. Chris pushed one of the doors open a fraction and peered out through the gap while Max went back into the house.

Consuela was waiting for him in the hall. They left through the front door and walked across to where Consuela's car was parked. Max glanced casually up the street. He could see the surveillance car seventy metres away and knew that the two men inside it could see him. They had a clear view of the front door and part of the drive. What they couldn't see, though, were the garage doors. There was too much vegetation – high shrubs and a birch tree – along the boundary next to the drive that hid the garage from their line of sight.

Max went round to the passenger side of Consuela's Nissan hatchback, where he knew he was invisible to the surveillance team. He opened the rear door of the car first and signalled to Chris. Chris pushed open the garage door just wide enough to squeeze through, closing it behind him. He scuttled out across the drive, crouching low, and dived into the back of the Nissan, lying down on the floor, where he was concealed by the front seats.

Max closed the car door and got into the front next to Consuela. She started the engine and they drove out onto the street, turning in the opposite direction to the watching men. Consuela checked her mirror. The dark blue car was pulling away from the kerb and coming after them.

'They're following,' she said.

Max resisted the temptation to look round, but he shifted slightly in his seat so he could catch a glimpse of the Avensis in the wing mirror on his door. It was fifty or sixty metres back. He could see the shapes of the two men in the front, but not the detail of their faces.

Consuela turned left at the end of the street and accelerated. The Toyota stayed with them, always about fifty metres behind. Consuela made no attempt to shake off the tail. She drove at a steady thirty miles an hour for ten minutes before slowing and turning into the car park of the supermarket where she did most of the shopping.

'There's a space over there,' Max said, pointing. 'Where that red car's just leaving.'

Consuela swung into the next lane and parked between a grey people carrier and a white van. She and Max got out, leaving Chris curled up on the floor in the back of the car. Max looked around. The Avensis was reversing into a space a couple of rows away. Max gauged its position in relation to the supermarket building. Perfect: it was exactly where he wanted it.

'OK?' he said to Consuela.

She nodded and they walked towards the supermarket entrance. As they entered the store, Max glanced back discreetly. One of the men from the Avensis was following them. He was in his twenties, a stocky guy in a brown sports jacket and green striped tie.

Max turned to Consuela. 'One of them is right behind us. I'll come and find you,' he said, then veered away from her and headed for the checkouts, walking quickly, but not so fast that he drew attention to himself.

The supermarket exit was at the side of the building, round the corner from the entrance. Max paused before he went through the automatic glass doors and looked back across the store. The man in the brown jacket was just coming in from the car park. He didn't look Max's way – he was concentrating on Consuela. He watched her disappear down one of the shopping aisles and set off after her. Max hurried out. He had to be quick, do what he had to do before Brown Jacket realized he wasn't inside the building.

The Avensis was in the front section of the car park, from where the driver could see the supermarket entrance, but not the exit. Max circled round in a wide loop to approach it from behind and slightly to the side so he wouldn't be seen if the driver happened to glance in his mirror.

When he was twenty metres away, Max bent down, pretending to tie his shoelace, and surveyed the car park. A few customers were transferring their shopping from their trolleys to their car boots, but none of them was taking any notice of him. Max ducked down behind a silver Volvo and snaked away across the tarmac, using his elbows and knees to propel himself. He slid underneath a Mitsubishi 4x4 with a high wheelbase and emerged immediately behind the Avensis. The driver was looking at Consuela's car and the supermarket beyond it, so he wasn't paying any attention to his rear. Even if he'd chanced to glance in his mirrors, he wouldn't have seen Max, for he was half underneath the Avensis's back bumper, working the nail carefully into the rear nearside tyre.

He took it slowly, piercing the rubber tread of the tyre and gradually enlarging the hole to let the air out a little at a time. He didn't want any loud hiss of escaping gas to give him away. Nor did he want the car to suddenly lurch down to one side. He had to do it by degrees so that the driver was completely unaware of what was happening.

Very gently, the tyre deflated until it was completely flat. Max withdrew the nail and slithered swiftly away under the neighbouring vehicles, standing up at the end of the row and walking back towards the supermarket exit. He went in through the sliding glass doors, past the checkouts, and started searching for Consuela. He glanced at his watch. He'd been absent for only about seven or eight minutes. The man in the brown jacket, presumably still following Consuela, wouldn't have had much time to wonder where Max was. Hopefully he would simply assume they'd split up to do the shopping more quickly and efficiently and that Max was in a different section of the massive store, picking up items for their trolley – an assumption that Max had every intention of confirming.

He grabbed a couple of packets of breakfast cereal,

then a bag of pasta and some rice, and carried them to the end of the aisle. He went past the deli counter and the in-store bakery and saw Consuela in the dairy aisle, picking up a packet of cheese. Brown Jacket was fifteen metres away from her, pretending to study the display of yoghurts and creams. Max walked past him, their shoulders almost brushing, and dumped the items he was carrying into Consuela's trolley.

'What else do we need?' he said, raising his voice a little so Brown Jacket would hear him.

'Washing powder,' Consuela said. 'Get a big box. And biscuits – whichever ones you fancy.'

'OK.'

Max moved off into the stacks again, collecting the washing powder and two packets of chocolate biscuits and bringing them back to the trolley.

'That's pretty much it, I think,' Consuela said.

They went to the nearest checkout and paid for their shopping, then returned to their car and loaded the bags into the boot. Max saw the man in the brown jacket getting into the Avensis.

'Successful?' Chris asked from the floor in the back of the Nissan.

Max climbed into the front beside Consuela. 'Piece of cake,' he said. 'If they're following us to Henley, they're going to have one hell of a long push.'

Consuela pulled out and headed for the exit. Two rows away, the Avensis was also on the move – although not for long. The driver could tell immediately that something was wrong. His car was tilted over to one side at the back and there was the sound of shredding rubber followed by the harsh clatter of metal wheel rims on tarmac.

Max looked round and saw the Avensis lurch to a stop in the middle of the car park. The two men got out and stared in dismay at their flat tyre. Then they looked up, watching helplessly as Consuela's Nissan turned out onto the main road and sped away into the distance.

SIX

They headed west out of London, taking the M4 past Slough before turning off near Maidenhead and continuing on to Henley. Consuela drove all the way, Max next to her. Chris sat in the back of the car, keeping an eye on the road behind in case they were still being tailed. They'd got rid of the Avensis, but there was always the possibility that there might be other surveillance teams watching them – teams that they hadn't managed to spot earlier. He saw nothing suspicious, however, and by the time they arrived in Henley they were sure they hadn't been followed.

Redmond Ashworth-Ames lived in a village in the Chiltern hills to the northwest of Henley. It was a small, picturesque place, an open green in the centre surrounded by a few red-brick cottages and a thatched pub. Ashworth-Ames's house was on the edge of the village, set back into the hillside with dense beech woods on the slope above it.

A middle-aged woman in black trousers and a blue cardigan greeted them at the door and said she was

Alicia Ashworth-Ames, Redmond's elder sister. She was a tall, thin woman with mousy brown hair and a tired face. Max, Consuela and Chris introduced themselves, then followed Alicia into the cottage. It was tiny – only two rooms and a kitchen downstairs and, Max guessed, no more than two bedrooms and a bathroom upstairs. There were exposed wooden beams in the ceilings, and doorways so low that Chris had to stoop to get through them.

Alicia glanced uncertainly at them, twisting her fingers together nervously. Consuela tried to put her at ease.

'Thank you for agreeing to see us,' she said with a smile. 'I hope we can do something to help your brother.'

'Yes, of course,' Alicia replied. 'I hope so too. Please, sit down.' She gestured at a threadbare sofa and an arm-chair. 'The kettle's boiled. Can I offer you some tea?'

'Thank you, that's very kind,' Consuela said.

'Three?'

'Not for me, thanks,' said Max.

Alicia smiled apologetically. 'I'm sorry, I don't have any soft drinks. We're not used to entertaining young people. Perhaps a glass of water?'

'I'm fine, thanks,' he replied.

He sat down at one end of the sofa and looked

around the room. It was small and cluttered, the sofa and armchair taking up most of the available space. There were two little tables covered with stacks of books and magazines, and paintings and framed photographs hung on the walls. Max recognized Alicia in several of the photos. She was on her own in a couple, but mostly she was pictured next to a studious-looking man in wire-rimmed spectacles who could only have been her brother. The photographs had all been taken outdoors – on the tops of mountains, Alicia and Redmond swathed in cagoules and woolly hats, or in what looked like tropical rainforest, both of them in shorts and T-shirts. One photograph showed them standing on a raised wooden platform with an orang-utan only a couple of metres away from them.

Alicia carried in a tray of cups and saucers from the kitchen and placed it precariously on top of a pile of magazines on one of the tables. Then she brought out a pot of tea. She filled cups for Consuela and Chris and handed them round.

'Redmond's just next door,' she said. 'We've had to convert the dining room into a bedroom for him. He can't manage the stairs any more. I'll get you settled before I introduce you. Too much noise and movement upsets him.'

'Are you sure he's up to seeing us?' Max asked.

'Well, you've come all this way. It would be a pity not to meet him. But what's this all about? You didn't say much on the phone.'

'Would you mind if we got to that a bit later? After we've spoken to your brother?'

Alicia looked at him doubtfully.

'Please, Miss Ashworth-Ames,' Max said. 'We want to help you. You have to believe us. We think we know what happened to your brother, but we need to speak to him first.'

Alicia thought for a moment, then gave a slight shrug. 'I suppose that would be all right. But I warn you, he's not able to talk much.'

'Thank you.'

She went across the hall and into the room on the other side. She came back a few minutes later, pushing a man in a wheelchair. Max was shocked by his condition. Redmond Ashworth-Ames was clearly very sick indeed. He was slumped sideways in the wheelchair, his head tilted over at an angle as if his neck muscles were too weak to support it. But it was his eyes that were most noticeable. They couldn't have been more different from the ones in the photos on the wall. In the pictures, Redmond's eyes were bright and alert, shining with life and intelligence. Now they looked vacant and dead, like stars that had burned out.

'Redmond, you have some visitors,' Alicia said. 'This is Max, and this is Consuela, and this is Chris.'

She went round all three of them, though it was clear that Redmond wasn't in any state to take in the information. His head lolled over, his eyes staring blankly at the sitting-room wall.

'I'm afraid he's in rather a bad way today,' Alicia told them. 'That happens. He has good days and bad days.'

'You said on the phone that he's been like this for the past year . . .' Max said.

'That's right.'

'Since he went to Peru.'

'The doctors think he might have caught something there. Some disease or virus. He's had lots of tests, but they haven't been able to establish what exactly is wrong with him. He's seen several specialists in London, but – as I told you on the phone – they're all baffled by his condition.'

'It must be very distressing for you,' Consuela said sympathetically.

Alicia nodded at her. She seemed reassured to have another woman there. 'It is. He used to be so energetic, so involved in things – and now look at him. How can a person change so drastically in such a short space of time?'

'Perhaps you could tell us what happened to him?'
Max said.

'Well,' Alicia replied, 'it all began last spring – April.
Redmond went to Peru. He's travelled all around the
world for his job, but he'd never been to Machu Picchu.
You know, the famous ruined Inca city – you must have
seen photographs of it. He'd always wanted to go there.
He was away for three weeks, and when he came back
he seemed the same as before. He was well; he'd had a
great holiday; he went back to work and everything
seemed fine. But then, after about a fortnight, he was
taken ill.

'At first it was just a fever – like a bad case of flu. He
went to bed with a raging temperature, rested, but the
fever got worse. I came over one evening – I didn't live
here then – and found him unconscious. I don't mean
asleep – he was in a coma. I couldn't wake him. I called
an ambulance and he was taken to hospital. He was in
intensive care for four, five weeks. I was sure he was
going to die. But then he pulled round. He recovered
consciousness, he came home, even though he wasn't
better. Physically he was very weak – he still is: that's
why he has to have a wheelchair – but mentally he was
even worse. He could barely speak most days, and when
he did, nothing he said made sense. His memory too
was affected. He can remember almost nothing about

the past few years. There are days when he doesn't even know who I am.'

Alicia broke off and blinked away tears. This was obviously a very painful subject for her.

'I'm sorry to put you through this,' Max said gently, 'but we think that when your brother went to Peru, he was kidnapped and taken to a place called Shadow Island, off the coast of Santo Domingo.'

'*Kidnapped?*' Alicia gaped at him incredulously. 'What are you talking about? Why would anyone kidnap my brother?'

'I know it sounds far-fetched,' Max told her, 'but hear me out, please. I saw the files on the island. Your brother's name was there. Date of arrival, April the sixteenth last year. Is that when he went to South America?'

'Well, yes, he went on the twelfth. But this is ludicrous. Redmond kidnapped? You must be mistaken.'

'You say that some days he's better than others, that he talks. Has he ever said anything about Shadow Island? Its name in Spanish is *Isla de Sombra*.'

As Max said the words there was an instant reaction from Redmond Ashworth-Ames. He let out a cry – a low, agonized cry that made Max's skin tingle, gave him goose pimples on his arms. He looked across at the figure in the wheelchair. Redmond's lips were moving as if he were trying to speak, but no words came out, just an incomprehensible series of moans. He tried to lift his head, straining visibly, putting in a superhuman effort. Slowly his chin came up. His eyes swivelled round, and for the first time Max saw some expression in them. There was a glint of something in those dark, empty orbs. Max realized with a shudder that it was a look of pure terror.

Alicia stood up and went over to her brother. She stroked his hair and face, trying to calm him. He was still moaning, a strange, disturbing sound like a wounded animal.

'It's OK, it's OK,' Alicia murmured soothingly. 'I'm here, there's nothing to fear.'

'I'm sorry,' Max said, averting his eyes from Redmond. It was too upsetting to watch him.

'It's not your fault – you weren't to know,' Alicia said. 'Yes, he has mentioned . . . that name . . . before. I didn't know what he was talking about. I thought he was just rambling.'

'What did he say about it?'

'Nothing I could understand. Just repeated those three words, usually at night. He wakes up a lot, sometimes screaming. He has very bad nightmares.'

She stroked her brother's head some more until,

gradually, he stopped moaning and was quiet. Alicia stayed by his side, holding his hand to comfort him.

'It's terrible to see him like this. If you can help me in any way, I'd be so grateful. What's wrong with him? You said your father had the same illness. Is he like Redmond?'

'I don't know. I don't think he's quite as ill,' Max replied. 'He managed to write me a letter to tell me he hadn't been well. But I know he was also held prisoner on' – he watched Redmond, not wanting to say anything that might agitate him again – 'on the island. I think both he and your brother were given a brainwashing drug.'

'A brainwashing drug?' Alicia said. 'None of this makes any sense. Drugs . . . kidnapping? It's crazy.'

Chris spoke for the first time. 'It may sound crazy, Miss Ashworth-Ames, but it's true. *I* was kidnapped too – abducted from the Amazon rainforest and taken to the island.'

Alicia stared at him, her brow furrowing. '*You?* You were kidnapped? Why? Who would do such a thing?'

'I think it has something to do with their jobs,' Max said. 'Chris was working for an environmental charity. Your brother was an ecologist – what kind of work was he doing?'

'He was in Borneo, studying the tropical rainforest,

which is rapidly disappearing. It's being cut down for oil-palm plantations. Animals are suffering as their habitat is being destroyed.' She pointed to the photograph on the wall. 'That was taken in Borneo – a place called Tanjung Puting National Park. I went out to visit Redmond there. The park is an orang-utan sanctuary. They're becoming almost extinct in the wild because of man's activities – logging, farming, bio-fuel production.'

She turned back to Chris. 'But you haven't answered my question. Who would want to kidnap you, or my brother?'

'The island is owned by a businessman named Julius Clark,' Chris replied. 'He's been carrying out experiments on prisoners there.'

'For what purpose?'

'We don't know.'

Alicia was silent for a time, deep in thought, her hand still entwined with her brother's. Redmond's head had tipped over to one side again and he was staring into space.

'I find this too incredible to believe,' Alicia murmured eventually.

'Look at your brother,' said Chris. 'Do you really think he's just got a virus? Look at the effect the name of the island had on him. He was there, believe me, and it was a terrifying experience for him.'

'Have you been to the police?'

It was Max who replied. 'We're still working out what to do. We don't know who we can trust. You're right, it's all very hard to believe. Julius Clark is a rich, powerful tycoon. The police would think we were raving mad, accusing him of kidnapping and drugging people.'

'Then what are you going to do?'

'Gather information, probe deeper, find some real, hard proof to back up our case and then we'll go public with it.'

Max eyed Redmond anxiously. He'd come here to talk to him, but it looked now as if that wasn't going to work. Still, he had to at least try.

'I don't want to upset your brother again,' he went on, 'but would you mind if I asked him a few questions?'

'Well, I don't know . . .' Alicia replied hesitantly.

'Please, I'll be careful what I say.'

Alicia nodded. 'All right, go ahead. But you must stop if he shows signs of distress.'

Max got up from the sofa and moved closer to Redmond, perching on the arm of Consuela's chair so that his eyes were on a level with Redmond's. He needed to see his face. Redmond might strugge to speak, but there were other ways of communicating with him, of gauging his response to questions.

'Hi,' Max said. 'My name's Max Cassidy. I'd like to ask you about your trip to Peru. Can you remember what happened there?'

Redmond didn't respond. He didn't look at Max, gave no sign that he even knew he was there, let alone that he'd heard the question.

Max tried again. 'Were you kidnapped? Did someone abduct you and take you to' – Max wanted to avoid saying *Isla de Sombra* – 'to that place – that island?'

Redmond still didn't look at Max. His eyes were dull and empty, rolling slightly in their sockets.

Max wasn't going to give up. He decided to try some of the names of the other prisoners who'd been kept on Shadow Island; see if he got a reaction.

'Have you ever heard of James Abbott?'

No response.

'Or Narang Anwar?'

Nothing. Not a blink.

'What about Erik Blomkvist?'

There was a flicker of something in Redmond's eyes. A tiny spark that flared for a moment and was then extinguished. Max felt a tingle of excitement. He'd got a reaction. Slight, but it was there nonetheless.

'You knew Erik?'

The spark came again, and this time it didn't die. Max knew he had to nurse it as if he were tending a fire, keep it glowing, blow gently on it until it grew into a flame.

'What do you know about him? Was he kidnapped too? Why was Erik taken to Shadow Island?'

Redmond's eyes turned towards Max, vague to start with, but then becoming more focused. He licked his lips and gave what sounded like a groan, a low rumble that came from deep inside him. There was emotion in the sound, but what was it? Discomfort? Pain? Something else?

Alicia started to intervene. 'I don't think this—'

'No, please, wait,' Max broke in. 'Listen, he's trying to say something.'

In the midst of all the incoherent noises, Max thought he could detect the outline of a word. No, *two* words.

'Eeee urr. Eeee urr.'

What was he saying?

'Eeee urr.'

What was it? Max ran the sounds around inside his head, trying to match the pattern to a known word or phrase. Something was missing. A letter; maybe several letters. *Add a consonant*, he told himself. *See what you get*. But which consonant?

'*Beee urr . . . deee urr . . . feee urr . . .*' He tried a few more. '*Seee urr . . .*'

The light flashed in Redmond's eyes.

'*Seee urr*,' Max repeated. '*See her*. Is that it?'

Then it dawned on him. It wasn't 'see her', but 'cedar'.

'Cedar? Cedar Alliance? That's what you're saying, isn't it? Cedar Alliance.'

He saw in Redmond's face that he had guessed correctly.

'What about it?' Max asked eagerly. 'Do you know what it is? Did Erik know?' He leaned towards Redmond, gazing intently into his eyes. 'I need to know. What is the Cedar Alliance?'

The moans continued, coloured now by an undertone of distress. Redmond's frustration and anger were getting too much for him.

Alicia, sensitive to all his moods, stepped in to protect him. 'That's enough,' she said sharply. 'You must stop, I insist.'

'OK, I'm sorry,' Max said softly. He pulled back, feeling frustrated himself now. The answer he was seeking was there in Redmond Ashworth-Ames, only it was buried too deep for him to find.

'Do you know what the Cedar Alliance is?' Max asked Alicia. 'Has he mentioned it before?'

'I've never heard of it. I think perhaps you should go now. Redmond needs a period of quiet before I put him to bed.'

'Yes, of course, we understand.' Consuela stood up and picked up her bag. 'Thank you so much for allowing us to visit. I'm sorry if we've upset your brother.'

'If he says anything about Shadow Island or the Cedar Alliance,' Max said, 'please would you get in touch with me? You have my number. In the meantime, could you tell his doctors that you suspect he might have been given a drug called Episuderon. It might help them treat him.'

'Episuderon?'

'That's right. But please don't say who told you about the drug – not for the time being anyway. And please keep our visit this evening a secret.'

'Is all this – this mystery – really necessary?'

'I think so,' Max said. 'If we find out any more about what happened to your brother, we'll let you know. Thank you for seeing us.'

He headed for the door. Before he left, he took a last look at Redmond, who was once more slumped sideways in his wheelchair, his arms dangling loosely down, his head flopping over. His jaw was moving as if he were chewing, and he was babbling quietly to himself, his eyes lifeless, his mind shut away behind a door that might never again be opened.

Max felt a chill pass through him. He had no doubt that Redmond's condition had been caused by

Episuderon, the same drug that Max's father had been given on Shadow Island. *Was my dad like this at some point?* Max wondered. *Is that why he disappeared for two years? Why he didn't get in touch with me or come home?* Alexander had mentioned the drug in the letter he'd left for Max in Santo Domingo. He'd said that he had good days when he could think clearly, and bad days when his mind seemed to go blank.

Max couldn't bear the thought of his father being sick and incapacitated, unable to speak or walk and with no one to look after him. It would have been easy to get upset, but that wasn't Max's way. He wasn't going to let it get him down; he was going to do something about it. More than ever now, he was determined to track his father down.

He was very quiet as they walked towards the car. Consuela put her arm around his shoulders and gave him a quick squeeze. She had an almost telepathic ability to sense his thoughts, to empathize with how he was feeling.

'I'll drive back,' Chris said.

'What if the surveillance team is outside the house again?' Consuela asked.

'We'll swap over before we get there. You can drive the last bit and I'll lie down on the floor in the back.'

Consuela handed Chris the keys. She was happy to

let him take over. Seeing Redmond Ashworth-Ames had upset her as well as Max. She didn't feel up to concentrating on the long drive home along unfamiliar roads.

Max climbed into the back seat and slouched down in the corner, still thinking about his father.

It was dark now. A bat flitted by overhead, just visible in the light from the windows of the house. Alicia Ashworth-Ames was silhouetted in the doorway. She raised a hand briefly to wave them goodbye, then turned away and closed the door.

They headed back through the village and down a narrow, winding country lane that had dense woodland on both sides, branches overhanging the road so that it felt as if they were driving through a tunnel. The headlamps picked out the trunks of beech and oak trees, their leaves shimmering in the bright light. A shape darted across the road in the distance, out beyond the reach of the headlamps – a fallow deer moving from one part of the forest to another.

Max felt as if he were in a cocoon, protected from the outside world. There was something unsettling, threatening even, about the woods, about their dark, hidden reaches, the wild animals creeping through the undergrowth. But Max was cut off from all that, safe inside the metal shell of the car. The low, monotonous hum of the engine was comforting. So too were Consuela and Chris in the front.

He closed his eyes and rested his head on the seat back, feeling the swaying motion as the car turned through the bends, left then right, then left again. It was soporific. Max felt himself getting drowsy.

Then he suddenly became aware of another sound – a louder, more intrusive engine noise. He opened his eyes. The interior of the car was lit up by the headlights of a vehicle behind. Max twisted round in his seat and looked out of the rear window. The vehicle was recklessly close, only a couple of metres back. Its headlights were high and dazzling. Behind the beams Max made out the shape of a big black four-wheel-drive Range Rover.

'Jeez, what's that guy doing?' Chris said, averting his eyes from the glare of the headlights in his rear-view mirror. He slowed a little. 'Go on, mate, go past if you want to.'

The Range Rover pulled out to overtake. Max watched it come alongside them. It had tinted windows so he couldn't see who was inside. He waited for it to zoom ahead, but it held its position next to them as if it didn't have the speed to get past.

'What the hell is he playing at?' Chris shouted.

The road was descending a steep hill now, twisting

and turning through the woods. Chris braked. Max expected the Range Rover to surge away from them, but it stayed level. The driver was braking too.

Max felt a jolt of alarm. Something wasn't right. Chris knew it as well. He swore under his breath and braked again. The driver of the Range Rover must have been anticipating it for he also slowed. The two vehicles sped down the hill only half a metre apart. Max looked across the gap. The Range Rover was much bigger and heavier than Consuela's Nissan. It seemed to tower over them, dark and menacing.

Then, suddenly, the Range Rover veered towards them. Max could hear the harsh roar of its engine. Its front wing smashed into the side of the Nissan. The Nissan swerved. Consuela screamed. Max hung on tight to the door handle next to him, his heart hammering.

Chris jammed on the brakes, but the other driver did the same. The two vehicles collided again. There was an ear-piercing screech of metal scraping against metal. This time, the Range Rover didn't pull away. It kept on coming, forcing the Nissan closer and closer to the edge of the road.

Chris turned the steering wheel, trying to hold his line, but the Range Rover was too powerful. It was like a tank, massive and unstoppable.

The road started to bend sharply to the right. The

Range Rover stayed in the middle of the carriageway. The two vehicles were still touching. Chris struggled desperately to force the other car away, but it was no use. The Range Rover increased the pressure, pushing the Nissan sideways. The screech of metal intensified. It was like a circular saw cutting through steel plate. Max could see the side of the other vehicle through his window, could see the door beside him starting to buckle with the pressure.

'Hang on!' Chris yelled.

He stamped hard on the brakes. The Nissan's wheels locked and it skidded, the tyres burning. Max lurched forward, but the seatbelt held him. The Range Rover shot past, tilting over almost onto two wheels as it careered round the right-hand bend. Chris wrenched the wheel over, fighting to control the Nissan, which was sliding rapidly to the left. For a second Max thought they were going to make it, then the nearside wheels hit the grassy verge and lost their grip. The car skidded over the edge and slithered twenty metres into the woods, narrowly missing a beech tree before coming to a halt in a clump of bushes.

Max sagged back in his seat and panted for breath. He felt sick. His pulse was throbbing violently.

'You OK, Max?' Chris called out.

'Yes.'

'Consuela?'

'I think so.'

Max pushed at his door. The metal was so crushed it wouldn't open. He slid across to the other side and got out.

There was no sign of the Range Rover. It had vanished into the night. The Nissan's headlights were still on. Max walked around the car and looked at the damage. The front wing and offside doors were twisted and bent, the bare metal showing through the scraped paintwork.

They'd been lucky. The edge of the road where they'd come off was soft earth which had helped slow the car down, and the forest here was less dense, the trees more widely spaced than up the hill. If they'd smashed into an oak, they would certainly have been badly injured, maybe even killed. Chris's driving, his quick reactions, had also helped save them. Max dreaded to think what might have happened with a less skilful driver at the wheel.

He leaned back on the car, trembling from head to toe, wondering if he was going to throw up. He took a few deep breaths, trying to shake off the nausea, and thought about what had just occurred, visualizing the Range Rover smashing into them, forcing them off the road. It could only have lasted a few seconds, but it seemed an eternity as it was happening. He hadn't noticed the Range Rover's number plate. He hadn't seen the driver. But whoever it was, Max was certain of one thing: he had been trying to kill them.

SEVEN

It was gone midnight by the time they got home. Extricating the car from the woods had proved more difficult than they'd expected. Chris had tried reversing it back out onto the road, but the ground was too soft. The wheels had simply spun round and round, digging the Nissan even deeper into the earth. It had been no better with Consuela in the driver's seat, Chris and Max pushing with all their combined strength. The car was stuck fast.

They called Consuela's breakdown service and had to wait an hour and a half for a van to come out to them. The mechanic – a large, cheerful man with a red, weather-beaten complexion – hitched the Nissan to a tow rope and pulled it out in ten minutes. He inspected the bodywork, curious about the damaged doors and paintwork. Chris told him the truth – said they'd been hit by another car and left it at that. The mechanic asked if they wanted to report the collision to the police. He seemed surprised when they said no, but didn't press them further. He checked the Nissan over to make sure it was fit to drive and sent them on their way.

Chris drove. Consuela was still too shaken by the crash to feel up to dealing with the roads and the other traffic. At the back of all their minds was the fear that something else might happen, that the Range Rover might be waiting for them up ahead, but in the end it was an uneventful journey back to London.

Half a mile from their house, Consuela took the wheel again while Chris lay down out of sight on the floor. Max kept a sharp eye out for the Toyota Avensis as they came down their street – and there it was, parked in its usual place, two men in the front.

Consuela reversed into the drive and Chris sneaked unseen into the garage and from there into the house. Max and Consuela went in through the front door. Consuela locked and bolted it behind them. Chris was already in the hall. He ran softly upstairs to check all the rooms, then came back down and gave them the thumbs-up: everything seemed normal, no intruders lurking in dark corners. They were all nervous. Although they were back in their home again, they felt vulnerable. Was the house safe? Could someone break in and attack them? They'd already decided that Chris would spend the night on the upstairs landing rather than in the basement. Max and Consuela would sleep a lot more soundly knowing that he was just outside their bedroom doors.

But Max couldn't sleep. The crash was too fresh, too vivid in his memory. *Someone had tried to kill them.* Was that really what had happened? It had certainly felt like it at the time, but maybe the intention had simply been to frighten them, to warn them off – a more obvious, more violent reminder of Rupert Penhall's warning not to meddle in things that didn't concern them.

And Max *was* frightened. The collision had terrified him. Where had the Range Rover come from? How did the driver know that Max and Chris and Consuela would be on the road near Henley at that particular time? Max was sure they hadn't been followed from London. He'd been careful when he first rang the Ashworth-Ames' house, ensured that he was using an untraceable mobile phone. That left only two other possible explanations: the Ashworth-Ames' phone line was being monitored so Max's call would have been recorded at their end, or their house was being watched – or both. A surveillance team in London, another one out in Oxfordshire – that was a serious operation requiring a lot of manpower. But who was behind it? Julius Clark? Rupert Penhall? Penhall claimed to be linked to the government. Would the British government really have authorized an attempt to kill Max and his companions?

He gradually dozed off into a troubled sleep that was

filled with nightmares about the collision and Redmond Ashworth-Ames. Conscious or unconscious, the same thoughts, the same sights tormented him, and he was glad when morning came and he could get up.

Chris was in a sleeping bag on the landing. He appeared to be asleep, but as Max stepped around him, he opened his eyes and gave Max an enquiring look – as if to ask, *Are you OK?*

Max nodded and went downstairs. Chris joined him in the kitchen a couple of minutes later and they had breakfast together in silence. It was Saturday. Max had a show at the London Cabaret Club that evening – his last of the current run. He and Consuela would need to go over there in the afternoon to prepare for the performance, but the morning was free. Max had an idea how he was going to fill the time. It had come to him during the night, when he'd been lying awake thinking about Henley and a phrase had come into his head that wouldn't go away: *Know your enemy.*

The phrase presumably had its origins in warfare, but Max had heard it applied to other things – to sporting contests, for example. It was a good maxim to apply to almost anything in life. Prepare yourself for your opponents, find out as much about them as you possibly can, and then you stand a better chance of beating them.

Know your enemy.
Know Rupert Penhall.
Know Julius Clark.

Max took Consuela and Chris into the basement and told them that he wanted to visit the local library and go online to search for information. He couldn't do it from home because their computer was almost certainly compromised, their emails and Internet activity being monitored by the surveillance team. But the library had terminals that would be safe to use.

Chris came with him. After the previous evening, he wasn't going to let Max go anywhere unaccompanied. They went over the wall at the bottom of the garden and took a long, circuitous route to the library just in case anyone was following them. Max sat down at a free terminal and clicked onto the Internet. Chris stood close by, where he could watch both Max and the library doors. Max typed in Rupert Penhall's name first and wasn't surprised to find nothing about him. Whoever Penhall was, he would make absolutely sure the details of his life were kept secret.

Max tried Julius Clark next and got nearly four million results – far too many to even begin searching through them. He added 'businessman' after Clark's name and narrowed the search down to 98,000. That was still too many to handle so he made it 'billionaire businessman'. He was down to fewer than 5,000 results now. He scrolled down through the entries. The search engine had focused on the word 'billionaire' as much as on Clark's name, and most of the entries concerned very rich people other than Julius Clark.

Max kept going through the pages. For a man as wealthy and apparently influential as Clark, there seemed to be very little about him on the Net. He clearly kept a very low profile.

Then something came up: *The Shadowy World of Reclusive Tycoon Julius Clark*. That had to be him. Max clicked on the entry and a newspaper article from the *London News Chronicle* appeared on the screen. It was a feature from the paper's financial section, written two months earlier by a journalist named Dan Kingston. Alongside the article was a grainy photograph of a man in a dark suit with rimless spectacles, which looked as if it had been taken with a long lens on a very dull day. It was a poor image, but Max had no trouble recognizing the man he'd met on Shadow Island. He gave a shudder. Clark's face didn't bring back pleasant memories.

Max read through the article. It was a thin piece, low on real, substantiated facts. The journalist had obviously struggled to find solid information about Clark and had resorted to speculation and rumour instead. But despite its shortcomings, the feature managed to give an effective impression of the billionaire businessman. 'A recluse', 'publicity-shy', 'secretive' were some of the ways in which he was described. 'Fabulously wealthy', 'well-connected' and 'utterly ruthless' were others.

Clark's background was vague. No one seemed to know where he'd been born or where he'd spent his youth. Even his age was unclear. 'Somewhere in his fifties' was about as close as anyone could get. His nationality too was uncertain. He might have been American, or possibly Canadian. There were rumours that he was really Swiss, and more than one source claimed he was Russian. The truth was he had no nationality, no ties to one particular country. Like many billionaires, he was effectively stateless. He lived out his life on a global stage, travelling ceaselessly from one country to another, never staying anywhere for long. He had houses in London, New York, Zurich and Moscow, and a luxury beachfront estate in the Bahamas where, it was said, he entertained politicians and business leaders from around the world.

No one was very sure what his political affiliations were because his whole life was shrouded in secrecy. His business interests were equally shadowy. Max had trouble understanding this part of the article. He didn't really know what 'shell corporations' or 'offshore holding companies' were, but he got the general idea that Clark had fiendishly clever ways of hiding his money-making activities. The only facts that everyone seemed to agree on were that Clark was a very private man, had a network of powerful political and business friends and was extremely rich – his personal wealth was estimated at somewhere between ten and twenty billion US dollars, depending on which source you believed.

Max printed off a copy of the article, tucked it safely away in his pocket, then he and Chris left the library.

His show in the evening went well. Max felt safe in the theatre and it was a relief to have something to take his mind off his worries; something over which he had absolute control. If only life were as simple as a stage show.

The next morning he went to visit his mother in prison. Consuela drove them out through the sprawling suburbs of London and on into Suffolk. The Avensis followed them all the way, but Max didn't let it unsettle him. He was sure they wouldn't try anything in broad daylight. He and Consuela didn't talk much. Max was preoccupied with his own thoughts. This would be the first time he'd seen his mum since his trip to Central America and he had a lot to tell her. He'd been looking forward to his visit all week, impatient to see her.

They parked in the fenced car park outside the perimeter wall of Levington prison and went in together. Max was used to the tight security measures – the bag checks, the metal detectors, the pat-down searches – but they annoyed him more than ever today. *Just let me in*, he wanted to yell at the warders, with their officious manner and bunches of keys dangling from their belts. *I'm not a criminal. And nor is my mum. She's innocent. She shouldn't be in here.*

They sat down at one of the tables in the visiting area and waited. Max fidgeted, unable to contain his irritation. It was all so humiliating, so wrong. Helen Cassidy was serving a twenty-year sentence for murder, for killing her husband in Santo Domingo. Her conviction – based on the thinnest of evidence, presented to a corrupt court in which Max was certain the judge had been bribed – had always been preposterous. It was even more so now that Max knew his father wasn't dead. The letter he'd found was proof of that. *But you don't have that letter any longer*, Max reminded himself. *Rupert Penhall has it.* The thought made his blood boil.

'Max, sit still,' Consuela said. 'The warders are watching us.'

'I don't care,' Max said defiantly. 'They can all go to hell.'

'Hey, calm down.'

'Why should I? I'm sick of being bossed around by them. *Do this, do that, take off your shoes, empty your pockets.* They're just a bunch of pompous bullies.'

'Keep your voice down,' Consuela hissed. 'If they hear you, they'll ask us to leave. And how would that help your mum?'

Max muttered something under his breath, but he didn't argue with Consuela. He knew she was right.

It was another five minutes before the door at the far end of the room opened and a group of about ten female prisoners came out, one warder leading the way, another bringing up the rear. Max scanned the group eagerly, searching for his mum. She was looking for him too. When their eyes met, her face lit up with delight.

Max leaped to his feet. He wanted to run across the room and meet her, but he knew the rules. Visitors had to stay at their tables. The prisoners were brought to them at the beginning of the visiting session and escorted away afterwards.

'Max!' Helen Cassidy threw her arms wide and hugged him tightly.

Max hugged her back, fighting to hold in the tears.

He hated this place. Hated it with a vengeance. He wanted to destroy it, to rip it apart brick by brick with his bare hands for what it had done to his mother.

'How are you, Mum?'

'I'm OK. You?'

'Fine.'

Helen embraced Consuela and sat down with them around the small table. She took Max's hand and squeezed it. 'I'm so glad to see you both. It seems ages since your last visit.'

She was looking thinner, Max thought. She'd always been slim, but now she was verging on the scrawny. Her complexion was pale and pasty from the poor prison food, and her hair was getting more and more grey. In her pre-prison days she'd coloured it, but not now. Hair dye wasn't allowed in Levington.

'What've you been up to?' Helen said brightly. 'How's school?'

'School's OK,' Max replied. 'But a lot's happened since I last saw you.'

'What do you mean?'

'We've been to Santo Domingo.'

Helen frowned. 'To *Santo Domingo*? What on earth for?'

'To find evidence to prove that you're innocent.'

'Oh, Max, you're such an optimist. What evidence?

It was two years ago. How can you find evidence now?'

Max took hold of his mother's hands and gripped them hard. 'Mum, I want you to prepare yourself for a shock. Dad's alive.'

Helen stared at him. Her whole body had gone rigid. '*What?*' Her voice was just a whisper.

'He's alive.'

'Max—'

'Let me finish, Mum. I found a letter he wrote – there's other stuff too. But I need to start at the beginning.'

He told her about their trip to Central America, about their ordeal on Shadow Island – everything that had happened. He spoke quietly so they weren't over-heard by the warders patrolling the room, and quickly, one eye on the clock on the wall. He had a lot to say and there wasn't much time.

Helen was silent when he finished. She didn't move, just looked at him in astonishment. Then tears welled up in her eyes. 'Oh, Max,' she murmured. 'Is this true? I can't believe it. Not after all this time.'

'It's true,' Max said.

'I was there,' Consuela added. 'I saw the letter.'

'You're sure it was from your dad?'

'It was his handwriting. It was from him all right.'

'What did he say? Where is he? What's happened to him?'

The letter had been taken away by Penhall, but Max had read it so many times he knew every word off by heart. He recited it to his mother as if he had the text there on the table in front of him.

Helen listened, tears pouring down her face. Max didn't like to see his mother crying, but these were tears of joy. Consuela found some tissues in her bag and passed them to Helen, who dabbed at her eyes and cheeks.

'He wrote that?' Helen said hoarsely. 'Alex said that?'

'Those were his exact words,' Max replied.

'I don't understand. Where's he been for the past two years?'

'I think he's been seriously ill. The drug he was given, it affects the mind and memory. He wrote me that letter recently, so I think – I hope – he's getting better, but I don't know for sure.'

'Then why hasn't he come home?'

'He said in his letter that he had work to do. He's frightened that if he surfaces, he will be killed.'

'Who would want to kill him?'

'The same person who drugged him – Julius Clark.'

'But why? Why would a wealthy businessman want to kill your father?'

'That's what I'm trying to find out,' Max said.

He waited a moment. One of the warders was

coming past – a big, hefty woman with the build of an Olympic shot-putter. She didn't give Helen a second glance. The prison staff were used to tears at visiting time: those precious contacts with family and friends were emotional moments for all concerned.

Max lowered his voice. 'Mum, I need to ask you about Dad.'

'Ask me what?'

'About his life. Julius Clark told me that Dad had a secret life; that his travels abroad to do his show were just a cover for other things. But he didn't say *what* other things.'

'That's ridiculous,' Helen said. 'He didn't have a secret life. He was an escapologist – you know that.'

'But was he something else as well?'

'Like what?'

'I don't know. A spy perhaps? Spies have covers, don't they? They pretend to be something they're not to hide what they're really doing.'

'A *spy*?' Helen said incredulously. 'You mean working for MI6, or the CIA, or something like that? Come *on*, Max.'

'What did Julius Clark mean then?'

'I have no idea.' Helen looked at Consuela, who had been Alexander Cassidy's stage assistant before she took on the role for Max. 'You travelled everywhere with him, Consuela. Did you see any evidence of a secret life?'

Consuela shook her head. 'I don't think so. Of course, I wasn't with him every hour of the day. We had free time on our trips. We didn't do the same things. I don't know what Alex did when I went off shopping or sightseeing.'

'Well, he did something,' Max said. 'He wasn't just an escapologist. That's why Clark had him abducted, then injected him with a brainwashing drug. Dad was some kind of threat to him, that's what I think.'

'A *threat*?' Helen said. 'In what way?'

'I don't know. There are a lot of things I don't know.'

The hefty warder walked past again. 'Two minutes!' she called out.

Max glanced at the clock. He was running out of time and there was still one other thing he had to ask his mum.

'This Cedar Alliance that Dad mentioned in his letter. Do you know what it is?'

Helen gave him a blank look. 'No.'

'Are you sure? He never said anything about it?'

'Not that I can recall. I'm sorry.'

Max took hold of his mother's hands once more. 'We'll have to go soon, but with any luck we won't have to do this many more times. Dad's alive, and I'm going to find him. I'm going to bring him home and get you out of here, Mum.'

Helen was crying again now, but smiling through her tears. All around them, the other visitors were finishing their conversations, getting ready to leave. Max stood up and gave his mother a long hug.

'He's alive. Thank God!' Helen whispered in his ear.

Max pulled away reluctantly. He always found these meetings distressing. His mum had spent the first eighteen months of her sentence in a Santo Domingo jail, but since her transfer to the UK six months ago, Max had come to see her every week. That was twenty-four visits. Each time he left, he felt as if he was abandoning her, leaving nothing behind except pain and loneliness. But this time was different: he was leaving her with hope.

In the afternoon, Max went upstairs to his room to finish off some homework – a history project on the First World War that had been hanging over him for weeks. But he struggled to concentrate on life in the trenches when his mother was foremost in his mind. He could still see her crying, could still feel the touch of her hands, hear the sound of her voice in his ears. The injustice of her situation made him furious.

But before he could get her out of prison, he needed

proof that his dad was alive; proof that a court would accept. He had to get his file back from Rupert Penhall.

Max's mobile rang. He picked it up off the desk. 'Hello?'

'Don't say my name. You know who this is, don't you?' a man's voice said.

Max went rigid. It was Chief Superintendent Richardson. 'Yes.'

'We need to meet. Can you make tomorrow evening?'

'Yes.'

'The same time and place as before. And be careful, Max.'

The line went dead. Max kept the phone in his hand for a few seconds, staring at the illuminated screen. *Well, that was short and to the point*, he thought. Not the warm, friendly chief superintendent he was used to. But what troubled Max more was not what Richardson had said, nor his uncharacteristically brusque manner, but the underlying tone and implications of the call. *Don't say my name . . . Be careful, Max.* The detective had sounded worried. More than worried. Max wondered whether he had imagined it, but Chief Superintendent Richardson had sounded scared.

EIGHT

Be careful, Max.

The chief superintendent's words echoed round and round inside Max's head all the next day. What had Richardson meant? Be careful of what? Be careful of whom? Did he suspect that someone was listening in to the call – that someone might follow them to their meeting and eavesdrop on their conversation?

Max thought about it obsessively at school, trying to work out what he should do. If a senior police officer like Richardson was worried – or even scared – then Max knew that something serious was going on and he had to take every precaution to make sure that their meeting was kept a secret.

During last period – a chemistry lesson in the science laboratories – Max decided to confide in Andy.

'You're kidding me?' Andy said in disbelief, after Max had told him about the bugs in his house, the men out at the front watching his comings and goings.

'I wish I were,' Max replied. 'I'm being spied on. I

think they follow me to school and back. That's why I need your help.'

'My help? How?'

'I've got a meeting after school, in town. It's vital that I'm not followed to it. Can you give me cover? You and maybe some of the footie guys? Get me out of the building so no one sees me?'

'Wow, this is serious stuff, isn't it?'

Max nodded. 'You don't know the half of it. I can't tell you any more, I'm afraid. I don't want to put you in danger.'

Andy stared at him. 'You're not kidding about that either, are you?'

'No.'

Andy glanced around the laboratory. 'Leave it to me,' he said. 'I'll rope in Sam, Matt, Joe and a few others. I'll ask Lucy too. She'll get some of the girls to come along.'

At the final bell Max collected up his books and went down to the school's front entrance. Eight or nine of his classmates accompanied him. They waited for the crush to build up in the foyer – hundreds of kids all pushing and shoving to get out – then moved off in a group, Max in the middle, the others surrounding him in a protective wall. He ducked down a little, so his head was hidden by his bodyguards as they left the building. Other pupils swarmed around them, all wearing identical black trousers and sweat-tops. If anyone was waiting outside, watching for him to come out, they would have a difficult job identifying him in the seething mass of teenagers.

The crowd surged through the school gates onto the street, splitting up into smaller groups, some going left, some right, some flooding across the road in a stream that was so dense and determined that the traffic was forced to give way to it. Max's friends stayed in a huddle around him, shielding him from view while they crossed the road, then held their positions to escort him down a side street and into the mouth of a pedestrians-only passage that cut between two houses.

'You're in the clear,' Andy said. 'Go!'

The cluster of friends broke apart at the front and Max sprinted clear, calling out his thanks as he dashed off along the passage. He was half a mile away before he slowed to a walk. He glanced back at intervals, but he saw no sign of anyone following him.

Ten minutes later, he reached the nearest tube station. Waiting on the platform, he looked carefully at all the other people around him, checking to see if anyone seemed to be watching him. He saw nothing to arouse his suspicions. The people all appeared to be wrapped up in their own affairs – reading the paper, talking to friends. Max noted faces and clothes and anything else he could, filing the information away in his head so that he would recognize these individuals if he saw any of them later in his journey.

Avoiding the more direct route, he went south a few stops before changing from the Northern to the Victoria Line at Euston. Then, at Victoria, he changed trains again and headed east on the Circle Line. At Westminster he got off and did what Chris Moncrieffe had done that day he'd been tailed from the airport – he swapped platforms and went back the way he'd come. At St James's Park he let all the other disembarking passengers off ahead of him and waited until the doors were just about to close before jumping down onto the platform. He loitered for a few minutes, but saw no familiar faces. As sure as he could be that he wasn't being followed, he went up to the surface and walked to the café near New Scotland Yard where he'd met Chief Superintendent Richardson the previous Friday.

It was twenty-five past four. The detective wasn't there yet. Max found a vacant table at the rear of the café and sat down with his back to the wall so that he could watch the entrance. On the dot of four thirty, Richardson came in. He saw Max immediately, but didn't go across to his table. Instead, he went to the counter and ordered a cup of tea, a Coke and two brownies. While he was waiting to pay, he turned round and surveyed the room. His gaze seemed casual, but Max knew he was taking note of every person in the café – just as Max himself had done when he'd first come in.

'Hello, Max. How are you?' Richardson said, putting his tray down on the table and pulling out a chair.

'I'm fine,' Max replied.

'I thought you could probably do with a drink and something to eat. I know how it is with you teenagers – always hungry. My two boys were, anyway.'

'Thanks. One of your sons is a policeman too, isn't he?' Max had a vague recollection of the fact from one of those dinner parties Richardson and his wife had attended at their house a few years earlier.

'That's right. Kevin. He's a detective sergeant in the Met now. Doing well for himself. My other boy's a teacher at a comprehensive in Nottingham. I don't envy him. Given a choice between a class of unruly teenagers and a bunch of hardened criminals, I'd choose the criminals every time.'

The chief superintendent seemed friendly enough, but Max detected a certain distance in his manner. He didn't seem as warm as last time. He wasn't smiling.

'Good day at school?' Richardson asked.

'Yeah, OK.'

'How was your journey into town?'

'That was OK too.'

'No problems?'

'No. I did as you advised. I was careful.'

'How careful?'

'I changed tube trains a few times, doubled back, kept an eye out for tails. I'm pretty sure I wasn't followed.'

Richardson broke open a sachet of sugar and added it to his tea. He stirred the drink slowly for a few seconds, then looked straight at Max. 'That's reassuring,' he said softly. 'But it's also a little worrying. You seem to know a lot about losing tails. You're a fourteen-year-old schoolboy, Max. Why would anyone be following you?'

The question made Max uneasy. 'Well . . .' He fumbled for a reply. 'I suppose it was what you said on the phone. You know, not giving your name, not mentioning the place where we were to meet, telling me to be careful. It made me nervous. Why would you do that? Why would you tell me to be careful?'

The chief superintendent smiled for the first time – a twitch of the lips that came and went in an instant. 'Answer a question with a question of your own, eh?' he said. 'That's an old tactic for avoiding awkward enquiries.'

'I don't understand,' Max said.

'I think you do. I've been a copper for a long time. Too long, I sometimes think. I've interviewed thousands of people – criminals, victims, witnesses. I have a nose for people who have something to hide. Have you got something to hide, Max?'

Max didn't reply. He took a bite of his brownie and drank some Coke to give himself time to think.

Richardson's mouth twitched again. 'That's another old tactic too. You could eat a ton of brownies, drink a thousand bottles of Coke, but at the end of the day I'd still be sitting here waiting for an answer.'

Max swallowed. 'I don't have anything to hide.'

'Don't you?' Richardson said. 'I want you to be straight with me. I can't help you unless you come clean and tell me what's going on.'

'I don't know what's going on.'

'That's your third evasive reply.'

'It's the truth. I *don't* know.'

'Maybe you don't know everything, but you *do* know something, don't you?' Richardson gazed at him seriously. 'You're not sure whether to trust me. Is that it?' he said.

'I don't know.'

'You can trust me, Max. I promise you that.'

The detective took a sip of tea and wiped his moustache with the edge of a forefinger. 'OK, I'll do you a deal,' he went on. 'I'll tell you what I know, and then, in return, you can tell me what you know. Agreed?'

Max hesitated. Then he nodded. Richardson was helping him. The least he could do was be honest with him. 'OK.'

'The search of your house first,' the chief super-intendent said. 'I've made some enquiries and discovered that the warrant was granted to the Met's Special Branch. Do you know what that is?'

'Not really.'

'Special Branch are a sort of political police. They deal with things like terrorism and subversion – people who want to overthrow the state. They work very closely with the Security Service, better known as MI5.'

Max's mouth went suddenly dry. He gulped down a mouthful of Coke. 'MI5 are interested in me?' he asked anxiously.

'So it would seem.'

'And Rupert Penhall? How does he fit in?'

'Mr Penhall is an interesting character. I had great difficulty in finding out anything about him. The only thing I know for certain is that he's bad news.'

'Bad news?' Max repeated.

'For you, and for me. Let me tell you what happened when I started asking questions about Penhall. I was called in to see the commissioner – he's the overall head of the Met – who told me to drop my enquiries. Well, he didn't tell me, he ordered me. He said that if I carried on asking questions, my career would be in jeopardy. Basically, he threatened to sack me. Now, in thirty-five years as a police officer, that's never happened to me before. Rupert Penhall, whoever he is, is clearly a man with friends in very high places. Which is why I was so mysterious on the phone. Partly for my own safety, and partly for yours, Max. I think it's better that no one knows we're having this meeting.'

Richardson broke off for a moment to look at the door. Two new customers were just coming in – two women, both elderly, both carrying bags of shopping. The detective relaxed – nothing to worry about there – and turned back to Max.

'It's your turn now. What exactly are you up to, Max?'

Max paused to collect his thoughts. Where did he begin? How much should he tell the chief super-intendent? How much should he leave out? It was a tricky one to call, and in the end he decided to be open and tell him everything.

'Last time we met,' Max began, 'I said I'd been to Santo Domingo to look for evidence to prove that my mum didn't kill my dad. I said her trial was rigged, the judge was corrupt, but I didn't tell you the most important bit. I found evidence that my dad's alive.'

Richardson gave a start of surprise. '*Alive?*'

Max nodded. 'I found a letter he'd left hidden for me. A letter written only a few weeks ago. He said he'd been ill for the past two years, had lost his memory. He was a lot better now, he said, but he couldn't come out of hiding because he was frightened he'd be killed.'

'*Killed?* Killed by whom?' Richardson asked.

'He didn't say. But I think he meant a rich business-man named Julius Clark.' Max paused again. 'This is going to sound incredible, but please believe me, it's all true.'

He told the detective about Shadow Island, about finding his father's medical file, about his confrontation with Julius Clark, about Chris Moncrieffe, about their eventual escape from the island – the whole story. As he finished, it felt as if a load had been lifted from his shoulders. Richardson was a police officer, a senior officer with a lot of authority. Having him on his side was an immense relief.

The chief superintendent was silent for a while. Max ate the rest of his brownie while he waited for a response. Then Richardson exhaled deeply.

'You're right, it does sound incredible.'

'But it all happened,' Max said quickly. 'I swear.'

'I believe you, Max, don't worry. But I've never heard of Julius Clark. Who is he?'

'Some kind of international tycoon, a billionaire. He's very secretive. I couldn't find out much about him. But he's got lots of connections with politicians.'

The detective fell silent again. He stroked his bristly moustache pensively, staring down at his half-finished cup of tea. 'I don't like the sound of any of this,' he said slowly. 'We're poking around in some very murky waters, and we don't know what we're going to find at the bottom.'

'There's something else you should know,' Max said.

He told the chief superintendent about their visit to Redmond Ashworth-Ames and their crash on the way home.

Richardson sat bolt upright in alarm. 'My God, Max! Someone tried to *kill* you?'

'That's how it seemed.'

'Did you get the number of the other vehicle?'

'No. It was dark, I was scared – everything happened so fast. I wasn't thinking about things like number plates.'

'You should have reported it to the police. They might have been able to trace the car. Why didn't you?'

Max hesitated. 'There were reasons,' he said awkwardly. 'Chris was driving. The police would have wanted his name, they'd have asked questions. And Penhall is after Chris. He asked about him when he searched our house. I think part of the reason for the search was to find Chris.'

'Why?'

'I don't know. Maybe because he's an ex-soldier and Penhall thinks he's more of a threat than Consuela and me.'

'Does Penhall know about Shadow Island?'

'I'm not sure. I think he must. I think Julius Clark must have high-up connections in the British government. Nothing else makes sense.'

'You mean Penhall is protecting Clark, working indirectly for him?'

'Something like that.'

Richardson swore softly, almost inaudibly. He was tense. The café door clicked open again and he glanced round hurriedly. But it was only a young, smartly dressed woman coming in. The detective gave her a cursory inspection, then turned his attention back to Max.

'What do you know about Chris Moncrieffe?'

'Only what I've told you. He was working for an environmental charity in the Amazon just before he was taken to Shadow Island, but he used to be a soldier, and also worked in the security business, whatever that is.'

'Security?' Richardson said. 'That can mean almost

anything. Bodyguarding, surveillance work, muscle for hire – you know what I mean? Working privately in trouble spots like Iraq and Africa. It's a dodgy business to be in.'

'Chris is a good guy.'

'You sure? Maybe the terrorism thing is true. You thought about that? Maybe Chris Moncrieffe is involved in something illegal, something that's got the attention of Penhall.'

'Not a chance,' Max said firmly. 'I'd trust him with my life. In fact, I probably owe him my life. Without Chris, I'd never have got away from Shadow Island. As I told you last time, all that stuff about terrorism is rubbish. Something else is going on here.'

He pushed his glass of Coke and plate to one side and rested his arms on the table, leaning earnestly towards the chief superintendent. 'Did you manage to find out anything about the documents Penhall took from me? Where they are . . . how I get them back?'

Richardson shook his head. 'I was told to drop my enquiries before I got that far.'

'So what do I do now? I need those papers – they're important.'

'Do you have a lawyer in London? Have you consulted anyone about your mum's case?'

'There's a guy named Malcolm Fielding,' Max said.

'He's been handling the case. Well, supposedly handling it. We haven't seen any results from him yet.'

'Talk to him. He can find out what's happened to your papers and make a formal application to get them back. And I'll keep digging around for more information about Julius Clark and Rupert Penhall.'

'Even though your boss told you to lay off?'

'Even more so since he told me to lay off. I don't like that. I'm a straight copper. I don't like being told what questions I can or can't ask. I'm going to get to the bottom of this, Max, take my word for it.'

The chief superintendent looked at his watch. 'I'd better get back to the office. You OK for getting home?'

'Yes, no problem.'

Richardson held out his hand. Max shook it.

'We'll keep in touch, Max.'

'Yes. Thanks for your help.'

NINE

They left the café one after the other, Chief Superintendent Richardson going first, Max waiting a couple of minutes before he went out into the street. He walked to St James's Park station and got on the tube. He was on his guard again, watching the other passengers carefully, but he saw no sign that anyone was following him.

Consuela and Chris were waiting for him in the kitchen when he got home, and they didn't look happy.

'Where've you *been*?' Consuela asked sharply. 'I was starting to get worried.'

'I'm sorry,' Max said. 'I got delayed. I should have called you.'

He took a couple of biscuits from the cupboard and poured himself a glass of juice, sticking to his normal routine, then nodded at them – signalling – and went down into the basement. Consuela and Chris followed.

'Where were you?' Consuela said, her voice concerned. 'I thought something must have happened to you.'

'I'm sorry,' Max apologized again. 'I should have phoned.'

'What do you mean, you got "delayed"?'

'I went to meet Chief Superintendent Richardson.'

'The policeman who took part in the show last week? Why?'

'I asked him for help,' Max said. 'To find out about Penhall; to get my papers back.'

He told them about the meeting, what Richardson had said, how worried the detective had been. There was a moment's silence when Max had finished. Then Chris let out an expletive.

'This doesn't sound good,' he said. 'Not good at all.'

'I don't understand.' Consuela frowned. 'This man, Penhall, what is he? A civil servant? A government bureaucrat?'

'Richardson didn't know,' Max told her. 'But whoever he is, he's dangerous. We need to get a move on, start following up our other leads.'

He took a few paces around the room. He was tense, bursting with pent-up energy. 'Those five names – the other prisoners who were kept on Shadow Island: James Abbott, Narang Anwar, Sergei Alekseev, Redmond Ashworth-Ames and Erik Blomkvist. The first three we know nothing about, so we need to focus on the remaining two. Their jobs are important. They both worked for environmental charities. So did you, Chris. You were in the Amazon, Redmond Ashworth-Ames worked in Borneo – both tropical rainforest areas that are under threat from development. Ashworth-Ames is too ill to help us. That means we have to concentrate on the Swede, Erik Blomkvist.'

'But Blomkvist is missing, presumed dead,' Consuela said.

'That doesn't mean we can't find out more about him. His background, his life, how he disappeared. If we can piece together that information, it might just give us a breakthrough, move our investigation on.'

Max paused, looking at Consuela, then Chris. 'We need to go to Sweden.'

'Max—' Consuela began.

'It's the only way,' he broke in quickly. 'Blomkvist is our only lead. We have to go, Consuela, and I'll need you with me.'

'I'm coming too,' Chris said. 'There's no way I'm letting you go alone.'

'The police are looking for you,' Max said. 'They'll have your name at all the airports – they'll be watching out for you.'

'Not if I travel under a different name, on a new passport.'

'You can get a false passport?'

Chris grinned. 'With friends like mine, I can get anything.'

Max turned to Consuela. 'We have to do it, you know that. What do you say?'

'I'm not sure,' she replied hesitantly.

'Look, someone tried to kill us on Friday night. Do you want to wait around doing nothing until they try again?'

Consuela was silent for a time. Chris prompted her gently. 'Max is right, you know.'

Consuela sighed, then gave a nod. 'OK, we'll go to Sweden.'

Rupert Penhall had been inside the house several times before, but its opulence still took his breath away. The big, high-ceilinged rooms with their ornate plaster mouldings, the cut-glass chandeliers, the thick Persian rugs, the antique furniture – everything reeked of money. A lot of money.

A maid in a black-and-white uniform showed him into the front room and left him there. Penhall looked around at the expensive furnishings. There was a mahogany sideboard in one corner, two richly upholstered sofas and three armchairs arranged around a low circular table whose surface was inlaid with gold and mother-of-pearl. A large, gilt-framed mirror occupied the space over the fireplace and there were paintings on the walls – a Monet, a Degas, a Matisse, all originals. The paintings alone must have cost fifty million pounds, but fifty million was small change to a man like Julius Clark.

Penhall went to the wide bay window and gazed out across the road at Regent's Park, the trees and lawns hazy in the evening light. He was on edge, which was unusual for him. His family background and his education had given him a confidence, an arrogance, that made him feel superior to almost everyone. But not to Julius Clark. Clark made him nervous.

'Ah, Rupert, it's good of you to come.'

Penhall turned to see Julius Clark coming through the door. The atmosphere, the temperature, seemed to change abruptly. The room felt distinctly colder, as if Clark had brought with him his own arctic micro-climate.

He looked at Penhall, his pale blue eyes glittering like winter frost behind his rimless spectacles. 'Can I offer you a drink?'

'No, thank you,' Penhall said.

Clark sat down in one of the armchairs. He was wearing a dinner jacket and black bow tie, diamond cuff-links sparkling on the sleeves of his white dress shirt. He crossed his legs carefully, adjusting the knees of his trousers to preserve their knife-edge creases, then gestured at the sofa. 'Please.'

Penhall didn't feel like sitting down, but he did as he was asked. There was something about Clark – his presence, his air of authority – that meant you didn't dare to disobey him.

Clark glanced at his watch, a silver Rolex with diamonds and rubies around the dial. 'You have ten minutes,' he said curtly. 'I have to attend a dinner in the City. Bankers, financiers . . . the Chancellor of the Exchequer will be there; the Governor of the Bank of England too.'

The message was clear – *I mix with powerful people, and don't you forget it.*

Penhall got straight to the point of his visit. 'Max Cassidy has been meeting a very senior policeman named John Richardson. My men followed them to a café near Scotland Yard last week and again today. Richardson has been making enquiries about me. I have no doubt that he's doing it for Max.'

Clark raised an eyebrow. 'He's a resourceful boy. A troublesome boy. But then we knew that already from his actions in Santo Domingo. Shadow Island is a useless, burned-out ruin, thanks to him.'

'But you're going to rebuild it, aren't you?'

'I could, but I don't intend to.'

Penhall's face registered surprise. 'You don't? But the programme, surely—'

'The programme will continue,' Clark interrupted tersely. 'That goes without saying. It will simply be moved.'

'Moved where?'

'To Kamchatka.'

'In Russia?'

'It will make an excellent location. Even better than Shadow Island. It's remote, inaccessible, and the Russians will turn a blind eye to our activities. Arrangements are already being made to move the scientists there. The lab should be up and running before the end of the month. But we digress. You were telling me about Max Cassidy.'

'He worries me. He's not giving up. He knows about Redmond Ashworth-Ames.'

'Ashworth-Ames is an invalid in a wheelchair, a gibbering wreck,' Clark said dismissively. 'What harm can he do us?'

'None now, but what if he recovers? What if his memory returns – his power of speech?'

'We will deal with that if and when we have to. You are still monitoring Cassidy's phones, I assume?'

Penhall nodded. 'Yes. But what else does Max Cassidy know? That's what concerns me. If he knows about Ashworth-Ames, perhaps he knows about the others.'

'He's heard nothing more from his father?'

'Not as far as we know.'

Clark removed his spectacles and polished them carefully with a silk handkerchief he'd taken from his jacket pocket. 'Alexander Cassidy is the real danger to us,' he said. 'I was hoping we could use Max as bait to lure his father out of hiding. But it doesn't seem to be working so far, and the boy is becoming an increasing nuisance.'

'My little warning – having his car forced off the road – doesn't seem to have deterred him,' Penhall said.

Clark replaced his glasses, then folded his handkerchief neatly into quarters and slipped it away into his pocket. 'Then perhaps stronger measures are required,' he said. 'A more effective warning.'

'He's not alone. He has allies. We have to think about them.'

'Allies? Who do you mean? The woman, Consuela Navarra – she is no threat.'

'But Moncrieffe may be. He was a soldier. He won't be easy to deal with.'

'You've found him?'

'Not yet. We suspect he may have been driving the car near Henley. But it was dark – impossible to be sure.'

'I'm not impressed, Rupert.'

Clark's piercing eyes bored into Penhall, who suppressed a shiver. He felt as if he were being impaled on an icicle.

'We're doing our best,' he said, aware that it was a feeble reply.

'Really? You disappoint me, Rupert. I expect results.'

'He's lying low somewhere. Don't worry, we'll find him and take care of him.'

'See that you do.'

'Then there's Chief Superintendent Richardson. He's been asking awkward questions. He's a senior police officer: he carries a lot more clout than a fourteen-year-old boy. What do you want me to do about him?'

Clark looked at his watch again and stood up. He adjusted his black bow tie in the mirror above the mantelpiece and smoothed back his hair. 'Take care of him too,' he said.

Detective Chief Superintendent John Richardson finished the crime report he was reading and put his signature at the bottom of the final page. He threw the report into the out-tray on the corner of his desk and leaned back in his chair, stretching his arms and yawning. There was a pile of paperwork a foot high in his in-tray, but he was too tired to tackle any of it now. It was gone ten o'clock at night. He'd been in his office since seven that morning and taken only one short break – to see Max Cassidy. The brownie he'd eaten in the café was the only food he'd had all day. He was starving.

He picked up the phone and rang his wife to let her know that he was on his way. She said she'd turn the oven back on to heat up his dinner. She was used to the long hours her husband worked. In the early years of their marriage he had made an effort to come home in the evenings – to see the children before they went to bed. But now the boys had both left home, he stayed late at the office almost every night. She didn't like it, but what could she do? His work came before everything else in his life.

Richardson took the lift down to the foyer and went out through the main entrance. He walked across Broadway into St James's Park Underground station and caught the tube home – the Circle Line to Notting Hill Gate, then the Central Line west. The carriage wasn't crowded at this time of night. That was one of the advantages of working such long hours – you missed the rush hour at both ends of the day.

Richardson slumped down in a seat and picked up a copy of the *Evening Standard* that someone had left behind. He flicked idly through the pages, too weary to concentrate much on the articles. Then he tossed the paper aside and closed his eyes. He didn't notice the young man in grey windcheater and trainers who had got on the train just behind him and was now sitting at the far end of the carriage, listening to his iPod.

The journey home took forty-five minutes. The chief superintendent dozed for most of the time, never quite dropping off to sleep completely in case he missed his stop. When he got off, the young man in the windcheater and trainers also left the train and followed him out of the station.

The road outside was always busy. Even now, there was a steady stream of vehicles speeding by. The chief superintendent waited on the kerb for a break in the traffic that would allow him to cross. A line of cars went past, then a couple of vans and more cars. A lorry loomed up in the distance, its headlights blazing through the night. Richardson watched it draw nearer. It was a high, articulated lorry, moving very fast. Richardson stepped back a little from the edge of the road. The lorry was twenty metres away when he felt a sudden, violent impact in the middle of his back. He toppled forward, his arms flailing, trying to recover his balance, but it was too late. He turned his head as he fell and saw the lorry bearing down on him, its engine roaring, its headlights dazzling, blinding him. Then the lights cut out abruptly and there was only darkness.

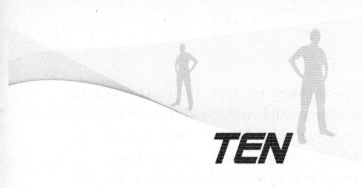

TEN

Max was having his breakfast when he heard the news. The radio was on in the kitchen, as it was every morning. He and Consuela were alone. Chris had slipped out through the garden before dawn to see about getting himself a fake passport. Consuela was drinking coffee, eating a piece of toast. Max was working his way through a bowl of cereal. He heard the headlines vaguely, registering that there had been a hurricane somewhere in the Caribbean and a plane crash in the Far East, but he wasn't really listening. It was only as the bulletin progressed that a few specific keywords made him sit up and pay more attention. *'Senior Scotland Yard detective ... road traffic accident ... sad loss to the force ...'* Max reached out and turned up the volume on the radio.

'... Chief Superintendent John Richardson was on his way home from work yesterday evening when he was hit by a lorry as he tried to cross the road. He was taken to hospital, but died later from his injuries.

'Chief Superintendent Richardson, the fifty-five-year-old

*head of Scotland Yard's Criminal Investigation Depart-
ment, had been a police officer for thirty-five years. A
Metropolitan Police spokesperson said that he was a well-
liked, highly respected officer. "John Richardson's tragic
death is a shock to everyone in the police force. He will be
sadly missed and we offer our sincere condolences to his
wife and family."*

'*And now, the sports news. Manchester United are to—*'

Max clicked off the radio. He looked at Consuela.
She'd put down her toast and had been listening
intently to the news report.

'Richardson—' she began, then broke off abruptly,
remembering the bug in the wall.

Max nodded. He'd gone cold. He felt sick. He
switched the radio back on as background noise and
went down the stairs into the basement. Consuela
followed him automatically. Her face was pale and
tense.

'A road traffic accident, they said,' she whispered.

'It wasn't an accident,' Max replied.

'You don't know that.'

'It's common sense. Richardson starts asking
questions about Rupert Penhall and is warned to stop.
Then, just a few days later, he's hit by a lorry and killed.
That's too much of a coincidence.'

Consuela licked her lips. 'Max, I'm frightened.'

'So am I.'

'What do we do? I wish Chris was here. I'd feel safer.'

'We stick to our plan. We need to go to Sweden as soon as possible. Tomorrow, maybe, or the day after.'

'But you have school.'

'School doesn't matter – it's irrelevant right now,' Max said quietly but forcefully. 'Someone rammed our car off the road, nearly killed us. Now the policeman who was helping us has been killed. We have to find out what's going on, Consuela.'

She gave a nod. 'OK. What do we do first?'

'Can you buy us some air tickets?'

'Do I buy one for Chris too?'

'He'll be travelling under a false name. We don't know what it is yet, so let him make his own arrangements when he gets back.'

'I'll book us a hotel too. Your father and I went to Stockholm a few years ago to do one of his shows. We stayed in a quiet little hotel in Södermalm – that's the island on the south side of the city. The Hotel Katarina, I think it was called.'

Consuela chewed on her thumbnail, looking uncertainly at Max. 'You're sure this is the right thing to do? You don't think we should go to the police, to one of Chief Superintendent Richardson's colleagues, and tell them what we know?'

'Richardson is dead because I got him involved,' Max said firmly. 'It's up to me to put it right now. I owe him that.'

Max walked to school in a daze. He couldn't stop thinking about Chief Superintendent Richardson. The detective's death had stunned him. Max had hardly known him, but he still felt a sense of sorrow at the loss. And he felt guilty. If Max hadn't asked him for help, he would still be alive. Indirectly, Max was responsible for his death. That was a terrible load to bear. He'd also lost an ally. Max felt more exposed, more vulnerable than ever before. He was sad and scared, but he was even more determined now to continue his investigations.

He was so preoccupied with his thoughts that he didn't notice the car pulling alongside him as he turned a corner half a mile from the school. It was only when the rear door opened that Max glanced sideways to see what was happening. But by then it was too late. Two men seized hold of him, one on either side, and bundled him roughly into the back of the car. Max had no time to react, no time to cry out before the door slammed shut and the car accelerated away.

He was sandwiched between the two men on the back seat. He tried to twist round, to look out of the rear window, to maybe signal to someone or shout for help, but the men pushed his head down onto his knees and threw a blanket over him, hiding him from sight as the car sped through the busy streets.

'What the . . . ? Who the . . . ?' Max struggled to speak with his face pressed tight against his legs.

'Shut your mouth, or we'll gag you. Understand?' one of the men snapped.

Max turned his head and attempted to sit up. The men pushed him back down and held him there. Max tried to resist, but they were too strong for him. He gave up the fight and lay still, his mind racing, thinking back over the previous few minutes. The car must have been shadowing him all the way from home, following him along the road, the men waiting for the right moment to strike.

Max was frightened. His spine was tingling, his stomach knotted. Who were these men? Where were they taking him? It was hot underneath the blanket, and difficult to breathe with his body doubled up. Max relaxed his muscles and tried not to panic. *Think of it like one of your stage tricks,* he told himself. *You're in control of your mind and body. You're caught, trapped in a moving car and these men have the upper hand, but stay calm and think clearly and you'll find a way to escape.*

The car turned left and came to a stop, the engine

still running. Traffic lights, Max guessed. There'd be other cars next to them, people on the pavement. If he could sit up and throw off the blanket, yell out at the top of his voice, he could attract attention, raise the alarm, maybe get someone to alert the police. But the two men clearly knew this was a dangerous moment, for they increased the pressure on Max's back, holding him down even harder than before.

The car pulled away again. Max felt the weight come off his back a little, but the men still kept hold of him. They were on their guard, vigilant. Max knew he had no chance of doing anything while he was in the car. He had to wait until they stopped, then make his move.

They turned right and went straight ahead for a few seconds before turning left. Max counted the time between each change of direction. He'd already lost his bearings and had no hope of working out exactly where they were going, but the mental exercise helped take his mind off his predicament, stopped him getting over-whelmed by fear.

After twenty minutes of erratic, stop-start motion, the car made a turn and increased its speed to what felt like sixty or seventy miles an hour. Max guessed that they'd left the traffic-choked metropolitan streets and were on a dual carriageway, or even a motorway. The car veered out into the next lane, presumably to

overtake, then pulled out even further. Three lanes –
that made it a motorway. But which one? The M1? It
had to be the M1. They hadn't gone far enough to reach
any of the others. So they were heading north. But
where north?

None of the men spoke; there was no idle conversation. Max was aware of the noise of the engine, the
tyres on the road, the throb of his pulse inside his head.
How far were they going? Were they taking him to
some remote spot out of London where they could kill
him and dispose of his body without any risk of it being
found? Max blotted the thought out of his mind.
Thinking the worst was a bad idea. He had to stay
positive, believe that he had a chance of surviving this
kidnapping.

The car slowed and forked to the left. They were leaving the motorway. Ten minutes later, they made a sharp
right turn and came to a halt. The engine was turned
off. Max heard the driver getting out and coming to
open the rear door, the two other men shifting in their
seats. One got out and pulled Max out behind him. Max
braced himself, preparing to throw off the blanket and
make a run for it. But the guards were ready for that.
They pinned his arms to his sides, then forced his
hands behind his back and handcuffed them together.
Max felt the cold steel on his wrists. He was used to the

sensation from his stage shows, but not in circumstances like this. On stage, he always knew he could release himself. Here – wherever they were – it would not be so simple.

The blanket was pulled down and held in tight at the waist to prevent Max from seeing the ground, then his arms were seized and he was led away. It was tarmac underfoot – Max could tell from the feel, the sound his trainers made: a road, or a car park. They paused. One of the men spoke into an intercom and a metal gate clicked open. They walked five or six metres, then another lock snapped back and they passed through a second gate. The locks, the obvious security – they had to be entering some kind of prison. Max felt a flutter of relief. A prison was better than some of the other possible alternatives.

The guard spoke into another intercom and Max heard a barrier open – not a metal gate this time, but what sounded like a wooden door. They were inside a building now, walking in a straight line. Max couldn't see through the blanket, but he picked up every other clue he could and processed it through his brain. The noise of their footsteps – that had to be lino on the floor. The slight echo that reminded him of school – they were in a corridor. The smell of something Max couldn't identify. Disinfectant? Floor polish? That reminded him of school too. He was in some kind of institution. More than ever now, he was sure this was a prison or a juvenile detention centre.

They stopped. Max felt hands frisking him, patting his clothes, feeling in his pockets. His loose change was taken away, and his wristwatch and belt. He heard a key being inserted into a lock, a door opening. His hand-cuffs were removed and he was given a hard shove in the back. As he stumbled forward, the blanket was whipped off his head. Max turned in time to catch a fleeting glimpse of one of the men and the blank wall of the corridor before the door was slammed shut and locked.

He was in the strangest room he'd ever seen. It was about three metres square, the same size as his bedroom at home, but there the resemblance ended. This room had no windows, no furniture, not even a handle on the inside of the door. The floor was made of some kind of squashy rubber that gave under the feet and the walls were covered in panels of what looked liked quilting. Max touched one of them. It was soft, like the cushions of a sofa. He could have punched his fist into the wall without hurting his hand.

He knew what the room was – a padded cell. He'd heard about them, but never seen one. They'd been installed in lunatic asylums in the Victorian era, for confining prisoners who might deliberately try to injure themselves, but he didn't realize they were still in use. There were no hard surfaces, no chairs or tables or sharp objects. A person could throw himself violently around the room and end up with little more than a few slight bruises.

Max looked up. The ceiling was too high to reach. In the centre, protected by a wire-mesh cage, was a single glowing light bulb. There was no switch on the wall so the light had to be controlled from somewhere else. He saw something else on the ceiling: in the corner opposite the door was a tiny CCTV camera spying on him. Max went to the door, which was also heavily padded on the inside. He didn't care whether the camera was watching him. Crouching down, he peered through the keyhole. He could see the wall of the corridor outside, but that was all. It was a solid lock, but Max knew he could pick it if he had the right tool. Unfortunately, he didn't. He had no tools at all.

He straightened up and paced around the floor. Down one side of the room was a mattress-sized piece of foam rubber that was presumably intended to be used as a bed. Max kept pacing next to the mattress, trying to work out where he was. Somewhere north of London, he was sure of that, but how far? It was six or seven miles from where he'd been picked up to the beginning of the M1. How long had they been on the motorway? Ten, possibly fifteen minutes. How many miles would they have covered in that time? Fifteen minutes at seventy miles an hour. Max did the arithmetic in his head – that was about seventeen miles. Plus the ten minutes after they'd left the motorway. They'd been going slower then, probably thirty or forty miles an hour so he could add on, say, another six miles in distance. That made about thirty miles in total. That wasn't far. He was thirty miles from home, but it might have been three hundred for all the good it did him. He was still locked in a padded cell in a secure prison.

He wondered who had brought him here. Julius Clark's men? Clark was a rich man, but even he wouldn't have had his own prison in the United Kingdom, which meant this was something to do with the British government. Rupert Penhall? It had to be Penhall who had organized Max's abduction. No other conclusion made sense.

But why? What was Penhall going to do with him now? Max thought about it over and over again until he decided that such speculation was pointless. All it did was sap his mental energy. *Just wait and see what happens*, he told himself. *That's all you can do.* He lay down on the foam-rubber mattress and closed his eyes.

He had no watch, so he could only guess at the time, but it seemed about three hours later that he heard a key turning in the lock. The door opened and a man in a navy blue uniform entered. He was tall and heavily built, with a big bunch of keys dangling from a chain on his belt. A typical prison warder, Max thought. He'd seen plenty of them at Levington, where his mother was being held. The Levington warders were all female, of course, but their gender made little difference. They all had the same arrogant air of the jailer about them.

Behind the warder came a second man – in the white outfit of a kitchen orderly. He was carrying a paper plate of food and a styrofoam cup of water. He placed the items on the floor just inside the door and retreated.

'Where am I?' Max asked the warder. 'Why've I been brought here?'

The officer didn't answer. He just walked out of the cell and locked the door behind him. Max slid off the mattress and crawled across the floor to the plate of food. It was some kind of stew and rice, all mixed together. He screwed up his nose. It wasn't quite the healthy Mediterranean food he was used to getting from Consuela, but it was better than nothing. He dipped the plastic spoon into the mush: the spoon was the only cutlery provided – no knife or fork, no metal utensils, no china plate or tray that could be used as a weapon.

Just a plastic spoon – even Max couldn't use that to pick a lock.

The food didn't taste too bad. Max cleared his plate in just a few minutes and drank the cup of water. Twenty minutes later, the lock clicked back and the door swung open. The warder came in first again, then the orderly, who picked up the plate, spoon and cup and withdrew.

The jailer looked at Max with blank, indifferent eyes. 'Stand up, turn round and put your hands behind your back,' he said, then handcuffed him and led him out of the cell.

The handcuffs seemed entirely unnecessary to Max. The man was twice his size. Did he seriously think that Max was going to overpower him? Or had the prison staff been told to be extra vigilant with this teenage inmate, warned that he was a slippery customer, a cunning, practised escaper.

They walked along the corridor, the warder gripping Max's left arm. Max glanced around, trying to appear casual, but taking note of everything he saw. It was a long, open corridor, heavy metal doors at both ends; brown lino on the floor, dirty cream walls, doors at intervals along both sides that Max guessed must be more cells; a CCTV camera high up near the ceiling towards the far end, monitoring the area.

Max saw an open doorway ahead on the left. Another prison officer came through it and gave a start as he saw Max and his escort. A start of surprise, and also, Max thought, of guilt. The two men nodded at each other, then the first warder took Max through the doorway. Inside was a washroom, an ancient, primitive washroom that looked as if it had barely been touched in a hundred years. There was a line of chipped enamel sinks along one wall, with a row of four toilet cubicles opposite. A small head-height window at the far end of the room was open, thick steel bars preventing anyone from climbing out of it. A cool breeze was blowing in through the gap, freshening the room, but Max's sensitive nose still detected a faint odour of cigarette smoke. So that explained the second officer's guilty start. As in every other public building, smoking would be forbidden here. The tight security must make it difficult – maybe impossible – for staff to go outside to smoke, so the warder had sneaked into the washroom, where there was no CCTV camera, for a crafty cigarette.

Max's escort unlocked the handcuffs. 'Do what you have to do,' he said sharply. 'And make it quick.'

Max went into one of the cubicles. There was an old-fashioned toilet inside, with a high cistern and a long chain flush that looked Victorian. *What* is *this place?* Max thought. *Padded cells, chain flushes – it's like stepping back into the nineteenth century.*

When he came out of the cubicle, he went across to the sinks and washed his hands. The warder watched him attentively. Max dried his hands on a paper towel and threw it into the waste bin.

'Hands behind your back,' the warder ordered.

He handcuffed him again and led him back to his cell. As the door swung shut and the key turned in the lock, Max lay down on the mattress and stared thoughtfully up at the ceiling. That had been a productive little excursion. Very informative. He had discovered a couple of useful things. Now all he had to do was work out how he could utilize those things to escape.

ELEVEN

Max did nothing except lie on his mattress and doze all afternoon and evening. Another meal was brought to him – a mixture of mince and mashed potato that was no doubt supposed to be shepherd's pie but looked and tasted nothing like the shepherd's pie Max was used to. This was a sort of bland slush that slopped around the plate and could be eaten only with a spoon. Max was beginning to see how the catering in this place worked – no food that required a knife and fork, or taste buds.

Afterwards he was handcuffed and taken along the corridor to the washroom. He saw no other people, no other prisoners and no sign in the washroom or toilets that anyone had used them before him. Max closed the cubicle door behind him – there were no locks on the doors – and sat down on the toilet seat. Just above his left shoulder was the dangling chain flush, its wooden handle polished smooth by countless prisoners' fingers. He reached up and took hold of the chain; then, ensuring that he made no noise that would carry to the warder standing guard outside, used his fingers to prise open two of the links in the chain. The metal was old, but it was tough. Max had to use all his strength to force open gaps of just a few millimetres – not enough to remove the links, but it was all he had time for right now. He'd open the gaps wider on his next visit.

He stood up and inspected the chain. At a casual glance, you couldn't tell that it had been tampered with. He pulled it, then went out and washed his hands and face at the sink. He asked the warder if he could have a toothbrush. The man shook his head.

'Why not?' Max said, hoping to start some kind of dialogue. If he could get the guard to loosen up a little, he might obtain answers to his other questions.

'How long am I going to be here?' he went on. 'I'll need a toothbrush. Where is this place, by the way?'

The officer ignored the questions and told Max to turn round and put his hands behind him. He handcuffed him again, led him back to his cell and locked him in. Max lay down on the mattress and stared at the ceiling some more. The worst thing about his incarceration, he realized, wasn't being shut away in a cell with nothing to do; it was not knowing why he'd been brought here and how long he was going to be a prisoner. He was worried, there was no getting away from that. Very worried. Most people who ended up in prison had gone through some kind of formal procedure. They'd been arrested, charged by the police, tried by a court. But Max had had none of that. There was no record of him in the system and that frightened him. It meant that no one knew where he was, and no one would know what had happened if he just disappeared for good.

The night was just as boring as the day. The only indication Max got that it *was* actually night was the light in the ceiling going out. He curled up on the mattress to keep warm – there were no sheets or blankets provided – and went to sleep. He slept surprisingly well considering where he was, and when he woke the light was back on, so he assumed it must be morning. He did a few exercises to loosen up, then lay back down and waited.

Some time later – Max had no real idea exactly how much later – the cell door opened and a warder entered. It wasn't the same warder as the previous evening, but he was just as large and just as reluctant to talk. Max tried asking him a few questions and met the same stone wall of silence. A kitchen orderly came in with breakfast – a paper plate bearing two thin slices of white toast and another styrofoam cup of water.

The routine followed the same course as the day before. Max ate the toast and drank the water, the jailer and orderly returned to collect the plate and cup, then Max was handcuffed and taken to the washroom, where he did more work on the toilet chain, prising open the links, but leaving them in place.

In the middle of the day he was brought a paper plate of pasta with a sloppy meat and tomato sauce on top of it, and a cup of water.

'Where am I?' he demanded when the warder and orderly came in. 'I want to know. I have a *right* to know.'

The warder took no notice.

Max walked over to him. 'Where the hell am I?' he asked fiercely. 'You can't keep me here. You can't keep me locked up.'

The man looked away as if Max were not there. That made Max even more angry. He made a sudden dash for the door – not because he had any serious hopes of escaping, but simply as an act of defiance: to show these people that he still had some fight in him. The warder grabbed hold of his arm and hauled him back easily.

Max glared up at him. 'What kind of a person are you?' he snarled. 'Keeping a fourteen-year-old kid locked up in a padded cell. You should be ashamed of yourself.'

The warder pushed him back. His face was flushed. *Good*, Max thought. *I've got a reaction at last.*

'Don't get lippy with me,' the officer said. 'There are worse cells than this. Just you remember that.'

He backed out into the corridor, banged the door shut and locked it. Max looked down at the plate of food on the floor. He was sorely tempted to hurl it at the wall and smear the pasta and sauce everywhere, but he controlled himself. That would achieve nothing, and besides, he was hungry. There was no point in throwing away his lunch. He sat down cross-legged and ate the meal.

When the warder and orderly returned for the plate and cup, Max was handcuffed and escorted along the corridor. He thought he was being taken to the toilet, but they went right past the washroom and through a locked door into a different section of the prison. This looked like the administrative area, where the prison staff were based. Through an open door on the left, Max saw a small kitchen containing a table and chairs, a sofa and a sink with a kettle and a microwave on the work-top next to it. On the far side of the room was a door and a barred window through which Max caught a glimpse of a courtyard enclosed by red-brick buildings.

They kept going along a hallway and paused by a locked steel gate for the warder to take out his keys. Next to the gate was what looked like the main control room of the prison – a cramped little space with a desk and chair facing a bank of CCTV screens. There were five screens, all showing different images from around the prison: the perimeter fence, the main gate, the external walls, the corridors inside, cells containing lone men – so there *were* other prisoners here. There were five screens, but clearly more than five cameras, for the pictures kept changing as the system jumped from one camera to another. On a notice board just inside the room was pinned a staff rota. Max saw that there were three eight-hour shifts a day: 8 a.m. to 4 p.m., 4 p.m. to midnight, and midnight to 8 a.m. The night shift had considerably fewer staff on duty than the other two shifts.

The warder unlocked the gate and pushed Max through ahead of him, locking the gate behind them. They walked ten metres along another corridor and stopped again. The officer opened an unlocked door and escorted Max inside. They were in a square room with a metal table in the centre and two metal chairs next to it, both bolted to the floor. Seated on the chair facing the door was Rupert Penhall.

'Hello, Max,' he said smoothly. 'Having a good time here?'

Max swore at him. It probably wasn't a wise thing to do, but he wasn't going to show fear in front of this man. He wanted his contempt to be crystal clear.

Penhall seemed amused rather than offended. He gave a smug smile. 'Well, I see your spirit hasn't been broken. Yet,' he added ominously.

'Why've you kidnapped me?' Max demanded. 'What's going on?'

'Sit down,' Penhall said.

He waited for Max to take the chair opposite and nodded at the warder. 'You can leave us now.'

'Are you sure, sir?' the officer asked doubtfully.

'He's handcuffed, he won't give me any trouble. I'll call if I need you.'

The warder went out of the room. Max adjusted his position on the chair. He couldn't sit back properly because of his manacled hands. 'Why don't you take off the cuffs?' he said.

Penhall shook his head. 'I don't think so.'

'You afraid of something? What? Are you afraid that I might escape? That I might attack you?'

Max was trying to rile him, to get him to drop his guard and maybe give away more information than he intended. But Penhall wasn't going to rise to the provocation. He had a styrofoam cup of coffee on the table in front of him. He took a sip. Max watched him, longing to throw the coffee in his face.

'You won't escape from here,' Penhall said.

'Where am I?'

'It's called Mount Pleasant. An interesting name, don't you think? Our Victorian ancestors aren't known for being a bundle of laughs, but whoever christened this asylum clearly had a fine sense of humour.'

'It's an asylum? For lunatics?' Max said.

'Built in the eighteen fifties to house the country's most dangerous – and most deranged – criminals. And still in use, as you've discovered, for people we want to detain without all the time-consuming complications of a court case.'

Max looked across the table. Behind Penhall's shoulder was a barred window through which he had a good view of the courtyard outside. Mount Pleasant had been built in the form of a square, with an enclosed garden in the centre – a patch of lawn and shrubs around the edges. The four sides of the building were three storeys high, with ornate gothic turrets on the corners Max could see. In the middle of the far side was a high arched entrance, big enough to get a lorry through, which gave access to the garden from the front of the prison.

'Why've you brought me here?' Max asked.

'Because you're a pain in the neck,' Penhall replied. 'And I'm getting tired of your pathetic little games.'

'My "pathetic little games"?' Max echoed. 'You mean trying to find out who framed my mum for a murder that was never committed, trying to get her out of prison, trying to find out why my dad was held prisoner on Shadow Island and drugged by Julius Clark? Is that what you're talking about? They're not games. They're my parents' lives.'

'And what a good little boy you are to want to help them,' Penhall sneered. 'The brave son coming to the rescue. It would be admirable, if it weren't so stupid.'

'You think looking for justice is stupid?'

'I'm a practical man, Max. I deal with realities, with the world as it is, not as people like you would have it.'

'What's that supposed to mean?'

'It means you're out of your depth. And you're out of your mind if you think you stand a chance against Julius Clark.'

'Why are you on his side? I don't understand. You work for the British government. Shouldn't you be protecting people like me? Shouldn't you be helping me get my mum out of prison instead of locking me up and threatening me? Clark must be paying you an awful lot of money.'

Penhall smiled and took another sip of his coffee. 'Don't be so naïve, Max. Julius Clark is a friend of the British people. His companies provide jobs, they create wealth. Political leaders love him – not just here but all around the world. They love the cash he gives to their parties, they love going to stay with him on his estate in the Bahamas, they love his private jets, the food and wine he gives them, the cruises on his yacht in the Mediterranean. He's a very popular man. And you, Max, what are you? A fourteen-year-old child with a missing father and a mother in prison.'

'How long do you intend keeping me here?'

'That depends on you. You cooperate, you get to go free. You don't, you stay locked up.'

'You couldn't get away with that. My friends would ask questions – someone would find out where I was.'

'I doubt it,' Penhall said. 'There are prisoners in Mount Pleasant who have been here for decades, who will die here without anyone knowing what's become of them.'

'I don't believe you.'

'People disappear in other parts of the world – vanish without trace. You think that doesn't happen in Britain too? This place is perfect for detaining troublemakers – people who haven't actually committed any offence, so they can't be tried and imprisoned in the normal way, but who nevertheless are a thorn in the side of the authorities. People like you, Max.'

Max licked his lips. His mouth had suddenly gone dry. He knew that Penhall was telling him the truth.

'You said if I cooperated, you'd let me go,' he said. 'Cooperate how?'

'By stopping what you're doing, by keeping your mouth shut, by telling your friends to do the same. You go to the press, or to the police, and we'll shut you away for the rest of your life. Imagine that – another fifty or sixty years in that padded cell. Nothing to do, nobody to talk to, no hope of release or escape. You're clever enough on stage with all your props and trick boxes, but you won't escape from here. This place is one hundred per cent escape-proof.'

Penhall drank the last of his coffee and held up the styrofoam cup. He squeezed it in his fist, crushing it until it disintegrated into pieces. 'You mess with me, Max,' he said, 'and I'll crush you as easily as I crushed that cup. Think about that over the next few days.'

Penhall got up from his chair, walked past Max and opened the door. 'He's all yours,' he said to the warder outside.

The officer came in and hauled Max to his feet. They went back out of the room and through the gate into the staff area. Max made a mental note of everything he saw: the control room, the CCTV screens, the kitchen, the keys the warder used to unlock the doors, including the door to his cell. All of it was important.

He lay down on the foam mattress as the jailer

locked him in. Looking around this empty cell and imagining years of captivity in it sent icy shivers through his whole body. Could Penhall carry out his threat to make him disappear for the rest of his life? Max had no doubt that he could. But that wasn't going to stop him doing what he had to do.

A lifetime in solitary confinement in Mount Pleasant was a terrible thought, but even more terrible was the thought of his mum being in prison for the next eighteen years. Max couldn't let that happen. And he couldn't let the people who had put her there get away with it. The same people who had kidnapped his father and Chris Moncrieffe, who had turned Redmond Ashworth-Ames into an invalid and had murdered John Richardson. Max was going to bring them to justice, whatever the cost to himself.

He pictured Penhall crushing the styrofoam cup in his hand and remembered what he'd said about Max to the warder – *He won't give me any trouble.*

Oh, won't I? Max said to himself. *Just you see. I'm going to escape from Mount Pleasant. And I'm going to do it tonight.*

TWELVE

The time passed incredibly slowly. Max was impatient to put his plan into action, but he knew he had to wait for the cover of darkness. He could do nothing until after nightfall. He lay on the mattress and dozed intermittently, grabbing as much sleep as he could now because he knew he wouldn't get much later.

He was bored, but also tense and keyed up. He kept running over the details of his plan in his mind, wondering if it was going to work. There were a lot of things that could go wrong, a lot of things that depended on timing and a big dose of luck, but it was the only plan he had. All he could do was take a shot at it and pray that fate was on his side.

In the early evening the tedium was broken by the arrival of his meal. The warder unlocked the cell door as usual, then stood guard as a kitchen orderly brought in the food. There'd been a change of shift since Max's meeting with Penhall. There was a different warder on duty now, the same one as the previous evening. He had kinder eyes than the day-shift officer. That gave

Max hope. There was a question he needed answering.

He smiled at the man. 'They took my watch away from me,' he said. 'Do you know what time it is, please?'

The warder hesitated, giving the question some thought and obviously deciding it was harmless, for he looked at his wrist and said, 'Seven o'clock.'

'Thanks,' Max said.

He'd established contact – that was what he wanted. He'd got the officer to see him as a person, to communicate with him. That was a beginning that Max could try to work on later.

He ate his food, and when the warder and orderly came back for the dirty plate and cup he said, 'Thank you,' politely and asked if he could go to the toilet. The warder handcuffed him and led him down the corridor to the washroom, then stood outside the cubicle while Max went inside.

Max sat down on the toilet and reached up to gently take hold of the chain. It took him only a few seconds to remove one of the metal links he'd prised apart earlier, then fasten the chain back together. As he did so, his fingers slipped and the chain rattled.

'What're you doing in there?' the warder called out suspiciously.

Max whipped his hands down just in time. The cubicle door banged open and the officer peered in.

'I'm just finishing,' Max said.

'Well, get a move on.'

The man glanced around the cubicle, then stepped back out. Max heaved a silent sigh of relief. The warder hadn't noticed that the chain was now a few centimetres shorter than before. Max had the chain link hidden in his hand. He squeezed the metal together to form a smooth ring and swallowed it. Then he stood up, flushed the toilet and went out to wash his hands.

Still suspicious, the warder took another look around the cubicle Max had just vacated, then told him to put his hands up against the wall. He frisked him thoroughly, checking his clothes, his pockets, even making him remove his shoes so he could look inside them. *Thank God I swallowed the chain link*, Max thought.

He gave the officer a puzzled, innocent look. 'What's the matter?'

'Nothing,' the warder growled. 'Put your hands behind your back.'

He handcuffed Max and escorted him back to his cell.

'There's not much to do in here, is there?' Max said conversationally as they walked along the corridor. 'I don't suppose there's any chance of something to read? A book, or a magazine.'

'That's not up to me, but I'll ask,' the officer replied, his tone gentler than before, as if he were trying to make up for his surliness in the washroom.

'Thanks,' Max said. 'Can I get my cell light turned off earlier too? I'm only fourteen – I'm not used to going to bed so late.'

Play on your youth, Max had decided. *Emphasize the fact that you're just a kid. Get their sympathy.* He hoped the officer didn't have teenagers of his own. If he did, he'd know that the idea of a fourteen-year-old wanting to go to bed early was utterly proposterous, and would suspect that Max was up to something. But the officer just shook his head.

'The lights are on a timer,' he said. 'Off at eleven at night, back on at seven next morning. It can't be changed.'

'OK, never mind,' Max said. He'd got what he wanted.

The evening passed even more slowly than the afternoon. Max sat on his mattress and stared vacantly into space, biding his time. Only when the light went out would he make his move.

He was aware of the CCTV camera up on the ceiling, but he made a point of not looking at it. Was someone watching him at this moment? Maybe, maybe not. He recalled what he'd seen in the control room: the screens chopping and changing between cameras, not lingering on any one location for more than a couple of seconds. There'd been no sound with the pictures. That was good. He didn't want anyone hearing him later.

Suddenly the bulb in the ceiling went out. *At last*, Max thought. *Eleven o'clock*. He started to count seconds and minutes in his head, clocking them off like a watch. After fifteen minutes he stood up, still counting. Now to retrieve the chain link. He arched his back slightly, took a deep breath and began the process of regurgitation that he'd practised for years for his stage act. Usually it was a key he was bringing up from his stomach, but a chain link was no different. He just had to concentrate, get his internal muscles to do exactly what he wanted. He focused on his stomach, making the top valve open, then his alimentary canal, squeezing the chain link slowly up the tube and into his mouth. It was easy when you knew how.

He took the link out. The metal was warm and wet. He held it in his fingers and straightened it out, leaving a tiny hook at one end. Then he went across to the door, knelt down and looked through the keyhole. The lights in the corridor had dimmed, but hadn't gone out completely. Max gripped the piece of metal between his thumb and forefinger and went to work on the lock.

It was a fairly simple mechanism, an old model that had not been changed or upgraded to make it more secure. In a prison like Mount Pleasant, with all its guards and cameras and fences, it probably wasn't thought necessary to have the highest quality locks on the individual cell doors. Max had seen many locks like this one. He had a collection of them, inherited from his father, in the basement at home, on which he regularly practised his picking skills. This one was well maintained, the moving parts smooth and recently oiled. In under thirty seconds Max had the tumblers inside disengaged. He could have opened the door then, but he delayed. He was still counting in his head, waiting for exactly the right moment.

Shift change for the prison staff was at midnight. At changeover time they would be distracted. They'd be busy talking to colleagues, passing on messages, maybe gossiping, talking about their social lives. Those few minutes would be when they were at their least alert, least likely to be watching the CCTV monitors carefully. That was when Max was going to break out.

He counted down the seconds. Every part of his plan had its risks. He just had to hold his nerve. He was pretty sure his cell door wasn't alarmed. The warders taking him in and out had never disabled an alarm first, as far as he could tell, but there were plenty of other things to worry about. The CCTV camera up on the ceiling for one. It couldn't see him in the dark, it wouldn't have heard the faint scrape of metal as he picked the lock, but the second he opened the door, it would no longer be pitch black inside the cell – a tiny amount of light would inevitably seep in from the corridor. Then there was the camera outside to negotiate. This was when Max needed luck on his side.

Eleven fifty-eight . . . eleven fifty-nine . . . midnight – or as close as he could estimate it. Max prepared himself; then, in one swift series of movements, he pulled open the door a few centimetres, slipped out through the gap, closing the door behind him, scuttled rapidly away along the corridor and ducked into the washroom. He leaned back against the wall just inside the doorway and waited, listening out for an alarm bell ringing, for the thud of feet as the prison officers came to find him. But nothing happened.

He was safe, at least for the time being. Max went across the washroom to the waste bin by the sinks and rummaged through the piles of used, screwed-up paper towels. *Please let it still be here*, he said to himself. He scooped some towels out of the bin and sifted carefully through them. At the bottom of the pile he found what he was looking for – the wooden match that he'd noticed the day before, thrown away by the warder who'd sneaked into the washroom for a surreptitious smoke. The match hadn't been used. The warder had obviously struck it, but the match hadn't ignited properly and he'd tossed it into the bin. On the head there was still some of the pink combustible coating that made matches catch fire. Max hoped there was going to be enough for his purposes.

Putting the match and a few clean paper towels in his pocket, he went back to the doorway and listened again. Still no sounds of activity anywhere. Would the night-shift guards have settled down to work by now? Would they be watching the CCTV monitors in the control room? Max knew the corridor camera would not be continuously transmitting pictures. That reduced the odds on him being spotted. Steeling his nerves, he crept out into the corridor and slid along the wall in the shadows where the camera – even if it happened to be online at that moment – would find it hard to pick him out. He made no sudden movements, kept his arms by his sides, his face pressed to the wall. He reached the door at the end of the corridor and exhaled with relief. He was underneath and behind the camera now, in the blind zone where he couldn't be seen. Crouching down, he used his metal pick to unlock the door.

This was probably the most dangerous part of the operation. On the other side of this door was the staff area – the kitchen and control room. If he was going to be caught, this was where it was most likely to happen.

There was no point in delaying now – he just had to take a chance. Grasping the handle, Max turned it as softly as he could and eased the door open a fraction. He peered through the gap, saw the back of a prison officer in the control room ahead, but no one in the hallway in between. The door to the kitchen was open, but it was impossible for Max to see if there was anyone in the room. Another chance he just had to take.

He opened the door wider and sneaked through, then closed the door quietly and darted across the hallway into the kitchen. His luck was holding – the room was empty. He pushed the door to behind him and looked around. It was a smallish room. The table, chairs and sofa took up most of the space. There was a refrigerator by the sink, and tea, coffee and sugar set out on the worktop near the kettle. Hanging from the wall was a mini fire extinguisher, and next to it a glass case containing a red button to set off the fire alarm. Max headed for the door on the far side of the kitchen that gave access to the courtyard. He was almost there when he suddenly heard footsteps in the hall outside. He reacted instantly, throwing himself to the floor behind the sofa.

Someone came into the kitchen. Max lay still and listened hard. Had he been spotted coming in? Had his disappearance from his cell been noticed? He heard the kettle being filled, the chink of a spoon in a mug, and relaxed a little. It was only one of the warders making a cup of tea. Would he stay in the kitchen to drink it? Max guessed probably not. The night shift had only just begun; the officer wouldn't be on his break already. And sure enough, a few minutes later, Max heard footsteps going back out into the hall. He looked out around the end of the sofa, making sure the coast was clear, then hurried over to the courtyard door and crouched down with his lock-pick.

This was a more sophisticated lock than the ones on the two internal doors, but nothing Max hadn't seen before. Most lock mechanisms were based on the same fundamental principles. Max had been practising cracking them since he was four years old. He knew exactly where to place the pick, how much pressure to exert and in what direction. One after one, the tumblers snapped back, unlocking the door.

Max didn't touch the handle. An external door like this would almost certainly have an alarm on it. He needed to cover the sound of it going off, and the best way to do that was to set off another alarm – like a fire bell.

He went back to the sofa and took the paper towels and unused match out of his pockets. He screwed up the towels, made a small mound out of them on the cushions, then struck the match on the rough surface of the wall. Some of the pink coating came off, but the match didn't ignite. Max felt a jolt of panic. He needed this to work – his whole plan depended on it. He turned the head of the match round, said a silent prayer and struck it again. For a split second it looked as if it wasn't going to light, then suddenly it burst into flame. Max applied it to the paper towels and they flared up immediately. Seconds later, the cushions caught fire. Max flitted across to the kitchen door and closed it. He didn't want the smell of smoke to alert the prison officers until the fire had really taken hold. He waited until the sofa was well ablaze, the flames licking up to the ceiling, then removed the fire extinguisher from the wall and broke the glass cover of the alarm with his elbow. An ear-splitting bell immediately started to clang. Max opened the door to the courtyard. A second alarm went off, but it was impossible to distinguish it from the fire bell. The two noises seemed to merge together into one deafening cacophony.

Max closed the door behind him and ran along the side of the courtyard garden, still carrying the fire extinguisher. He dived behind a clump of bushes and lay flat on the ground, looking back the way he'd come. The kitchen window shattered and flames shot out through the broken pane, getting larger and more ferocious as they were fanned by the breeze. Huge clouds of smoke billowed up into the air, much to Max's satisfaction. The blaze was too big now for the staff to tackle on their own, particularly as Max had made off with the nearest fire extinguisher. That was just how he wanted it.

For five or six minutes he lay in the bushes watching the asylum burn, then he heard the sound of sirens drawing nearer, getting gradually louder. The arched wooden doors in the front wing swung open, and three fire engines raced through into the courtyard and came to a halt.

Firemen jumped out and the courtyard came alive with activity. Hoses were unrolled and connected up to hydrants, then the jets of water were directed onto the burning kitchen. In only a few minutes, the blaze was under control. Max was pleased with himself. He'd got it just right: the incident was serious enough to warrant calling the fire brigade, but localized enough for the prison not to be evacuated, and Max's empty cell discovered.

He waited until all the firemen were occupied, then slithered out from the bushes on his belly and snaked underneath the nearest fire engine. He lay on the ground out of sight for the next half-hour while the firemen extinguished the blaze and then began to pack up their gear. He saw legs moving around the fire engines, the firemen's thick protective boots tramping across the courtyard. The air was heavy with the smell of smoke and burned wood.

A fireman's feet stopped only a metre away from Max's face. The man slid open the locker on the side of the fire engine to stow away some item of equipment. Max let him finish, then wriggled across underneath the chassis and looked out cautiously. The fire was completely out now, a few plumes of smoke drifting up into the sky. The firemen were rolling up their hoses, removing their helmets and clambering back into the fire engines. Max prepared himself. He had to time this just right. He checked in all directions. There was no one looking his way, no one close to the fire engine. Squirming out quickly from under the vehicle, he pulled open the roller door of the equipment locker on the side and scrambled inside, pulling the door down after him.

He was in complete darkness, surrounded by buckets and cylinders of compressed air for the firemen's breathing apparatus. Trying not to make any noise, he slid to the back of the locker and curled up, arranging the pieces of equipment so that he couldn't be seen if anyone opened the door. His heart was in his mouth, his stomach churning with anxiety. He needed just a few more minutes, that was all. He'd got this far. *Please don't let them find me now*, he whispered to himself. *Please.*

The engine turned over and the vehicle set off slowly, circling around the courtyard and heading for the exit. Then it stopped. Max heard voices, but not what they were saying. Footsteps scraped on the concrete close by. Had the prison officers discovered that Max was missing? Were they searching all the fire engines? The locker door rattled open. Max buried his face in his arms and held his breath. Someone was looking inside the locker. Max could sense their eyes peering around. He waited for the shout, the hands reaching in and dragging him out, but all he heard was the noise of something being thrown in – a piece of equipment that must have accidentally been left behind – then the locker door clattered shut.

The vehicle moved off. Max started breathing again. He listened to the sounds from outside, the pitch of the engine. They were passing through the exit, crossing the prison forecourt. An outer gate opened, the fire engine picked up speed, then it turned and accelerated some more. They were out on the open road, speeding away from Mount Pleasant.

THIRTEEN

It wouldn't be a long journey, Max knew that. The fire engines had got to the prison less than ten minutes after the alarm had gone off, so it couldn't be far to their station. They were driving slower on the return trip, of course, their sirens silent, but Max reckoned they would still be back at base in less than fifteen minutes.

He pressed his back to the wall of the locker to stop himself sliding about as the fire engine went round corners. He was feeling jubilant. He couldn't believe he'd pulled it off. He'd got away. 'A hundred per cent escape-proof' was how Penhall had described Mount Pleasant. Well, Max had shown him how wrong that was. He wished he could see Penhall's face when they told him that Max had broken out. That would be quite something. But when would they actually discover that he'd gone? Very soon, if they decided to check the cells – though why would they do that in the middle of the night? No, seven o'clock was the earliest they'd notice his absence. When the lights came back on, the prison officers would certainly spot the empty cell on the

CCTV monitors. It was probably about one o'clock now, maybe half-past. That gave Max five and a half hours before they came looking for him.

The fire engine slowed to a crawl, turning sharply to the left. Max heard the clatter of a big door sliding open and knew they'd reached the station. The vehicle moved forward a few metres and stopped. Max stayed where he was until he was sure that all the firemen had left the immediate area, then very quietly pushed up the roller door of the locker and clambered out. The garage was deserted, the three fire engines parked next to one another. HERTFORDSHIRE FIRE AND RESCUE SERVICES, it said on their sides. So he'd been right. He was just north of London. Now all he had to do was find a way home.

The main doors at the front of the fire station were closed, but Max went through into a storeroom and found an unlocked door that opened onto the car park at the side of the building. He went across it and walked quickly away. He was in a built-up area: residential streets leading off a main road that, even at this time of night, had a fair amount of traffic moving along it.

After about four hundred metres he reached a round-about and signs pointing to Hatfield, St Albans and the M25. He took the exit for the motorway and stood in a lay-by with his thumb out. He knew hitch-hiking was a risky business, but he had no money, no other way of getting back home. He had to wait ten minutes before a large white bakery van pulled in.

'Where're you going?' the driver asked.

'London,' Max replied.

'I'm making a delivery to the South Mimms service station, junction of the M25 and A1. Will that do you?'

'Yes, thanks,' Max said.

'You're out late, a young lad like you,' the driver said as he swerved back out onto the road.

'I missed the train from St Albans and decided to hitch home,' Max improvised. 'It's taking me longer than I thought.'

'There are loads of lorries at South Mimms. One of them will give you a lift.'

The driver was right. When they reached the service station, Max wandered around the lorry park and quickly found a trucker who was willing to take him into London. Max told him the same story about missing his train, and the trucker, taking pity on him, went out of his way to drop him off just a couple of miles from home. Max walked that final bit of his journey, climbing over the garden wall to approach the house from the rear. He used his home-made lock-pick to open the basement door and stepped inside. As he fumbled in the darkness for the light switch, he suddenly felt an arm hook around his neck, squeezing his windpipe.

'It's me,' he managed to croak feebly.

The arm pulled away and the light snapped on. Chris stared at him. 'Jeez, Max, I'm sorry. Did I hurt you?'

'I'm OK.'

'I didn't know who it was. I just heard someone fiddling with the lock. Thank God you're back. Where've you been? We've been worried sick.'

Max gave him a brief explanation, then said, 'I'll tell you the rest later. Right now, we have to get a move on. Do you know if Consuela booked our tickets for Sweden?'

'Yes, she did. For this afternoon. The two of you.'

'You're not coming?' Max asked, suddenly alarmed.

'Not on the same flight. I'm going via Copenhagen. It's safer if we don't travel together.'

'Good. We'd better wake her, get our passports.'

'What's the hurry? The flights aren't—'

'We have to go *now*,' Max interrupted urgently. 'Get an earlier flight. I have to be out of the country within the next few hours.'

It was nearly five o'clock when they arrived at Heathrow. Despite the early hour, the terminal building was already starting to fill up with passengers. It was two hours until the cell lights at Mount Pleasant came on. Max hoped that was sufficient time for them to change their flights and get out of the country.

He and Consuela went to the British Airways ticket counter and Consuela worked her charm on the male clerk, asking him whether there was space on an earlier flight to Stockholm. The clerk checked his computer and found them two spare seats on the 6.45 a.m. departure.

Chris wasn't with them. They'd already split up outside the terminal and he was killing time in a coffee shop before flying out later in the day, as originally arranged. He was travelling on the new passport he'd acquired from one of his contacts – in the name of Alan Montgomery, supposedly a thirty-three-year-old sales executive whose photograph, at first glance, looked nothing like Chris – until he put on the pair of clear-lensed, horn-rimmed spectacles he'd also acquired – and suddenly he *was* Alan Montgomery.

Don't overdo your disguise, Chris said. *Don't even think about wigs or false beards, they're too easy to spot. Stick with your basic shape and appearance and add a small change – spectacles, dyed hair – to make yourself look different.* Airport security would check names first, in any case, not photographic likenesses. They'd be looking out for a Chris Moncrieffe, not an Alan Montgomery.

Max had butterflies in his stomach as they went through passport and security control, wondering if he was going to be stopped. Had his escape from Mount Pleasant been discovered? Had Penhall alerted the airports to look out for him? If he had, it certainly wasn't obvious. The official checked his passport and boarding pass and let him through without a word.

The plane left dead on time. Max had put on his spare wristwatch at home and he checked the dial every few minutes after take-off. By seven o'clock they had passed over the Essex coast and were out over the sea, heading northeast towards Scandinavia.

FOURTEEN

Max had never been to Sweden before. In his imagination, it was a strange, wild northern region, covered with snow and ice and thick pine forests and populated by tall blond people who wore fur hats and got around on skis or reindeer-drawn sleighs. So he was surprised – and maybe a little disappointed – to find that Arlanda Airport, twenty-five miles north of Stockholm, was just like every other airport he'd visited. It could have been Heathrow, except it was smaller and cleaner and the signs were in Swedish as well as English. There were certainly plenty of tall blonds in the arrivals area, but none of them was wearing a fur hat, and as for snow and reindeer, well, there was no sign of either, unless you counted the stuffed toys in the airport shop.

On the *flygbuss* into the centre of Stockholm, Consuela told Max a bit about the city – how it was known as 'the Venice of the North' because it was built on a series of islands, connected by bridges. She'd done some sightseeing when she'd come with Max's dad and thought it was one of the most beautiful cities she'd ever visited. She'd loved the fresh sea air, the architecture and old houses, and the fact that wherever you looked there was water, either at your feet or gleaming in the distance between the distinctive Scandinavian buildings.

Max saw it for himself when they got off the bus outside the central railway station and took a taxi to their hotel, driving along the edge of what Consuela described as the oldest part of the city – the Gamla Stan – with water on one side of the road and a row of ancient houses on the other, with occasional glimpses of a tall red-brick church tower and an elegant stone façade that Consuela said was the Royal Palace.

The taxi crossed a busy traffic intersection that formed a bridge to the island of Södermalm, then passed the Tunnelbana – Underground – station at Slussen and began to climb up a hill. Over the stone parapet at the side of the road, Max saw boats in the port, and green, wooded shores along the shipping channel that led out towards the sea.

The taxi turned left up another hill and stopped outside a five-storey brick building with a sign outside that read HOTEL KATARINA. Across the road was a small public park with rocky outcrops, patches of grass and a path leading to a stone church that was topped by a green copper spire. On the slope in front of the church nestled a ramshackle little wooden cottage that looked as if it belonged in a fairy tale.

Consuela paid the taxi driver with some of their Swedish kronor, then they picked up their luggage – they'd travelled light: just a small overnight bag each – and went into the hotel. The foyer was bright and modern: a varnished wooden floor, a reception desk made of pine, a seating area with steel-framed armchairs and a glass-topped coffee table covered with colourful magazines. The receptionist was a young man in his mid-twenties with spiky blond hair and a gold ring in one ear. He was wearing jeans and an open-necked casual shirt. He glanced briefly at Max, then gave Consuela a longer look and smiled.

'Señorita Navarra, it's good to see you again,' he said in excellent English.

Consuela was surprised. 'You remember me?'

'Of course. How could I forget? How long ago was it that you were here? Two, three years? Welcome back to Stockholm.'

The receptionist smiled again, unable to take his eyes off Consuela. Max watched with amusement. Consuela had that effect on men. Max was used to feeling completely invisible when he was with her.

'It was two single rooms, wasn't it?' the receptionist asked.

He clicked a mouse and studied the computer screen behind the counter. 'I've put you in number eight, one of the rooms overlooking the garden at the back. It's much quieter there. And the young gentleman . . . Mr Cassidy.' The receptionist looked up. 'I'm guessing, but you are Alexander Cassidy's son, no?'

'Yes,' Max said.

'I remember him too. I was sorry to hear about . . . about what happened. You are in room number four, just across the landing from Señorita Navarra.'

He handed Consuela a couple of key cards. 'Breakfast is in the dining room between seven and nine. Do you have any luggage?'

Consuela held up her small bag. 'Just this.'

'Would you like a hand with it?'

'Thank you, but I think I can manage.'

'Your rooms are on the first floor.'

The young man went ahead of them and pressed the button to summon the lift. 'Enjoy your stay. If there's anything else I can do to help, please let me know,' he said to Consuela.

'Thank you, I will,' she replied politely.

Max waited until the lift doors had closed behind them before he grinned at Consuela and said, 'You should have let him carry your bag. It would have made his day.'

'He was only being friendly.'

'Then he could've polished your shoes with his tongue.'

'Stop it, Max. He was a very nice young man.'

'*Very* nice,' Max agreed.

Consuela gave him a hard stare. 'That's *enough*.'

They went to their rooms. Max's was small, but comfortable, the window overlooking the street that ran down the side of the hotel. He didn't care what it was like. It was only for one night. He dumped his bag on the floor – there was no point in unpacking it – and went back downstairs. He borrowed a Stockholm telephone directory from the receptionist and went to Consuela's room. It was twice as big as his, with a floor-to-ceiling window that provided a view over the garden – a lawn and a small patio with tubs of flowers and a few chairs on it.

Max looked up the number of Grön Värld, the environmental charity that had employed Erik Blomkvist, and punched it into the phone next to Consuela's bed. A man answered, speaking Swedish. Max didn't understand what he'd said.

'I'm sorry, but do you speak English, please?'

'Of course. What can I do for you?' the man said in faultless English.

'My name is Max Cassidy. I wanted to talk to someone about Erik Blomkvist.'

'Erik? Erik is no longer with us, I'm afraid.'

'I know. That's what I want to talk about. His disappearance, the work he was doing before he went missing.'

There was a short silence. When the man came back on, his voice was guarded. 'Did you say Cassidy?'

'Yes, Max Cassidy.'

'You are related to Alexander Cassidy?'

'He's my father.'

'Give me your number. I'll call you back in five minutes.'

'But can't I—'

'Five minutes,' the man said urgently. 'What's your number?'

Max thought about giving the name of their hotel, then changed his mind. The man's tone had unnerved him. He gave his mobile number instead. The line went dead. Five minutes later, his mobile rang.

'Max?'

'Yes.'

'I'm sorry about that. My name is Axel Svensson. I'm out of the office now, on a different phone.'

'Your phones aren't safe?' Max said.

'Let's say we have our suspicions. Our work is sometimes controversial, sometimes political. There are people who don't like what we do. Now tell me, why are you interested in Erik?'

'I think I might know what happened to him. I'm in Stockholm. Can we meet? I could come to your offices.'

'Not our offices.' Svensson's voice was wary. 'I'm busy all day, but I can meet you this evening. Where are you staying?'

'The Hotel Katarina, in Södermalm.'

'There's a restaurant not far from your hotel. The Sista Styvern, on Fjällgatan. I will meet you there for dinner at nine.'

'OK.'

'Until then.'

'Just one more thing,' Max said quickly. 'You asked if I was related to Alexander Cassidy.'

'Yes.'

'Do you know my father?'

'I'll tell you tonight,' Svensson said, and hung up.

Max and Consuela spent the afternoon in the hotel. Max went to bed for a few hours. He'd had no sleep the previous night and was dog-tired. When he awoke it was still only six o'clock. There was a lot of time to kill before they went to meet Axel Svensson.

Max wondered about going out and exploring the city, but they'd agreed that they would remain in their rooms, at least until Chris arrived. Stockholm was a peaceful, civilized place, but after their experience on the road near Henley and Max's incarceration in Mount Pleasant, it made sense to be careful, particularly given Svensson's manner on the phone – his reluctance to talk, his suspicions that their call might be being monitored. If Svensson was worried, then Max and Consuela needed to be extra-cautious.

Max was restless. There was nothing to do in a hotel room. He read a book he'd brought with him for a while, then switched on the television. Maybe there was a good film on that he could watch. He flipped through the channels, but found only game shows and soaps, all in Swedish. He watched one of the game shows for a while, trying to work out what was going on, then gave up and switched off the TV.

He wasn't used to inactivity. At home, at about this time of the day, he would normally be training, working out on the exercise machines in the basement or practising his escapology techniques. He could do a few exercises now – some press-ups, some pull-ups on the doorframe of the en-suite bathroom – but he couldn't be bothered. For once his self-discipline had deserted him. Instead he lay on the bed and thought about his escape from Mount Pleasant. Rupert Penhall would know by now that Max had flown to Stockholm. Would he contact the Swedish authorities, get them to arrest Max, maybe put him on a plane straight back to London? Max didn't know. Sweden was a foreign country. Did Penhall have that kind of influence here? There was no point wondering. If it happened, it happened.

Max looked at his watch again. It was seven fifteen. He went into the bathroom and took a long shower to give himself something to do. He was fully dressed, drying his hair with a towel, when there was a knock on the door. Max went to the peephole and looked out. There was a man in the corridor; a tall man with horn-rimmed spectacles.

Max unlocked the door and swung it open. Chris came in, glancing around the room.

'Everything OK?' he asked.

'Fine. How was your trip?'

'No problems. You?'

'Easy.'

'No questions at the airport?'

'No.'

'Or tails at this end?'

'I don't think so.'

Chris went across to the window and stood to one side, peering down warily into the street. 'I'm in room fourteen, on the floor above,' he said. 'Have you been in touch with Grön Värld?'

'We're meeting a guy named Axel Svensson for dinner at nine.'

Chris checked his watch. 'Where?'

'A restaurant. Consuela was going to look up the street on her map.'

'Let's go and find her.'

Max tossed his towel into the bathroom and they went across the landing to room eight. Max knocked. Consuela opened the door, then stood aside to let them enter. She'd tied her hair back and changed into black trousers and a plain white top.

Chris went through the same procedure again – crossing to the window and looking cautiously out into the garden.

'Nice view,' he said. 'You seem to have ended up with the best room.'

'The receptionist fancies her,' Max said.

'Yeah?' Chris said.

Consuela coloured slightly. 'Max, be quiet.'

She turned away and picked up a map of Stockholm from the desk. 'I found Fjällgatan,' she said. 'It's not far from here. A ten-minute walk, maybe.'

She spread out the map on the bed and pointed to an area on the southern edge of central Stockholm. 'This is Södermalm,' she said. 'We're here, near Skånegatan, and Fjällgatan is here, just half a kilometre or so away.'

Chris looked at his watch again. 'I think we should leave now, get there early. That will give us time to check out the area, see who else is in the restaurant.'

Consuela folded up the map and put it in her handbag. They went downstairs and across the foyer. The receptionist barely glanced at Max and Chris, but beamed warmly at Consuela and wished her a pleasant evening.

Outside on the street, Chris turned to Max and said, 'You're right, I've never seen a more lovesick guy in my life.'

'Oh, shut up,' Consuela said irritably and set off along the street.

Chris and Max had to run to catch up with her.

'Hey, wait for us,' Max cried.

Consuela stopped. 'No more jokes, OK?' she said. 'They're not funny.'

'OK, we're sorry.' Max could see that she wasn't in the mood for humour. Being in Stockholm was making her edgy.

'Yeah,' said Chris. 'It's not the poor guy's fault that he has terrible taste in women.'

Consuela's mouth tightened. She spun round and kept on walking.

'OK,' Chris called after her. 'I'm sorry, no more jokes.'

Consuela slowed a little, appeased by the apology.

Max and Chris drew alongside her. She consulted the map and they turned right down a hill, going past apartment blocks, and shops and offices that were closed up for the night. At the foot of the hill they skirted a children's playground and climbed up a steep flight of stone steps onto a ridge occupied by a massive red-brick building that looked like a school or a hospital. Consuela led them past, then down a narrow flight of wooden steps onto a street that seemed to be suspended above the harbour on the very edge of a cliff.

'This is Fjällgatan,' she said.

They saw a sign reading SISTA STYVERN hanging from a bracket outside one of the buildings at the western end of the street, but they didn't head for it immediately. They went in the opposite direction, walking towards the eastern end, where there were buildings only on the right-hand side. On the other side was a long, narrow strip of public gardens that gave a magnificent view out over Stockholm.

There were one or two people sitting on benches, enjoying the warm evening air. It was almost nine o'clock, but it was still very light, much lighter than it would have been in London. Max vaguely remembered from his geography lessons that the summer days got longer the further north you went.

At the edge of the gardens was a metal railing, then a forty-metre drop to the road along the waterfront. There was a ferry terminal on the far side of the road, a huge white ship moored alongside it, its side emblazoned with the words VIKING LINE and the vessel's name – *Cinderella*.

They stood there for a few minutes, gazing out across the city – the Old Town away to their left, a funfair on an island across the water. Max could see the bright lights on the rides, just make out the shapes of the cars careering around the roller coaster. The faint sound of music carried across the harbour. Then they went back along Fjällgatan to the Sista Styvern.

The restaurant was down some steps, built into the hillside above the port. Max smelled the enticing aroma of onions and garlic and spices as they went down into a vaulted reception area containing a counter and glass cabinets of drinks and chilled desserts. In a room to the right were two large wooden tables laden with food – the smörgåsbord eat-all-you-like buffet for which the Swedes were famous.

It must have been obvious that they weren't Swedish, for the young woman behind the counter spoke to them in English. 'Hi, welcome to the Sista Styvern. There are more tables outside on the terrace.'

Consuela looked at the customers helping

themselves to food from the big tables. 'So how does this work?' she asked. 'Do we serve ourselves?'

'You pay a set charge for the food of ninety-eight kronor each,' the young woman replied. 'Eat as much as you want. Drinks are extra.'

'We're meeting someone here. I'm not sure if he's arrived yet.'

'No problem. Find a table, then pay when you're ready to eat.'

They went outside onto the terrace and sat down at a table. It was like a conservatory, with glass walls on three sides, the panes slid open to let in a cooling breeze. Max looked around at the other customers. Most were casually dressed, some just in T-shirts and jeans. There were big groups of young people talking and laughing, and one or two couples seated at the smaller tables. There was no man on his own who might have been Axel Svensson.

Below the terrace, the ground dropped away steeply to the road by the waterfront. Max saw a small passenger launch crossing the harbour from one of the outlying islands and pulling in to a jetty near the Gamla Stan. The streetlights of the Old Town were on, illuminating the pink-, red- and orange-painted walls of the ancient buildings.

A little after nine o'clock, a man came out onto the

terrace and scanned the tables, as if he were looking for someone. He was in his thirties with shoulder-length blond hair and a close-trimmed blond beard. He saw Max – the only teenager in the restaurant – and came across to their table.

'Max?'

Max nodded.

'I'm Axel Svensson.'

Svensson held out his hand. Max shook it, then introduced Chris and Consuela.

'Let's get something to eat,' Svensson said. 'Then we'll talk.'

They followed him back inside. Consuela paid for their meals and they were given a large plate and some cutlery each. It was Max's kind of restaurant. No waiters fussing around, no menu to read, just a mountain of food and no restrictions on how much you could take. He went round the table, helping himself to the various dishes – rice, potatoes, stews, salads, smoked salmon, a couple of large chunks of crusty bread – until he needed both hands to take the weight of his plate.

Consuela looked disapprovingly at his mound of food. 'Max, you can't possibly eat all that.'

'You just watch me,' Max replied.

Chris bought beers for himself and Consuela and Svensson, and a large juice for Max, and they went back out to their table. Svensson looked around discreetly, examining the other customers. He seemed tense, nervy. They made small talk to begin with, Svensson asking them how they were finding Stockholm, what their hotel was like – boring stuff that didn't interest Max. He concentrated on his food for a few minutes – he hadn't had a decent meal for days. Then Svensson turned to him. He had bright blue eyes, but they weren't a cold blue. They were more like the blue of a Mediterranean sky: clear and warm.

'You said you might know something about Erik's disappearance.'

Max nodded. 'That's right. But could you tell me first what exactly happened to him. I don't know the details.'

'He went camping on Gotland last September. That's an island in the Baltic, to the south of Stockholm, about three hours by ferry. His clothes and rucksack were found on the beach one evening by walkers who thought it was a bit strange and reported it to the local police. The police looked everywhere for Erik, but found no trace of him. They concluded that he must have gone swimming and got into difficulty, been swept out to sea by the currents and drowned.'

'But his body hasn't been found?' Max said.

'Not so far.'

Max tore off a chunk of bread and chewed it. 'Did

you ever think that it might not have been an accident?'

Svensson gave a slight start. 'That is a strange question. Why do you ask it?'

'Because of your reaction when I called you – leaving your office and finding another phone, not wanting to meet me there. Also, you keep looking nervously around the restaurant. You seem worried about something . . .'

Svensson took a moment to reply. He smoothed his beard with his fingertips, his brow furrowing pensively. 'As I mentioned on the phone,' he said, 'the work we do is sometimes controversial, sometimes political. We have opponents – enemies who do not agree with us.'

'What kind of enemies?' Max asked.

'People in power; businessmen. Environmentalists are a nuisance to the big multinational corporations that want to continue drilling for oil, mining for minerals, chopping down trees, selling petrol-guzzling cars and all the rest of it. They don't like people getting in their way, and that is what we do. We question them, we challenge them, we oppose them. That doesn't make us popular.'

'And you think your phones are being tapped by these businesses?'

'Or by the security services, yes. We've also had a couple of suspicious break-ins at our offices. Files and laptops have been stolen. And only last month, one of my colleagues was set upon and beaten up by a gang of thugs as he left the office late in the evening. So we're careful about what we say on the phone, where we go, who we meet.'

Max glanced around the table. Chris was wolfing down a plate of food that was almost as big as Max's; Consuela was toying with a green salad and a small slice of ham. They were listening to the conversation, but leaving all the talking to Max.

'And my question about Erik's disappearance . . . ?' Max asked.

Svensson looked steadily at him for a second before replying. 'Yes, I wondered about it. The whole thing was very odd. The pile of clothes on the beach, Erik missing. At first the police thought it might have been suicide, but that was ridiculous. Erik wasn't the type to take his own life. So it had to have been an accident. The other alternatives were just too far-fetched to believe.'

'What other alternatives?'

'Well, if he didn't commit suicide and it wasn't an accident, that only leaves abduction or murder. Erik was an ecologist studying orang-utans and trees. Why would anyone kidnap him or kill him? That wouldn't make sense.'

'But it's what happened,' Max said.

Svensson stared at him. '*What?*'

'It's what happened,' Max repeated. 'Erik was kidnapped and later killed.'

'Are you serious? Kidnapped by whom?'

Max told him about Shadow Island, about what he'd seen there; how he'd found Erik Blomkvist's name in the files in Julius Clark's office. Svensson listened intently, his eyes opening wide with shock and horror. When Max had finished, the Swede took a long gulp of beer.

'My God, is that true?' he asked.

'It's true,' Consuela confirmed. 'I was there too.'

'So was I,' Chris added. 'I'm not a scientist, but I was working for an environmental pressure group like yours in the Amazon when I was kidnapped and taken to Shadow Island.'

'But why?' Svensson said. 'Why would this Julius Clark kidnap people?'

'To brainwash them,' Max said, 'using a drug called Episuderon. There were other prisoners too, including a British ecologist named Redmond Ashworth-Ames. And my father.'

'Your *father*?' Svensson blinked a couple of times and gaped at Max. 'But I read it in the papers. Your father was killed, wasn't he? And your mother—'

'My mother was framed and wrongfully imprisoned,'

Max interrupted. 'My father is alive. He somehow escaped from Shadow Island, then vanished. I'm trying to find him. You knew him, didn't you?'

Svensson hesitated for a moment as he ate a piece of smoked salmon with some mustard and dill sauce. Then he nodded. 'I met him when he was in Stockholm three years ago.' He glanced at Consuela. 'I recognize you from his stage show. You were his assistant, weren't you?'

'Yes,' Consuela replied. 'Did we meet back then? I don't remember you.'

'No, we didn't meet. Alex came to Erik's flat alone one morning. I was there too.'

'My dad went to Erik's flat?' Max said incredulously. 'He knew Erik?'

Svensson didn't reply immediately. He studied Max, then looked at Consuela and Chris. He seemed to be weighing something up in his mind, deciding whether to confide in them.

'Please, you must help us,' Max said imploringly. 'If you know something about my dad, something that could help us find him, you must tell us.'

Svensson held Max's gaze for a few seconds. Then he said quietly, 'Did your father ever mention the Cedar Alliance?'

Max sat bolt upright, as if he'd had an electric shock. 'The *Cedar Alliance*?'

He pushed his plate to one side, his food half finished, and leaned forward over the table. Suddenly he wasn't hungry any more. 'Dad mentioned it in a letter he left me. But he didn't say what it was.'

Svensson looked around the restaurant terrace, scrutinizing the other customers. No one was paying them any attention: they were all engrossed in their own groups, their own conversations. But he obviously didn't want to risk being overheard, for when he spoke again, his voice was low and discreet.

'You must know how mankind is destroying the environment – it's common knowledge. We're over-fishing our seas, we're polluting the oceans and the soil with poisonous chemicals. We're stripping the forests, we're turning farmland into deserts. We're threatening dozens of species of animals with extinction by our activities. We can't seem to stop ourselves. We have to find new reserves of oil to extract, new mineral deposits to mine, new products to make and sell, all to fuel our insatiable need to consume and make money.

'Greed – that's the root cause of all the problems. Most of the world's population lives in terrible poverty, but we in the West have never been richer, and our economies, our lives, are controlled by businesses that seek only to make bigger and bigger profits, regardless of the cost to the environment. The rich and powerful don't care what happens to the Earth so long as they still have their big houses and their yachts and their private jets.'

Svensson broke off and gave a rueful smile. 'I'm sorry, this sounds like a speech. What I'm saying is that our planet is sick, and it's going to get sicker unless we change our ways and start taking better care of it. But that isn't an easy task because these greedy business-men and their friends are making too much money out of exploiting the Earth. And their money talks. It buys them political support, it buys them influence and power – more power than many of the world's govern-ments. They allow nothing to stand in the way of their profiteering. No one can stop them.'

He paused again. 'But the Cedar Alliance is trying.'

'How?' Max said. 'What is it? What does it do?'

'It's a secret global organization dedicated to protect-ing the Earth from over-exploitation,' Svensson replied. 'I say "organization", but it's not like most other organizations. It doesn't have a headquarters, it doesn't have any offices or a staff of employees. It's what its name suggests – an alliance of people and groups around the world who share the same beliefs and aims. Many of them work for environmental groups like mine, but not all. It's far bigger than that. There are scientists and students in the Alliance. Journalists, teachers, lawyers, doctors, farmers, politicians; all sorts of other people too. We're all different, but we all share the same overriding objective: to save the planet for our children to enjoy, as we have enjoyed it.'

'My dad said it had the "conscience of the world on its side",' Max said.

'It does. How could any responsible, thoughtful human being not want to protect the world we live in?'

'But what does my dad have to do with the Cedar Alliance?'

'Your father was – *is*,' Svensson corrected himself, 'one of the leaders of the Alliance.'

'My *dad*?' Max said in disbelief. 'But he's a professional escapologist.'

'So? As I said, there are many different people in the organization. Hundreds, probably thousands. There is no membership list, you see. The Alliance is organized into very small groups – cells, we call them – like a spy ring. The members of each cell know their fellow members, maybe only half a dozen people, but they don't know who is in other cells or how many people are above them in the organization. It's safer that way. It means that no one person can betray the Alliance, and our enemies don't know who to attack.'

'You're sure my dad is one of the leaders?' Max said.

He was still finding it hard to take in what Svensson had said.

'No doubt about it. That's why he came to Erik's flat. To meet the members of our cell. A big multinational mineral corporation was trying to get permission for a huge new mine in Lapland – that's the area that runs across the north of Norway, Sweden and Finland. We were trying to stop them. Your dad had visited the other Alliance cells in Norway and Finland to coordinate the campaign to stop the mining corporation. He gave us money from a central fund to help pay for publicity and research.'

'The Alliance has a central fund?'

'Donations from supporters, some small, some big. Not all wealthy people are the same. There are many who are concerned about the environment.'

Max turned to Consuela. 'You didn't know anything about this?'

Consuela shook her head, bewildered by Svensson's revelation. 'Nothing. I remember the tour. We did shows in Oslo and Helsinki as well as Stockholm. But I had no idea that your dad was meeting environmental campaigners, or that he had anything to do with this Cedar Alliance.'

'How could you not know? You were with him,' said Max.

'Not all the time. There were plenty of opportunities for him to have secret meetings.'

Max sat back in his chair. His head was swimming. He felt as if he'd been tipped upside down and spun round and round. He was in a daze, his whole world topsy-turvy. So this was the secret life his father had been leading; the secret life he'd kept hidden not only from Max, but from Max's mother and Consuela too.

'I can see this has come as a bit of a shock to you,' Svensson said.

Max nodded. 'I knew none of this. My mum didn't know either.'

'Your father had to keep it secret,' Svensson said. 'You must see that. The Cedar Alliance's strength is its invisibility. It operates quietly, stealthily, guiding affairs from a distance. If our enemies knew who the leaders were, they would try to eliminate them.'

'Julius Clark found out about my dad,' Max said. 'That's why he kept him a prisoner on Shadow Island.'

'But you said your father escaped.'

'He did.'

'Then that's good. He must be out there somewhere, still working for the Cedar Alliance.'

'But where?' Max asked. 'Where would he go? Where would he hide? Do you know?'

'I'm sorry, I don't . . . Maybe he will try to contact you, or send you a message.'

'Maybe,' Max said, but he didn't think it likely. His father had gone underground – to protect himself, but perhaps also to protect Max. He wouldn't make contact in case he put Max in danger.

Consuela put her hand gently on Max's arm. 'I didn't know any of this, Max, believe me,' she told him. 'It's as big a shock to me as it is to you.'

'I know.' Max smiled at her, though there was a heaviness in his heart. He'd thought he was close to his dad. Now he was beginning to wonder how well he'd really known him.

'Can I ask you one more thing?' he said to Svensson. 'What work was Erik doing before he disappeared?'

'He was working in Borneo.'

'In *Borneo*?' *Just like Redmond Ashworth-Ames*, Max thought. That had to be important.

'Yes. In Tanjung Puting National Park. Do you know much about bio-fuels?'

Max shook his head.

'They're fuels made from plants, like maize, sugar beet or the seeds of the oil-palm tree. They can be used in cars and machinery instead of petrol. Some people see them as a greener, cleaner fuel that will help slow down global warming. But things aren't that simple. To produce bio-fuels you need land, a lot of land. In Borneo, for example, they've been clearing vast areas of rainforest to plant oil palms. Land has been stolen from the local people, trees have been felled illegally and the wild animals – like orang-utans – driven out or killed. People are going hungry because land that was once used for growing food is now being used for bio-fuel production. Erik was studying the impact of oil-palm plantations on wildlife and plants and campaigning to stop the destruction of the rainforest.'

'Thank you for telling us this,' Max said.

'I'm glad I could help,' the Swede replied. 'Your father is a good man. He's doing important work. I hope you find him.'

They left the Sista Styvern shortly after that. Max didn't finish his plate of food – he'd lost his appetite. On the street outside, they shook hands with Svensson and parted company. He went one way along Fjällgatan, Max, Consuela and Chris went the other. It was late, but it still wasn't fully dark yet. The sky was dusky, the street shrouded in a gloomy twilight.

Chris and Consuela talked quietly about what Svensson had told them, but Max didn't join in. He didn't feel like talking. He was distracted, thinking about his father.

They were nearing the end of the street when the

attack came. Two shadowy figures erupted suddenly from a doorway to their right, another two from a doorway across the street. They moved swiftly, going for Chris first. A knife blade flashed as it scythed up towards his chest, but he reacted instinctively, twisting out of the way and kicking one of the assailants in the groin, then spinning round and head-butting another.

'Run, Max!' he yelled, shielding Consuela from the thugs.

Max hesitated, watching Chris lash out at the men, punching, kicking, trying to drive them back.

'Run!' Chris shouted again.

A figure lunged towards Max, a knife glinting in his hand. Max dodged sideways and felt the knife rip through the folds of his jacket. The thug was off balance, unsteady on his feet. Max kicked the knife out of the man's hand and heard it skitter away across the ground. Then he took off down the street, running flat out. Not caring where he went. Just running.

FIFTEEN

At the end of Fjällgatan, Max paused for a second to look back, taking in the chaotic turmoil of shapes and figures – the dark bodies ducking and dodging, arms flailing, fists lashing out, the street resounding with the hard, aggressive grunts of brawling men. And in the thick of it, Chris was holding his own against the attackers, his army training giving him an edge in a fight. Consuela was joining in too, to back him up.

Then Max saw something that made his blood turn cold – two of the thugs breaking away from the brawl and racing down the street towards him. Coming after him.

He turned and glanced around rapidly, trying not to panic. The street curved away to his right, sweeping down to join the main road to the waterfront. Max sprinted round the bend and headed down the hill towards the harbour, vehicles speeding past him. He thought about stopping one of the cars to ask for help, but they were all moving too fast. If he ventured out into the road, he knew he'd just be knocked down. So he kept running – running as fast as he could. He was young and fit, but the two men behind him were also young and fit. When Max glanced over his shoulder, he saw that they were only fifty metres back. He could tell from the way they moved that they wouldn't tire easily. They'd keep going until they caught him.

Max gritted his teeth and dug in, just as he did on his training runs around the park in London. Legs pounding, arms pumping, heart and lungs fighting for that extra bit of speed. He was nearing the bottom of the hill now, approaching the busy junction near the waterfront where the traffic swept in from all directions. There was a Tunnelbana station on the other side of the road. For an instant Max wondered whether he could get across to it and lose his pursuers underground, but he quickly abandoned the idea. The traffic was far too heavy. The thugs would be on him before he got anywhere near the station.

They were still fifty metres back – Max was relieved to see that the gap hadn't narrowed. But how long could he keep up this punishing pace? He could already feel the pain in his chest and legs. What should he do? Find help, protection? But where? There were no police cars around and very few pedestrians. He could stop a passer-by and ask for assistance, but he didn't speak

Swedish. And he didn't have time to explain himself. He couldn't afford to stop for even a few seconds, so he kept going, through the junction and across the bridge into the Gamla Stan – the Old Town.

He looked over his shoulder again and felt a surge of hope. His pursuers had dropped back a little. Maybe they were tiring. Max put on a burst of speed, trying to widen the gap, and ducked down the first side street he came to. It was narrow, with tall, four-storey buildings on both sides, uneven cobbles underfoot. The buildings shut out the sky, the last traces of daylight, turning the street into a dark corridor.

Max ran to the end and stopped. He was in a small square where several streets all came together. He looked back. There was no sign of the thugs yet. He turned left and saw a narrow opening between two buildings. He dived into the gap and tore up a steep flight of steps, his shoulders almost brushing the walls. At the top of the steps he emerged into another cobbled square. He dashed across into a side street, running twenty metres before he noticed an archway to one side. Plunging through it, he found himself in a courtyard surrounded by high buildings. There was a light on in a second-floor window – an apartment, Max guessed – that sent a golden glow out into the courtyard, illuminating the tubs of flowers around the edges and a fenced structure housing a collection of household refuse bins.

He edged behind the bins and crouched down, trying not to pant too noisily. His heart was hammering – from exertion, but also from fear. Where were the men? Had they seen where he'd gone? He knew he couldn't remain where he was. If the men came into the courtyard, he was trapped.

He waited a couple more minutes, until he'd recovered his breath, then crept back to the arch and peered cautiously out into the street. There was no one about. He stepped out and strode quickly away. He crossed another small square and turned left.

And walked straight into one of the thugs.

The man was waiting just round the corner, so close that Max almost collided with him. The thug was taken by surprise too. He lunged forward and grabbed hold of Max's jacket. Max tried to get away, but the man held on. He was bigger and stronger than him. Max knew he couldn't escape or beat him in a fight. He had to use his brains. He stopped struggling for a second, as if he were giving up. The thug relaxed his guard, and Max struck back, smashing the heel of his shoe as hard as he could into the man's knee. The man screamed and clutched at his leg in agony.

Max darted round him and sprinted away down the

street. But he'd gone only a short distance when the second man burst out from another side street just in front of him. Max swerved to avoid him, lashing out with his fist and catching the man on the nose, throwing him off balance long enough to get away. He turned sharp right and accelerated down another street. Then, suddenly, he emerged onto the broad boulevard that ran along the water's edge on the eastern side of the Old Town. Looking back, he saw the second thug giving chase, a mobile phone pressed to his ear.

Max paused briefly to get his bearings. The island of Södermalm, where the Sista Styvern and the hotel were, rose up to his right, about half a kilometre away. There was light traffic on the boulevard, big gaps between vehicles. Max let a van go past, then ran out across the road and onto the quayside. The area was cobbled, scattered with parked cars. Max turned right, heading towards the bridge to Södermalm. Beside him, three metres lower than the quay, was the sea. Max could hear the water lapping against the stone wall.

A car turned onto the far end of the quayside and came racing towards him. Its headlights caught him full in the face, dazzling him. He heard the squeal of brakes and the car slewed to a stop. Two men jumped out. One of them raised his hand. Max saw a flash. Something hissed past his ear. A bullet. The man fired a second shot, but by then Max was already diving sideways, out over the edge of the quay and into the sea.

As he entered the water, he pulled back with his arms and kicked hard, swimming out as far and as deep as he could. The water closed over him, dark and impenetrable. Max knew he couldn't be seen from the land. His hand grazed something coarse and rough – a rope that was attached to the sea bed at one end and at the other to a mooring buoy. Max clung onto the rope to stop himself floating up to the surface. The men would be watching from the quay, waiting for him to come up for air. His only hope was to stay underwater for long enough to convince them that he was dead – hit by the second bullet – or drowned. Max tried to relax, so that he used less oxygen. He'd been practising holding his breath for years as training for his escapology act. He was never going to need that skill more than now.

He let out a little air to ease the pressure on his lungs and counted slowly to himself. *Twenty seconds . . . thirty seconds . . .* How long would the men wait? Most people could only hold their breath underwater for half a minute or less. Max could hold it for three minutes. He prayed that was going to be enough. *Sixty seconds . . . seventy . . .* Max felt comfortable. *Eighty . . . ninety . . .* He pictured the men up on the quay, staring hard at the water, looking for a body, for any sign of him. Two minutes passed. Would they give up and walk away now? Max let out more air – just a bit: he didn't want any telltale bubbles rising to the surface. The vice was tightening around his chest. *Two and a quarter minutes ... two and a half ...* The pain was getting worse. This was the really dangerous point. Much longer and Max risked blacking out. He had to judge it perfectly. Get it wrong and he would die as surely as if one of those bullets had hit him.

Two and three quarter minutes ... There was no choice now. He would have to take his chances.

Letting go of the rope, he kicked upwards. His eyes were open, looking towards the quay as he broke the surface. He was ready to snatch a mouthful of air and dive back down if the men were still there. But they weren't. The quay was deserted, the car and the men gone.

Max gulped in the night air, almost sobbing with relief. He'd made it! Then he swam slowly back to the quay and found an iron ladder bolted to the wall. The land was only a few metres above him, but he was so exhausted it took him three attempts to haul himself out. He climbed to the top of the ladder, water pouring from his clothes, and stumbled away.

*   *   *

He was lucky it was dark. In daylight, the sight of a soaking wet teenage boy walking through the city streets would have drawn curious glances, maybe even the attention of the police. But at night Max's bedraggled condition was less noticeable. There were fewer people about, and most of those were too intent on finding the next bar or getting home to their families to take much notice of a kid who'd been for a nocturnal dip in the sea.

Max walked quickly but vigilantly, his eyes constantly roving the street, looking out for danger. He thought he was probably safe – if the thugs suspected he was still alive, then surely they would simply have waited around on the quay to finish him off – but he couldn't be absolutely sure. Every person who passed him, every car, was subjected to the same wary inspection. Anything suspicious and Max was ready to run again.

He walked across the bridge to Södermalm and headed back up the hill he'd run down earlier. His feet squelched in his trainers; water trickled down his back and legs. He was shivering with cold. He reached the end of Fjällgatan. The area was deserted. There was no sign of Chris or Consuela, or the men who'd attacked them. Max felt an icy tremor of fear pass through his body. What had happened to his friends?

He didn't know what to do. He was alone in a foreign city. He'd been chased, almost killed. It was dangerous to remain on the streets. He had to get back to the hotel.

He remembered the route they'd taken, the landmarks they'd passed on their way to the Sista Styvern. He made a couple of wrong turns, but corrected himself, and in less than fifteen minutes he rounded a corner and saw the Hotel Katarina ahead of him. He saw something else too and stopped dead, then ducked quickly out of sight into a doorway. Just along the street, two figures were running towards him. For one heart-stopping moment Max thought it was the men from the quayside, but then he realized that one of the figures was a woman. They drew closer, crossing a pool of light under a streetlamp, and Max felt an overwhelming flood of relief as he realized it was Consuela and Chris. They were safe!

Max stepped out into the open and ran to meet them.

Consuela let out a cry as she saw him. 'Max! Thank God!' She threw her arms around him and held him tight. 'We've been looking everywhere for you. We thought—' She didn't finish the sentence. She broke away and looked at him. 'You're soaked. What happened? Are you OK?'

'I'm fine,' Max said.

'You don't look it. Those guys—'

'I dived into the sea to get away from them.'

'The *sea*? Oh, God, I can't tell you how relieved we are to see you.'

'I'm OK. Just a bit wet.' Max glanced at Chris and noticed the dried blood on the side of his face. 'You're hurt.'

'Just a graze,' Chris said. 'And a few bruises.'

'What happened to the men?'

'Chris drove them off,' Consuela said. 'Let them go so that we could find you. That was more important.'

'They tried to kill me,' Max said. 'They had a gun. They fired a couple of shots . . .' His voice trailed off. He was suddenly aware that his whole body was shaking.

Consuela took hold of his arm. 'Come on, let's get inside.'

They walked along the street, Max in between Consuela and Chris. Just before they reached the hotel, they paused. Max straightened his dishevelled clothes and combed his hair with his fingers to make himself look more presentable. Consuela took a handkerchief from her bag and wiped the blood off Chris's face. Then they went into the hotel. There was a night porter on duty behind the reception desk. He glanced up, but didn't pay much attention to them; didn't seem to notice Max's damp appearance. He just nodded and looked back down at the magazine he was reading.

They took the lift upstairs and went into Consuela's room, locking the door behind them. Max slumped down onto the edge of the bed.

'Get in the shower, Max,' Consuela said. 'You can use mine.'

'I can go to my own room,' Max said.

'It's better that we all stick together.'

'You think those men will come here?'

'I don't know. But I don't want to take any chances. Go on, get those wet clothes off and warm yourself up.'

'Do you have the keycard for your room?' Chris asked. 'I'll get your things.'

Max rummaged in his trouser pocket and was relieved to find that the keycard was still there. He hoped the immersion in the sea wouldn't stop it working. He passed the card to Chris and went into Consuela's bathroom, stripped off and got in the shower. He stood under the jet of hot water for a long time, not bothering to soap himself, just letting his body warm up. Then he scrubbed himself thoroughly, getting rid of all traces of seawater.

Max was wrapped in a towel, the bathroom misty with steam, when Chris tapped on the door and passed in a fresh set of clothes. Max dressed and went out into the room. Consuela and Chris had been busy during his absence. They'd gone into both Max's room and Chris's, removed the mattresses and duvets from the beds and brought them back to Consuela's room. The mattresses were laid out on the floor now, pretty much taking up all the space.

'We're staying together tonight,' Chris explained. 'It'll be safer.'

'Do you think we should go to the police?' Max asked. 'Tell them about the attack?'

Consuela and Chris exchanged glances.

'We were discussing that while you were in the shower,' Consuela said. 'We don't think it's a good idea.'

'They'll want to know who we are, why we're here,' Chris said. 'We don't want that. I'm travelling under a false name, on a forged passport. I don't want them making enquiries about me.'

'We also don't know whether we can trust the Swedish police,' Consuela added. 'Remember what Svensson said about their phones being tapped, their offices burgled, files taken; the possibility that the security services might have been involved.'

'Now stop worrying and get yourself into bed. It's very late,' Chris said.

It was an unsettled night for Max. He couldn't stop thinking about the evening's events. He was terrified that the thugs would come to the hotel, break down the door of their room and finish the job they'd failed to complete on the quayside. Everything merged together into one petrifying nightmare – a waking nightmare and a sleeping one too, for even when he finally dozed off, the frightening images kept recurring, repeating themselves over and over again until he woke in a cold sweat, trembling with fear and panic.

The final time he was jolted awake, shortly after dawn, he decided he'd had enough of this torment and, throwing back his duvet, got up and went into the bathroom. He washed and dressed quietly, then returned to the bedroom and sat on the chair in the corner, watching the room getting gradually lighter. Chris was the next to wake. He opened his eyes, saw Max on the chair and sat up quickly, instantly alert.

'You OK?' he said.

Max nodded. 'I couldn't sleep.'

Chris turned his head to check Consuela. She was sleeping restlessly, one bare arm sticking out from beneath her covers. He slipped out from under his duvet and put on his clothes. Then he and Max took the mattresses and bedding back to their own rooms. By the time they returned to Consuela's room, she was awake and dressed.

They could have had breakfast in the hotel, but they were impatient to be on the move. They wanted to get away from Stockholm, from the traumatic memories of the previous evening. The hotel receptionist, a young, auburn-haired woman this morning, ordered them a taxi and they drove directly to Arlanda. Outside the terminal, they split up so they wouldn't be seen together. They had breakfast at the airport coffee shop, Max and Consuela sitting at one table, Chris at another several metres away.

Chris's was the first flight to go – SAS to London via Copenhagen – then, an hour and a half later, Max and Consuela were called to board their British Airways direct flight to Heathrow. Max lined up by the gate with butterflies in his stomach again. They'd had no problems getting through passport and security control, but they were still on Swedish soil. There was still time for the police to arrive and take them away for questioning. Max braced himself as he neared the gate. The BA flight supervisor checked his boarding pass and passport for what seemed like an eternity. Then she smiled and waved him through.

Only when the plane was in the air, climbing steeply above the houses and countryside surrounding the airport, did Max sit back and relax. They were on their way home. For a couple of hours at least, they were safe. He stared out of the window, watching the lakes and woods below get smaller and smaller, disappearing completely as the plane soared above the clouds. He was still suffering the after-effects of being attacked and chased, of nearly losing his life to an assassin's bullet. But he tried to shut all that out, obliterate it from his mind, and focus on the one positive thing that had come out of their visit to Sweden. He had discovered what the Cedar Alliance was. Now he had to expand his knowledge, find out more about the Alliance and, most importantly, about his father's secret life.

SIXTEEN

It was early afternoon when they landed in London. Max's stomach was a tight ball of nerves. Would the police, or Penhall, be waiting to pick them up the moment they arrived? But they got through passport control and customs without incident. As they emerged into the arrivals area, Max was on red alert, looking around for danger. He didn't think even Penhall would be stupid enough to try anything in broad daylight in a busy airport, but he wasn't going to let his guard down for even a second. He studied the other people in the concourse. There was the usual collection of taxi and limousine drivers holding up cards bearing the names of the passengers they'd been hired to collect, and one or two individuals meeting relatives or friends, but no one appeared to be paying any attention to Max or Consuela.

They went down the escalator into the Underground station and boarded a Piccadilly Line train that was waiting to depart. Other people got on after them – a couple of women pulling suitcases on wheels, a pair of backpackers with rucksacks almost as big as them-selves, a young man in a windcheater and trainers. Max half hoped to see Chris, but he knew that was unlikely. Chris's connecting flight from Copenhagen would have got in forty minutes earlier than Max and Consuela's flight. He would be halfway home by now.

The tube journey took more than an hour, the train getting gradually more crowded as they got closer to central London. Max watched the other passengers carefully, noting their faces, their clothes, checking whether any of them were taking an obvious interest in him, and getting ready to resist if they made a move towards him. He'd been snatched once by Penhall's men. He wasn't going to let it happen again without a fight.

They walked the last quarter of a mile from the tube station. The dark blue Toyota Avensis was no longer parked in the street, but Max noticed a maroon Ford in almost the same location, two men sitting in it. Consuela unlocked the front door of the house and they went inside. Max was extra-vigilant, pausing in the hall to listen for any sounds. Consuela too was on edge. Chris should have been there already. Max had expected him to be waiting for them, but the house was deathly quiet. Maybe he was downstairs in the basement.

Max went warily through into the kitchen and down the stairs. The basement was deserted. Alarmed now, Max tried the door to the garden for which Chris had the key. It was still locked. Where *was* he? Max found the spare key and unlocked the door. He was just in time to see Chris drop nimbly over the wall at the end of the garden and come running across the lawn, his travel bag slung over his shoulder.

Max heaved a sigh of relief. 'I thought you'd be here before us,' he said as Chris reached him. 'Was your flight delayed?'

Chris shook his head. 'It was bang on time. I waited around at Heathrow for you and Consuela to arrive.'

'You did? I didn't see you.'

'That was the idea. I wanted to check if anyone followed you home.'

'I looked, but I didn't spot anyone,' Max said.

'But they were there all the same.'

'They were?' Max was stunned. 'Who?'

'A youth in a grey windcheater and trainers to begin with. Then he got off the train and a woman took over. She was on your tail until the moment you turned the last corner. Then I assume the guys in the car were watching you. The car is still there, isn't it?'

'Yes. Not the same one. It's a maroon Ford now.'

'Where's Consuela?'

'Inside.'

'You checked over the house?'

'No.'

'Let's do it now.'

They went into the basement and locked and bolted the door behind them. Then they went upstairs and did the same to the other external doors. Max went into all the rooms, Chris accompanying him but keeping well back so he wouldn't be seen from outside, and made sure the window locks were engaged. He saw no sign that anyone had been inside the house during their absence.

Feeling more secure now, Max left Chris and Consuela in the kitchen and went upstairs to do something he'd planned on the flight home from Sweden. At the far end of the landing was the small bedroom that his father had used as an office. Max went in and paused. This had been the place where Alexander Cassidy had done all the paperwork for his escapology shows. Max had never really thought of his dad's stage act as a business, but that was exactly what it had been. Alex had kept invoices and receipts, drawn up accounts and paid tax just like any other businessman.

Max had never taken much interest in that side of his father's work – it was the escapology, the performing, that had fascinated him, that had made him want to follow in his father's footsteps. Since he'd become a performer himself, Max had learned only too well how much preparation and organization had to go on behind the scenes, but when he was growing up and watching his father on stage he'd known nothing about all that boring administrative stuff, and cared even less. What mattered was the next trick, the next illusion, the next escape his dad was going to perform.

Now Max was realizing that there was a lot more about his father's life that he didn't know. He sat down at the desk and pondered for a moment on what Axel Svensson had told them. The Cedar Alliance was a secret organization dedicated to saving the Earth from over-exploitation and destruction, a partnership between groups and individuals who shared those aims. It worked quietly and without publicity, coordinating action between its many diverse supporters, organizing protests, galvanizing opposition and funding campaigns to protect the environment. That had surprised Max. He'd never had any inkling that there was a guiding hand working out of sight behind all the world's great environmental action movements. But what had stunned him more was Svensson's revelation that Alexander Cassidy was one of the leaders of the Alliance. How could that be? How could Max's father, a world-famous escapologist, be a part of such an organization? And how had he kept his role in it hidden from his family for so long?

Max now recognized how little he really knew about his father. He was fourteen years old; his dad was forty-eight. When Max was born, Alexander Cassidy had been thirty-four. He had lived for thirty-four years before Max had even appeared on the scene. That was a long time, and Max knew almost nothing about it. His father's past was a mystery to him.

What had Alexander done during those thirty-four years, particularly during those adult years after he'd left school? He'd been learning the skills of escapology, building himself a career, Max knew that. But what else had he been doing at the same time? Max was realizing that his father was like the two-faced Roman god, Janus. Max had seen one of his faces, but his other face had always been hidden from view. What he had to do now was take another, harder look at his father's life and try to catch a glimpse of that second face. But where did he begin?

He looked around the office. The walls were covered with framed posters for Alexander Cassidy's shows – 'Alexander the Great', as he was billed. And in between the posters were photographs of Alex, sometimes on his own, posing in the black suit he wore for his act, sometimes with Consuela or Max's mum. One or two photographs showed them all together, Max included. Max got up and went over to stare at one of the prints – a shot of the four of them outside the Coliseum in Rome, Max ten years old, grinning for the camera with his dad's arm around his shoulders. Max remembered the trip well. His father was away a lot, touring the world with Consuela to assist him. Max and his mother usually stayed at home, but the Rome trip had been during the school holidays so, for once, Max and Helen had gone too. They'd stayed in a hotel near the Spanish Steps, gone sightseeing to St Peter's, the Forum and the Castel Sant'Angelo, and in the evenings Alexander had performed on a stage in a gigantic marquee that had been erected in one of the public parks. Thinking about it all brought a lump to Max's throat. That was why he didn't often come into his father's office. It brought back too many painful memories.

Max forced himself to turn away from the photographs. He hadn't come to wallow in the past. He had a purpose: to see if his father had left any clues that might give Max a clearer idea of his activities for the Cedar Alliance and help him find out where he was now.

Max sat at the desk again and pulled open the drawers, one by one. They contained nothing but stationery and office materials – a stapler, a hole punch, pads of writing paper and envelopes. He stood up and moved on to the two big filing cabinets against the wall. They should have been crammed with papers – Alexander's business records – but they were completely empty. Max stared in puzzlement at the bare drawers, then he remembered Rupert Penhall and the police search. The officers had been in here, sifting through documents. Max hadn't realized until now that they'd taken such a lot away. He closed the drawers, feeling suddenly depressed. There was probably nothing left in the office – the police would have cleaned it out, taken everything.

Max opened one of the cupboards. It was empty. He tried the adjoining one. That too had been stripped clean. Max was angry now. How dare they take away all his dad's papers! They had no right to them. He wondered whether the police had overlooked anything. Was there anywhere else in the house where his dad might have stored documents? The basement? The loft? But the police had been in both those places. They'd searched everywhere.

Thoroughly dispirited now, Max took one last look around the room – and noticed a cardboard box on the floor in the corner. He knelt down and opened the lid. His hopes rose as he saw it contained papers, then fell again as he realized they were just publicity posters and flyers for his father's shows. That was why the police had left them behind: they were little more than waste paper. Max pulled out a few of the flyers and spread them out on the carpet. They related to a tour of the United States that his dad had undertaken four years earlier – New York, Washington DC, Philadelphia, Baltimore, Cleveland, Chicago, San Francisco: he'd gone across the entire country over a three-week period.

Max pulled out more leaflets. They were a mini-record of his father's career. Posters for shows in Sydney, Melbourne and Perth, Australia, for Auckland in New Zealand and – closer to home – Paris, Brussels, Hamburg, Berlin and Vienna. His dad had certainly got around. There could hardly have been a major country in the world he hadn't visited at some point. Max leafed through flyers advertising shows in Moscow and Prague, Budapest and Warsaw, Thailand and Borneo.

Max stopped.

Borneo? Of course. His dad had been to Borneo.

Max looked more closely at the flyers. They advertised a series of shows in Kuching, Brunei and Kota Kinabalu. He didn't know where any of those places were. He turned one of the flyers over. There were a few scribbled notes on the back of it in his father's handwriting:

*Kalimantan Air Charters – Kuching to Pangkalan Bun.
11 a.m. 3,500 RM.*

Then he saw two words that made him suck in his
breath quickly:

Narang Anwar.

That was one of the five names Max had found in the
files on Shadow Island – the names of prisoners who'd
been held captive there.

Narang Anwar. Who was he? Why had Max's dad
written his name on the back of the flyer? And what did
the other notes mean?

Keeping hold of the piece of paper, Max went downstairs. On the bookshelves in the sitting room he found
an atlas and opened it to the page for Borneo. It was a
big island between Southeast Asia and Australia. Most
of the northern part of the island belonged to Malaysia,
divided into two provinces called Sarawak and Sabah.
The southern, larger part was Indonesian and was
known as Kalimantan. Max found Kuching, Brunei and
Kota Kinabalu along the north coast. Pangkalan Bun
was harder to locate, but eventually he found it in
southwest Kalimantan. He found something else too;
something that set his pulse racing. Very close to

Pangkalan Bun was Tanjung Puting National Park – the place where both Erik Blomkvist and Redmond Ashworth-Ames had worked.

Max took the atlas with him into the kitchen, almost shaking with excitement. Consuela and Chris weren't there so he went down into the basement and found them sitting on one of the exercise mats, Chris drinking tea, Consuela strong black coffee. They were close together, chatting quietly, but broke off as Max came in, closing the door behind him.

Max showed Consuela the flyer he'd found in the office. 'Do you remember that trip?' he asked.

Consuela studied the glossy leaflet. 'Yes, I remember it.'

'Spring, two thousand and seven. That was the year Dad disappeared. This was probably the last trip he did before he went to Santo Domingo.'

'I think it was,' Consuela said. 'What about it?'

'Look on the other side.'

Consuela turned the flyer over and read the scribbled notes, frowning as she got to the name at the end. 'Narang Anwar,' she said, looking up enquiringly at Max. 'Isn't that . . . ?'

'One of the prisoners on Shadow Island, yes.'

'Why would your dad write his name here?'

'I was hoping you might tell me. I know you've

always said you've never heard of Narang Anwar, but are you absolutely sure? You didn't encounter him in Borneo? Dad didn't mention him?'

'No, I'd remember.'

'Tell me about the trip. Dad seems to have done three shows, with two days in between each one.'

'That's right. We did Kuching first – that's the capital city of Sarawak. Then we went to Brunei, a tiny, independent state just along the coast, and finally to Kota Kinabalu, in Sabah, on the northeastern tip of the island.'

'That's all? You didn't go anywhere else in Borneo?'

'Well, *I* didn't.'

'But Dad did?'

Consuela shrugged. 'I'm not sure what he did. At the end of the tour we returned to Kuching. You couldn't fly direct from Kuching to Britain so I went on alone to Singapore for a few days' holiday, and your dad stayed on in Kuching. He joined me in Singapore later and we flew back to London together.'

'Do you know what my dad did during those few days you were apart?' Max asked.

Consuela shook her head. 'He stayed in Kuching, as far as I remember. He said he liked it there – it was more relaxing than Singapore.'

Max indicated the first part of the note on the flyer.

'*Kalimantan Air Charters – Kuching to Pangkalan Bun.* It looks to me as if Dad chartered a plane and flew down here to Pangkalan Bun.' He pointed to the place in the atlas. 'Eleven a.m.: that was the time of the flight – and three thousand five hundred RM – I'd guess that was the price. What currency do they use in Sarawak?'

'The ringgit, abbreviated to RM,' Consuela said. 'But why would he do that?'

'The national park where Redmond Ashworth-Ames and Erik Blomkvist worked is very close to Pangkalan Bun,' Max said. 'There can only be one possible reason why he went there. He was doing work for the Cedar Alliance.'

No one said anything for a time. Then Chris drained his mug of tea and gave Max a serious look. 'You want to go to Borneo next, don't you?'

'It's the only lead we have,' Max said. 'Blomkvist and Ashworth-Ames were there. So was my dad. And this Narang Anwar has some connection to Borneo too, I'm sure of that. We have to find out what.'

'Borneo is a long way, Max,' Consuela said gently. 'And it could be very dangerous.'

'Staying here could be dangerous too,' Max retorted.

'What about school? You've already missed a lot.'

'We've been over all that,' Max said. 'I'm not going back to school. We have to find out what the hell is going on, and we're not going to do that if I'm stuck in a classroom learning French grammar.'

'When?' Chris asked.

'As soon as we can.' Max turned to Consuela. 'We can't afford to wait here doing nothing. Penhall, Clark – they're closing in on us. We have to stay one step ahead of them.'

'Borneo's not like London, you know,' Consuela pointed out. 'It's a wild, untamed kind of place. Who knows what might happen to us there?'

'Don't forget that I was snatched from the streets of London by Penhall's men,' Max said. 'We're not safe here. Not until we find enough evidence to nail Julius Clark. And we're not going to do that by sitting on our backsides. We have to go looking for that evidence.'

Chris looked at Consuela. 'I agree with Max,' he said. 'We're running out of time.'

'But even if we do find evidence – and who's to say we will? – what use will it be against a man like Clark – a man who appears to have the authorities in his pocket?'

'I've thought of that,' Max replied. 'Just wait a minute.'

He dashed upstairs, picked up the telephone directory from the hall table and returned to the basement. He looked up the number of the *London News Chronicle* and punched it into his mobile.

'Dan Kingston,' he said when the switchboard answered.

It took a few seconds for him to be put through.

'Yes?' It was a low, man's voice.

'Dan Kingston?'

'That's right.'

'I need to talk to you about Julius Clark,' Max said.

Kingston took a moment to respond. 'Who is this?' he asked curtly.

'My name's Max Cassidy.'

'Cassidy? Not the Half-Pint Houdini?'

'Yes, that's me.' Max had forgotten that he was a minor celebrity. 'I read a piece you wrote about Clark. I have some information that you might find interesting.'

'What information?'

'Not on the phone. I need to meet you in person.'

'I'm intrigued. When do you want to meet?'

'Are you free today?'

'Come to our offices. You know where they are?'

'I can find them.'

'I'll be here until eight tonight.'

The line went dead. Max put the phone away in his pocket.

'What are you up to, Max?' Consuela asked suspiciously.

'I'm taking out an insurance policy,' Max replied.

'Would you mind taking care of the travel arrangements again? The air tickets to Borneo? I'll be back later.' He looked at Chris. 'I'd feel safer if you were with me.'

'You don't have to ask,' Chris replied. 'After what happened in Stockholm, I'm not letting you out of my sight.'

Dan Kingston wasn't Max's idea of a newspaper reporter. He'd expected some overweight, red-faced hack with a fifty-a-day cigarette habit and a fondness for malt whisky, but Kingston was small and neat, wearing a smart suit and tie and a pair of round wire-framed glasses that gave his face an owlish appearance. He looked more like an accountant or a librarian than a journalist.

He met them in the ground-floor foyer of the *London News Chronicle* offices and took them upstairs to the newsroom – a huge open-plan area divided up into smaller workspaces by chest-high partitions. Each workspace contained four or five desks and the same number of computer terminals. Reporters were talking on the phone or working on stories, tapping away on their keyboards; in the central section, where the desks were grouped together in two rows, sub-editors were hunched over screens, designing the layout for the following day's edition.

Kingston led them across the newsroom to a glass-walled conference room containing a long, polished wooden table and a dozen chairs. The journalist sat down at one end of the table and gestured for Max and Chris to join him.

'It's a pleasure to meet you,' he said to Max. 'I've never seen your show, but I know people who have and they say it's terrific.'

'Thanks,' Max said, shifting uncomfortably in his seat. Compliments always embarrassed him.

'Your phone call surprised me,' Kingston went on. 'Why would Max Cassidy, the teenage escapologist, be interested in Julius Clark?'

Max took a moment to assess the journalist before he replied. He liked the look of Kingston. He had a serious manner and inquisitive, intelligent eyes. Max felt instinctively – as he had with Chief Superintendent Richardson – that he could trust him; that Kingston could keep a secret.

'That article you wrote about Clark,' Max said. 'I read it on the Internet. You seem to know quite a bit about him.'

Kingston pulled a wry face. 'Well, I wouldn't say that. No one knows very much about him – no journalist, at any rate. Clark has made sure that his activities aren't subject to public scrutiny.'

'You think he has things to hide?'

'He has a lot of things to hide. Most people who are as wealthy as he is don't like anyone enquiring about the source of their money. But even by those standards, Clark is exceptionally secretive. He loathes any kind of publicity.'

'You said in your article that he had lots of different businesses.'

'He does, though it's impossible to say how many. He keeps everything very complex so that no outsiders can really see what he's doing.'

'And he has powerful friends.'

'Very powerful friends, yes,' Kingston agreed.

'In Britain?'

'Everywhere he does business.'

'He pays them?'

Kingston smiled. 'Some of them.'

'Bribes?'

Kingston pursed his lips, gazing thoughtfully at Max. 'I don't want to patronize you, Max. You're a teenager, but you seem like a bright kid, quite well clued up about the world. Yes, Clark bribes people. In some countries around the world, that's how you do business. You pay people off to get what you want. But even in the West, where we think we're more honest, you can buy influence.'

The journalist paused, glancing from Max to Chris, then back to Max. 'Why don't you tell me what this is all about? You said on the phone you had some information for me.'

'I have,' Max said. 'But I'll only give it to you on the condition that you don't use it straight away. You can only use it if anything happens to me.'

Kingston blinked behind his glasses. 'That sounds very melodramatic. Why should anything happen to you?'

'Because someone's already tried to kill me,' Max said.

The journalist stared at him. '*Kill* you? You're joking! Who? Why?'

'I don't know for certain. But Julius Clark is involved, I know that.'

'Just wait a minute,' Kingston said. 'I think we need this on the record. Let me get my notebook and my file on Clark.' He stood up and left the conference room.

Chris glanced uneasily at Max. 'I hope you're doing the right thing here.'

'We can't trust the police or the security services,' Max said. 'I want someone to know what's been happening, and I think this guy is the right person.'

Max looked out through the glass wall into the news-room. Dan Kingston was bending down by a desk, taking a folder out of a drawer. He picked up a few other items from the desktop and came back to the conference room.

'You don't mind if I record our conversation, do you?' he asked as he resumed his seat. 'I'll take notes too, but a verbatim record would be useful. I like to get my facts right.'

'No, I don't mind,' Max said.

Kingston placed a small digital recorder on the table, switched it on and adjusted its position so that the microphone was facing Max. Then he opened his notebook to a clean page and picked up his pen. 'OK, fire away.'

Max collected his thoughts for a couple of seconds, then told the journalist all about Shadow Island: why he'd gone there, what had happened to him, what he'd seen, how he'd escaped – pretty much word for word the same account he'd given Axel Svensson. Kingston listened carefully, taking a few notes but mostly watching Max with a mixture of shock and disbelief registering on his face.

When Max had finished, the journalist sat back and let out a long, deep breath. 'You know, Max,' he said, 'if I didn't know your name, your reputation, I'd think you were mad. I've never heard such an incredible story in my life.'

'But it's true,' Max said.

'I can corroborate every word of it,' Chris added. 'I was there.'

'Let me get your details down,' Kingston said.

He made a note of Chris's name and asked him a few questions about his background and his experiences on the island. Then he turned back to Max.

'Let's go over a few things again. You say there were other prisoners on this island. How many?'

'I don't know how many had been kept there at one time or another,' Max replied, 'but there were a lot of files in Julius Clark's office. Dozens. We only saw one other prisoner – a man who looked Middle Eastern. I think his name was Arhat Zebari.'

Kingston's jaw dropped open. He gaped at Max in utter astonishment. 'Arhat Zebari?' he repeated.

'Yes. Have you heard of him?'

In reply, Kingston rummaged in his folder and pulled out a newspaper cutting. He put it on the table and turned it around so that Max and Chris could see it more clearly. It was a black-and-white photograph from an Arabic newspaper. In the foreground was a group of three men standing a few metres in front of an oil derrick. One of the men was Julius Clark.

Kingston pointed with his finger to a second group of people in the background of the photograph – four men standing almost directly underneath the derrick. 'Do you recognize a face?'

'That's him!' Max gasped. 'The one on the left. Isn't it, Chris?'

Chris leaned closer and nodded. 'That's the man we saw on Shadow Island,' he confirmed. 'Who is he?'

'He's a Kurdish journalist. This photo was taken near Kirkuk, in northern Iraq, earlier this year. Julius Clark was there to oversee the signing of an agreement giving one of his companies a large part of the oil fields in the area. The other two men are the chairman and the chief executive officer of the company, Rescomin International.'

'*Rescomin?*' Chris said sharply. 'That's one of Clark's companies?'

'Yes,' Kingston replied. 'It stands for Resources, Commodities and Minerals. It drills for oil and mines minerals and metals all over the world.'

'It's also the company I was monitoring in the Amazon rainforest – for illegally felling trees, clearing the jungle to graze cattle for beef production.'

'Arhat Zebari's a journalist?' Max said.

'A very good one,' Kingston said. 'I spoke to him a few months ago, when I was researching my article on Clark. He was doing similar research, investigating Rescomin's activities in Iraq.'

'You haven't spoken to him since?'

'He disappeared in the late spring. He hasn't been seen since. Now I know why.'

'You believe us then?' Max said.

'I believe you. But one thing I don't get. Julius Clark is a rich, successful man. Why would he be doing any of this?'

'That's what we're going to find out,' Max said. 'And that's why we don't want you to publish anything yet. It all sounds too unbelievable. We need to collect more information, find evidence to back up our story.'

Kingston nodded. 'I couldn't write anything without that, in any case. With a man as powerful as Julius Clark, it would be crazy to publish without cast-iron proof. But can you get it?'

'We can try.'

The journalist regarded Max with concern – and something else that might have been admiration. 'You've got guts, I'll give you that,' he said. 'But are you sure you're not biting off more than you can chew? Julius Clark is a formidable opponent.'

'I know,' Max said. 'But it's too late to worry about that now. He's hunting my dad, he's got my mum put in prison for a murder she didn't commit and he's tried to kill us. There's too much at stake for us to give up now. But if anything does happen to me, I'd like you to use what we've just told you; make sure Clark doesn't get away with it. Will you do that?'

Kingston held out his hand. Max took it in his own.

'Yes, I'll do that, Max.'

Rupert Penhall was lounging back comfortably at his desk, drinking coffee and reading a sheaf of intelligence reports, when his assistant – a hatchet-faced young man in a grey suit – came into the office and handed him a fax message.

'This just came through, sir. I thought you'd want to see it immediately.'

Penhall glanced at the sheet of paper and stiffened. He sat up abruptly, tossing the intelligence reports to one side. 'Thank you, James.'

He waited for the young man to leave the room, then punched a number into his phone. 'Julius, it's Rupert. I've just had word from my monitoring section. Max Cassidy and Consuela Navarra have booked flights to Borneo. What do you want me to do?'

There was a pause before Clark responded. 'Do nothing, Rupert,' he said. 'Let them go.'

'But Borneo, that's—'

'I know what it is,' Clark interrupted sharply. 'I said let them go.'

'You're sure you don't want me to take care of it?'

Clark gave an icy laugh that, even over the phone, made Penhall shiver.

'You haven't had much success so far, have you, Rupert? The boy is still at large, still a problem. I think it's time *I* stepped in.'

'You're going to deal with him?'

'Oh, yes. Make no mistake about it: I'm going to deal with him.'

SEVENTEEN

The suffocating heat hit Max the moment they stepped off the plane in Kuching. It was so intense it was difficult to breathe. His chest felt tight, as if a very large boa constrictor had wrapped its coils around him and was slowly squeezing him to death. Then, as if that wasn't bad enough, there was the humidity to deal with. Just seconds after their arrival, Max's whole body was dripping with sweat. If he'd taken a warm shower fully clothed he could hardly have been much wetter.

Chris saw the expression on his face and grinned. 'First time in the tropics it's always like this,' he said. 'But you soon get used to it. When I was in the army, the first three weeks in the jungle were hell – leeches sucking your blood, mosquitoes chewing you up alive – but after that you got to love it and never wanted to come out.'

Max grimaced. 'I hope we're not here for three weeks.'

They walked across to the small terminal building, collected their baggage and went through immigration and passport control. Max looked on anxiously as the uniformed officer examined his passport. There'd been no problems in Singapore, but he was steeling himself for trouble now they'd landed in Sarawak. Penhall would have had access to the passenger records at Heathrow and would know where they'd gone. It would have been simple for him to contact the Kuching authorities and ask for Max and Consuela to be detained. But the immigration officer clearly hadn't been instructed to watch out for them. He simply stamped their passports, wished them a pleasant stay and let them through the barrier.

At the information desk on the airport concourse Max asked where they could find Kalimantan Air Charters and was directed out of the building and two hundred metres along the road to a small group of cabins housing businesses linked to the airport – catering services, fuel supplies, car hire and a couple of air charter companies.

Kalimantan Air Charters had the smartest-looking premises – a one-storey wooden shed with a brightly coloured sign over the main door and a plastic replica model of a twin-engined plane sitting on the flat roof as if it were about to take off.

Behind the reception desk inside, a smiling young woman wearing a crisp white dress welcomed them in excellent English and asked how she could help. Max explained that they wanted to charter a plane to take them to Pangkalan Bun. But of course – that would be simple to arrange, the receptionist said, and took out a booking sheet. Max gave her Consuela's name, then Chris's alias of Alan Montgomery, spelling them out letter by letter when it became clear that they were unfamiliar to her. Then he gave his own name. He started to spell that out too, and was surprised to see her write it down perfectly without any prompting.

She looked up at him. 'Cassidy – that must be a common English name, no?'

'Why do you say that?' Max asked.

'We had another Mr Cassidy who chartered one of our planes. A very nice gentleman.'

Max gave a start. 'His name wasn't Alexander Cassidy, was it?' he said.

'Yes, it was.' The receptionist gazed at him curiously. 'You look very like him, actually.'

'You remember him? You must have a good memory.'

'Good memory? No, I don't think so.'

'But it was more than two years ago.'

The young woman frowned. 'I'm sorry, I don't understand.'

'Alexander Cassidy chartered a plane two years ago,' Max said.

The receptionist shook her head. 'No, not two years ago. It was only last week.'

The room fell so silent that Max thought he could hear the beating of his heart. He stared at the woman. '*Last week?* He chartered a plane *last week*?'

'Yes.' She smiled uncertainly. 'Is everything all right? This Mr Cassidy, he is a relative?'

'He's my father,' Max said. He leaned across the counter so eagerly that the receptionist shrank back from him, as if she feared he might attack her.

'He chartered a plane *last week*?' Max repeated. '*When* last week? Where did he go? You must tell me.'

The woman glanced around nervously. 'Perhaps I should not have said so much. The information is confidential. I should not talk about other customers.'

'No!' Max exclaimed. 'You can't do that. I need to know. I need to know *now*. It's vitally important.'

Consuela pulled him away from the counter. 'Take it easy, Max – you're upsetting her.'

She smiled at the receptionist. 'I'm sorry, but we really need your help,' she said sweetly. 'We're trying to find Alexander Cassidy. If you have any information about him, please tell us.'

The young woman looked at her, then at Max. 'Information?' she said hesitantly.

'Can you tell us where he went?'

'Well . . .'

'Please.' Consuela smiled at her again. 'Wherever it was, we would like to charter one of your planes to take us there too. We'll pay cash, in US dollars.'

Max took a wad of money out of his pocket and peeled off a few notes. The receptionist eyed the money greedily and seemed to forget her worries about talking to them.

'He went to Pangkalan Bun,' she said. She brought out a file and checked through the papers in it. 'Last Monday. He flew out at two fifteen in the afternoon.'

'Thank you,' Consuela said. 'Do you know where in Pangkalan Bun he was headed? What he was planning to do there?'

'He didn't say. You could ask the pilot. He might have told him.'

But the pilot – a slim young Chinese Malay named Sammy Lin – didn't know either. He flew them south from Kuching in a six-seater Cessna. Max was allowed to sit up front in the cockpit next to Sammy and took the opportunity to ply him with questions. But Alex Cassidy had clearly not been in a talkative mood the previous week.

'He say nothing,' Sammy told Max.

'What, nothing at all?'

The pilot shook his head. 'He was only passenger. I say he can sit next to me, but he no want to. He sit in back and say nothing the whole trip. He have things on his mind, I think.'

'He never mentioned why he was going to Pangkalan Bun?'

'No. I fly him in, then bring tour group back to Kuching. That is all.'

Max didn't press him further. He gazed out of the window, trying to contain his excitement. His father had been here in Borneo just the week before. Perhaps he was still here, still in Pangkalan Bun. The mere thought made his heart beat faster. He was on his father's trail, and the scent was still fresh. He was getting closer by the hour. Surely he would find him soon.

The plane flew low the whole journey, cruising beneath cloud level and giving Max a good view of the ground below. He was astonished at how green the terrain was, how sparsely populated. The dense, impenetrable rain-forest seemed to stretch for hundreds of miles in all directions, a thick carpet of trees and other vegetation unbroken by towns or cities. Occasionally he saw a clearing containing a village or the shimmering ribbon of a river twisting its way towards the distant sea. They flew over mountains, their rocky peaks poking up through the jungle like islands in a vast green ocean. Then, suddenly, the scenery changed. The thick canopy of rainforest disappeared and Max saw nothing but bare open ground, some of it blackened as if a fire had swept across it.

'What's happened down there?' he asked Sammy. 'It looks as if it's been burned.'

'It has,' the pilot replied. 'They clear land, chop down all trees, then burn off other vegetation.'

'What for?'

'For that. You see it?' Sammy pointed down through the window to where the cleared ground had given way to trees – not the solid cloak of the rainforest, but rows of trees arranged in straight lines with gaps in between. 'Oil-palm plantations,' he explained.

Max stared down at the trees, remembering what Axel Svensson had told him in Stockholm – about how the Borneo jungle was being destroyed, the wildlife killed or displaced to make way for oil palms for the bio-fuel industry. He saw what the Swede had meant now. The plantations below were enormous. Max had never seen anything like them. They seemed to go on for ever, thousands and thousands of trees reaching all the way to the horizon.

'Every time I fly over here, is more and more clear

ground,' Sammy said. 'Sometimes smoke from burning is so thick I have to change course.'

'How many of these plantations are there?' Max asked.

The pilot shrugged. 'Who knows? Thousands, probably. There are more to the west – big area near coast where rainforest has all gone completely. None left. But they start to spread inland. Ten years ago I fly across whole island, hundreds of kilometres, and see only a few plantations. Now they everywhere.'

On the descent into Pangkalan Bun, Max saw more oil-palm plantations, then the plane turned and touched down on the landing strip.

Sammy handed Max a business card with his name and phone number on it. 'You want plane, give me a call,' he said. 'Any time, day or night.'

The sun was low in the sky as they took a taxi from the airport into Pangkalan Bun. There were flooded paddy fields on either side of the road, the water shimmering in the twilight, and dotted around the landscape were wooden houses on stilts. Max saw a small monkey swinging idly beneath one of the houses, then the taxi pulled out to overtake a cart pulled by a bullock. The hot, humid air gusted in through the open windows, laced with sweet foreign scents. Max had never been to the tropics before and he marvelled at how different it was. How serene and exotic.

The taxi driver had recommended a hotel and dropped them off outside it. It was a short distance from the river, a two-storey building with a veranda on the ground floor and a long wooden balcony running along outside the first-floor bedrooms.

Max and Chris shared a twin; Consuela had a single next door to them. They took it in turns to have a shower in the bathroom down the landing. Max swilled away the sweat and grime of their long journey with tepid water, but it was so humid that by the time he'd dressed he was damp with perspiration again. They ate in a nearby restaurant – a simple meal of fried fish and rice – then went to bed early.

Max was weary, but he couldn't sleep. He lay on his bed – it was too hot to slip beneath the sheet – and listened to Chris's heavy breathing for a while before getting up and going out onto the balcony.

He could see lights, hear some creature – a gecko, he thought – chirping up on the roof. A motor scooter rattled by, two young men on the back of it. A scrawny dog, its ribs showing through its skin, dodged out of their way, then crossed the street and slunk away down a dark alley.

Max wondered where his father was. Pangkalan Bun

was only a small place. *Are you here somewhere, Dad?* he thought. *I hope so. Don't let me lose you again. Stay around for at least one more day, because in the morning I'm coming looking for you.*

EIGHTEEN

Max was up early the next day, woken by the traffic on the street outside the hotel. He lay on his bed, staring into space and planning how he was going to track down his father. Where in Pangkalan Bun might he have gone? A hotel? Max could go round all the hotels in town and see if Alex had stayed in one, but that would take a long time and might not produce a result. In any case, his dad might not necessarily have stayed in Pangkalan Bun. He might have flown in to the airport and gone somewhere else straight away. But where? Max recalled the notes on the back of the flyer he'd found in his father's office – in particular, the name Narang Anwar. That had to be important. Who was Narang Anwar?

Max slid off the bed, dressed and crept quietly out of the room, trying not to disturb Chris. Downstairs, he borrowed the local telephone directory from the hotel manager and sat on the veranda looking through it.

There were a large number of Anwars listed, but only one with the forename Narang. There were two numbers and two addresses for him, one obviously business, the other residential. Max made a note of them both on a scrap of paper. Then he stretched out his legs and leaned back in his bamboo armchair, waiting for Chris and Consuela to get up. It was pleasantly warm on the veranda. He was in the shade, but he could see the line of the sun creeping gradually across the ground, feel his skin getting damp in the already humid air. In an hour or two it would be insufferably hot.

After ten minutes he began to get impatient. He didn't want to be lolling around on a veranda, he wanted to be getting on with his search. Going back upstairs, he roused Chris and Consuela, then returned to the veranda. Chris came down first, crumpled and unshaven. Consuela took a little longer, but she looked fresh and clear-eyed, her skirt and top uncreased, her make-up immaculate.

They went to a *kedai kopi* – a coffee shop – along the street for breakfast. Chris had been in Borneo with the army – though not this bit of the island – and he warned Max about the food.

'Don't expect cornflakes and toast, or a nice pastry. They're much more likely to serve us noodles or rice.'

Some of the locals were indeed eating bowls of noodles, but Chris and Max had a *roti* each – a sort of griddled flatbread that came with a small bowl of curry in which to dip it. Consuela just had black coffee.

Max told them what he'd found in the phone book and suggested that tracing Narang Anwar should be the first thing they did. They didn't argue with him.

'That sounds like a good idea,' Chris said. 'But after what happened in Sweden, and what happened to Max before that in London, we stick close together at all times.'

'You think there's any danger here?' Consuela asked anxiously.

'There's danger everywhere.'

They headed for Narang Anwar's business address first. It was near the centre of the town, in a narrow street that was crammed with brightly coloured market stalls selling everything from pots and pans to beds. They squeezed through the throng past live chickens squawking in cages, rolls of silk and other cloths hanging from racks, huge baskets of nuts, and exotic-looking fruits and vegetables that Max had never seen before. The sultry air was heavy with the scents of cooking and oriental spices.

Anwar's office was on the first floor of an old two-storey commercial building which, like their hotel, had a wide wooden balcony running all the way along the front. From the balcony, doors opened into small office units housing various businesses – an accountant and book-keeper, an insurance broker, an estate agent – their professions advertised on signs in both the local language, Bahasa Indonesia, and English. Outside Anwar's office was a discreet plaque identifying him as an ATTORNEY-AT-LAW. But the door was shut – and locked, as Max discovered when he tried the handle.

'Anwar not there,' said a man in a short-sleeved white shirt who'd come out of the adjoining office.

'Do you know where he is?' Max asked.

'He gone.'

'Gone? What do you mean?'

'He not there for many weeks now. No one know where he is. He disappear.'

'Does he have any family?'

'He have wife. She live out of town.'

Max read out the address he'd written down from the phone directory.

'That right,' the man said. 'That where wife live. Rita.'

'Is it far?'

'Ten minute on foot, less in car. Go south along Jalan Abdullah Muhammad.'

'Thank you. Has anyone else been here looking for Mr Anwar? Another foreigner, maybe – an Englishman?'

'Yes, man come here last week. I tell him same thing.'

'What did he look like, this man?' Max asked.

'Tall, grey hair, that all I remember.'

'He didn't give a name?'

'No. No name.'

Max thanked the man again, then led the way back down the wooden steps to the street. 'It had to be my dad,' he said. 'Who else could it have been?'

'And Anwar?' Consuela wondered. 'What's happened to him?'

'He never came back from Shadow Island.'

They headed south out of the town centre along a wide road fringed with palm trees and ferns, Max mulling over what they'd found out. Narang Anwar had disappeared. That didn't surprise Max – he knew, after all, that Anwar had been a prisoner on Shadow Island. Some of those prisoners, like Redmond Ashworth-Ames, had come back. Others, like Erik Blomkvist and Arhat Zebari, hadn't. Max had hoped that Anwar might have been in the first category and was disappointed to find he wasn't. But he'd discovered one interesting fact – Anwar was a lawyer. That was intriguing. Zebari had been a journalist, Blomkvist and Ashworth-Ames both ecologists. How did they all fit together?

It was a gruelling walk in the merciless glare of the sun. Max wished he'd brought a hat and sunglasses and a bottle of water. The heat was sapping, and by the time they reached Narang Anwar's home they were all flagging and desperate for a drink.

The house was smaller than Max had expected. He thought lawyers were generally well-off, but Narang Anwar's home was just a modest bungalow with a tiny patch of garden in front. Rita Anwar answered the door. She was a petite woman in her mid-thirties, with straight, jet-black hair and facial features that were a mixture of Indonesian and Chinese. She wore a pale blue dress and sandals, her toenails varnished pink. Max introduced himself and his companions.

Rita stared at him in astonishment. 'You're Alex Cassidy's son? My goodness, what brings you here? Come in.'

She beckoned them into the house and closed the door. Max noticed the temperature change immediately – and with great relief. The place was air-conditioned.

'You look hot. Would you like a drink?' Rita asked.

'Please, that would be nice.'

'Ari?'

A boy about Max's age appeared in the kitchen doorway. He had short black hair, dark skin and a broad face with high cheekbones.

'Ari, would you mind helping with some drinks for our guests, please?' Rita asked. 'This way.'

They went through into a sitting room at the back

of the house and Rita gestured at the chairs. 'Please.'

She waited for them to make themselves comfortable, then turned to look at Max. 'You're Alex Cassidy's son,' she said again, as if she couldn't quite believe it.

'Has my dad been here?' Max asked.

Rita frowned. The question seemed to confuse her. 'Been here?' she said hesitantly. 'You mean recently?'

'In the last week or so.'

'The last *week*?' She paused. 'I don't understand. I thought your father was dead. It was in the papers. Somewhere in Central America. And your mother, isn't she . . . ?'

'My mum's in prison, yes,' Max said. 'But my dad isn't dead. He flew from Kuching to Pangkalan Bun last Monday. I thought he might have come here to see you.'

Rita shook her head in bemusement. 'No, he hasn't been here. You say your father is *alive*?'

'I only found out a couple of weeks ago,' Max replied. 'I haven't seen him, but he sent me a letter. He's in hiding, on the run.'

'*On the run?* From whom?'

'I was hoping you might be able to help me there.'

Rita looked bewildered. '*Me?*'

'He knew your husband. You seem to have met him too.'

'But that was more than two years ago.'

'Why did he come here then?'

'To see my husband. Narang brought him home for dinner one evening. He was a very nice man, very good company.'

'To see your husband about what?' Chris asked.

'They were discussing the possibility of Alex doing a show in Kalimantan. Not in Pangkalan Bun – that's too small – but maybe in Banjarmasin or Pontianak – they're both big cities.'

'A show?'

'I think it was going to be a charity show. To raise funds for a local wildlife project – an orang-utan sanctuary near here. Narang was always doing things for charity. He was a very good man.' Her voice cracked and Max saw her blink away a tear.

'What happened to your husband, Mrs Anwar?' he asked as gently as he could, sensing that the question might upset her.

Before Rita could reply, the sitting-room door opened and Ari came in with a tray of drinks. He placed the tray on a low table next to Rita's chair and went back out.

'Tea?' she asked Chris and Consuela.

She filled three cups with pale Chinese tea, then handed Max a glass containing some kind of soft drink. He took a tentative sip. It was cold and tasted of lime. He took a bigger gulp. It was delicious.

Rita composed herself, her cup and saucer perched on her knee, then answered Max's question.

'I don't know what happened to him,' she said calmly. 'He just disappeared.'

'Disappeared?'

'He flew to Jakarta on business in April – a meeting at one of the government offices. His plane arrived safely, with Narang on board, but he never made it to the meeting. Somewhere between the airport and Jakarta city centre he vanished. He hasn't been seen since.'

'The police have investigated it?' Consuela said.

'So they say,' Rita replied, her tone sceptical.

'You don't think they have?'

Rita took a delicate sip of tea, considering her response for a moment. 'You know my husband was a lawyer?' she said. 'His work didn't make him popular, with either the police or anyone else in authority.'

'Why not?'

'How much do you know about Kalimantan? You must know that it is covered with rainforest, with hardwood trees that sell for a lot of money when they are felled. It becomes even more profitable when you turn the cleared land into oil-palm plantations.'

Max nodded. 'We saw some of the plantations when we flew down from Kuching.'

'Much of the forest has been cleared illegally, but the local police and politicians have turned a blind eye to it. Many of them have been bribed by the big corporations that are doing the logging. The forest has been destroyed, with all the implications that has for wildlife and the environment, but there is a human cost to it all too. Local people have lost their land – the land they depended on for their food. It has been stolen from them by the corporations, who employ security guards and armed thugs to frighten and intimidate anyone who tries to oppose them. Sometimes they kill their opponents. Ari, the Dayak boy you saw just now – his parents were both murdered by militias working for an oil-palm corporation called Rescomin International.'

'Rescomin!' Chris exclaimed. 'Julius Clark's company.'

'That's right,' Rita replied. 'They have a massive oil-palm plantation and processing plant upriver from here. Narang was fighting them, representing the poor, defenceless people whose land had been stolen, whose families had been threatened or killed. But he was fighting a powerful enemy. Rescomin have teams of lawyers working for them, powerful people in their pocket both here and in Jakarta. It was an immensely difficult task for Narang, but he wouldn't give up. He was determined

PAUL ADAM

to get justice for his clients. And that has cost him his life.'

'You think he's dead?' Max asked.

'He must be. There were death threats: phone calls, letters warning him to drop his cases. But Narang wouldn't be frightened off. He was a very brave man.' Rita looked away, her lower lip quivering, her eyes glistening. 'He stood up for what was right. He stood up for the weak against the strong. And they killed him. I don't know who – the militias, some hired thugs working for Rescomin. I can't prove it – Narang's body hasn't even been found – but I know that's what happened.'

'You're right, I think your husband *is* dead,' Max said softly. 'I'm very sorry. And I think I know how he died.'

He told her about Shadow Island, about finding Narang's file in Julius Clark's office and his suspicions about the drug Episuderon, which he believed had killed Narang and many others. Chris backed him up, telling of his own experiences too.

Rita listened intently, her face screwed up in horror. 'You are sure about this?'

'Absolutely.'

'Then this man Clark is a murderer. How can he get away with it?'

'He won't,' Max said. 'That's why we've come here: to find evidence against him. Did your husband have

273

anything we might be able to use – statements, documents, files?'

'He did,' Rita replied. 'But the week after he disappeared there was a break-in at his office. All the paperwork was taken.'

Max's heart sank. 'Everything?'

'I'm afraid so. There is evidence at the Rescomin processing plant, Narang was sure of that – documents that would show the corporation had stolen land, had been logging illegally, maybe even records of which politicians, which police officers they have bribed. But the plant is heavily guarded. Narang was trying to get the courts to order Rescomin to hand over their papers, but the case was getting nowhere. And now Narang is gone there is no one else to continue his fight.'

'He had no partners?' Consuela said.

'No, he always worked alone. Most lawyers here are not interested in fighting multinational corporations. They are only interested in making money. That's why we have a two-bedroom bungalow rather than a six-bedroom mansion with a swimming pool. Narang followed his conscience, not his wallet.' Rita shook her head in despair. 'What can anyone do against a corporation like Rescomin?'

'Have you ever heard of the Cedar Alliance?' Max asked.

'No, what is it?'

'An organization dedicated to protecting the environment, to fighting the people who want to destroy it. My
father was part of it. I think your husband was too.'

'He never mentioned it.'

'My dad came back here last week,' Max said. 'I need
to know why. Is there anyone he might have visited? Do
you know if he met any other people when he was here
two years ago?'

Rita thought for a moment. 'I don't know. The only
person I can think of is a man named Jaya who runs the
local charity for which your father was going to do a
show – the orang-utan sanctuary.'

'Where do we find him? Where is this sanctuary?'

'The sanctuary is out in the rainforest, but Jaya has
an office in town – not far from Narang's.'

'Do you have the address?'

'Ari will take you there.'

'No, that's not necessary.'

'There are some things he can do for me in town at
the same time.' She turned her head and called, 'Ari!'

The Dayak boy came in, stealing a curious glance at
Max, Consuela and Chris, then waiting while Rita gave
him instructions.

At the front door Rita shook hands with them, holding onto Max's hand with both her own. 'If you find

anything, you must let me know. I do not want Narang's death to go unpunished.'

'I will,' Max replied.

They went back out into the sweltering heat and headed towards the town centre. Ari walked alongside them in silence. Max tried to make conversation with him.

'Do you live with Mrs Anwar?' he asked.

'Sometimes,' Ari replied.

'Where do you live the rest of the time?'

'Here and there.'

'In Pangkalan Bun?'

'And upriver.'

'Upriver?'

'Where I come from.'

Max wanted to ask him about his parents, but decided not to. He didn't know the boy at all and it was probably a very sensitive subject. So he asked him how old he was instead.

'Fourteen,' Ari replied.

'The same age as me. Don't you have to go to school?'

Ari's face broke into a wide grin. 'Don't you?' he fired back.

Max laughed. 'Mrs Anwar said you were a Dayak. What does that mean?'

'Dayak is word for forest peoples. Who live here a

long time. Before Chinese and Malays and others come.'

'You grew up in the rainforest?'

'Yes. Rainforest was my home.'

'"Was"?'

Ari shook his head – this wasn't something he wanted to talk about – and Max moved swiftly on to a different topic.

'You speak very good English. Where did you learn it?'

'Here and there,' Ari said again. It was obviously one of his favourite phrases.

'In school?'

'I pick it up from tourists. Some days I am guide in orang-utan sanctuary.'

'This one run by Jaya?'

'Yes. I speak English to tourists. Show them forest, orang-utan being fed.'

'That must be fun to watch.'

'Yes, orang-utan is very funny, very good to watch. You want to go there? I take if you like.'

'Thank you, but I'm not sure if we'll have the time.'

'You look for father, yes?' Ari must have been listening outside the door at Rita's house.

Max nodded.

Ari nodded back, as if he understood. 'I hope you find him,' he said.

They went back through the market by Narang Anwar's office. The street was still thronging with people, stallholders yelling their prices, measuring out their wares on brass scales – big ones for fruit and vegetables, smaller ones for spices. A man staggered along carrying a huge bag of rice; youths passed by eating Chinese dumplings with their fingers, their lips smeared with grease. Glistening fish and chunks of meat were laid out on slabs beneath gaudy red and green canopies; women bustled around the stalls, pushing and jostling, their arms laden with bags; and drifting over everything was a cloud of smoke from the grills where chicken was being barbecued.

Beyond the market, the streets were less crowded but still busy, cars and bicycles and belching lorries competing for space. Ari led them away from the main road down a narrow side street that was shaded from the sun by the surrounding buildings. He stopped outside a doorway screened by strings of beads to keep out the flies.

'This where Jaya work,' he said.

He pushed aside the bead curtain and they followed him inside. A slightly built, mahogany-skinned man was sitting behind a desk, speaking into the telephone. He waved a hand at Ari, acknowledging their arrival, and continued his conversation.

Max looked around the office. The walls were covered with photographs of rainforest animals and plants – trees, flowers, monkeys, lizards, snakes, lemurs. But dominating the display was the orang-utan. Max studied the pictures. He'd seen orang-utans in zoos back home, clowning around in their enclosures, and always found them fascinating: their long arms, all that ginger hair, those big eyes and expressive faces. He knew they were an endangered species and was glad to see that someone was fighting to ensure their survival.

Jaya came off the phone and exchanged a few words in Bahasa with Ari, the boy obviously explaining who Max, Consuela and Chris were. Jaya started with surprise and stared hard at Max for a moment.

'I have to go now,' Ari said. 'Maybe I see you around.'

'Yes – thanks for bringing us here,' Max replied.

The Dayak boy flashed a quick smile and left the office. Jaya stood up behind the desk and said in English, 'Hi, I'm Jaya.'

He shook hands and found chairs for them, then went back to his own seat, giving Max another stare that was so intense he had to look away. 'So how can I help you?'

'You met my father a couple of years ago,' Max said.

'That's right.'

'You haven't seen him again in the last week, have you?'

Jaya blinked, then frowned with puzzlement.

'He's alive,' Max went on quickly, anticipating Jaya's next question. 'I know he came to Pangkalan Bun. Did he come to you?'

Jaya shook his head slowly. 'He has not been here. Perhaps Mrs Anwar . . .'

'He didn't go there either,' Max said. 'Who else might he have gone to see? Have you any idea?'

'No idea at all. I met your father only once, with Narang. I have not seen him since.'

Max was disappointed. He'd been so optimistic that he would pick up his dad's trail in Pangkalan Bun, but every lead he'd found – Narang Anwar, Rita Anwar and now Jaya – had proved to be a dead end. He looked at Chris and Consuela. He could see that they were as deflated as he was.

'Your father talked about doing a show for us,' Jaya said. 'For our orang-utan sanctuary. It's a shame it never happened.'

'I was looking at your photographs,' Consuela said. 'You're doing good work.'

'I only wish we could do more. The tide is against us, I'm afraid. Every week, more and more rainforest is being destroyed. Soon there will be no orang-utans left in the wild.' He gave a weary shrug of resignation. 'What are orang-utans compared to palm oil? What can a small charity like ours do against the multinational corporations?'

'Narang Anwar was fighting them,' Max said.

'And look what happened to him.'

Jaya got to his feet. 'I have to go out to the sanctuary now. I'm sorry I haven't been able to help you.'

'That's OK. Thank you for your time.'

Max walked out of the office and paused to let Consuela and Chris join him. 'We didn't get far there,' he said despondently. 'I was hoping for more.'

They headed off down the street. No one said anything. They were all thinking the same thing: *Where do we go from here?*

They turned onto the main road, heading back towards the street market. Two hundred metres further on, they were waiting to cross at a busy junction when Max saw a blue-and-white police car speeding towards them from the town centre. Some sixth sense told him to look over his shoulder and he saw a second police car coming in the opposite direction. The hairs on the back of his neck stood up. Something was wrong – he could feel it instinctively.

The police cars slewed towards the kerb and came to an abrupt halt. Two officers jumped out of each vehicle.

Chris and Consuela didn't even notice what was happening until the policemen had surrounded them.

'You're under arrest,' one of the officers said curtly.

'*What?*' Chris stared at the man, then spun round to find two more policemen behind him. His arms were seized, Consuela's too.

For a split second everyone seemed to have forgotten about Max. He didn't think twice, didn't hesitate. He took off across the junction, weaving his way through the traffic, and sprinted away along the road. He didn't look back – he knew the police would be coming after him.

NINETEEN

The pavement was crowded with people – shoppers and other pedestrians sauntering along slowly, in no hurry to go anywhere. Max couldn't afford to get trapped in the middle of the throng so he stuck to the road, running along in the gutter next to the streaming lines of traffic. It was dangerous, but not as dangerous as allowing the police to catch him.

At the next junction he glanced back. The two officers were still in hot pursuit, though he'd opened up a gap of fifty or sixty metres. They were young, trim men, but they were hampered by their uniforms and all the equipment they carried on their belts – radios, pistols, batons. Max, on the other hand, was carrying no extra weight and he was fast and fit, all his hours of training paying dividends now.

He shot across the road, dodging recklessly through the traffic, which had to brake or swerve to avoid him. Car horns honked, drivers yelled insults at him, but Max was oblivious to everything. Everything except escape.

He headed for the street market. He could shake off the policemen there, or find somewhere to hide. He looked back. They weren't giving up the chase. One of the officers had his radio to his mouth as he ran – calling for reinforcements, Max guessed. The other was yelling out and gesticulating furiously, apparently ordering the pedestrians to stop the fleeing boy. But no one intervened. People paused and turned to stare curiously at Max as he hurtled past, but they made no attempt to catch him.

Max smelled the smoke from the barbecues before he saw the market. He careered round a corner and there it was in front of him. A whole street blocked by stalls and dawdling shoppers. He glanced over his shoulder again. The two officers hadn't come into sight yet. Max's heart leaped. He was going to make it.

He ran into the market, squeezing through the crowds, looking back over people's heads. Still no sign of the policemen. He couldn't move very fast here and had to slow to a walk, ease his way past all the shoppers. Their bodies were all around him, a pulsing mass of flesh that he had to force apart to keep going. He hit a wall of people and came to a stop, trying to find a way through. He took another quick look behind, but couldn't see the police officers. He prised apart two large men and slipped quickly through the gap. The

PAUL ADAM

police would be encountering the same obstacles, the same dense jam of people. If Max could only get to the other side of the market, he'd be home and dry.

The crowd began to thin out. The stalls were coming to an end. Max burst out of the market, already starting to accelerate. And skidded to an abrupt halt.

There were two more policemen waiting for him. Max stared at them, feeling suddenly sick. They were five metres away, blocking his path. He knew he had no chance of getting past them. He was trapped. Police officers in front of him, two others closing in from the rear. Max did the only thing he could: he spun round and plunged back into the market.

The officers yelled at him in English to stop, but he was already twisting and turning through the crowd. He looked around desperately for another way out, but couldn't see one. There were stalls all along the street and buildings behind them – no side streets, no exits. In the distance, Max caught a glimpse of two peaked caps gliding towards him. He stopped. Whichever way he went he'd be caught.

The policemen were closing in, still shouting, pushing and shoving people out of the way. Max threw himself to the ground and snaked away underneath one of the stalls. As he emerged on the other side, he felt a pair of hands take hold of his arms. He stiffened, getting ready to fight, then looked up and saw Ari.

'This way,' the boy said softly.

He helped Max to his feet, then kept hold of his arm and guided him away from the stalls and into a narrow alley that Max hadn't noticed. They ran along it and out into another street. Ari turned left and Max followed. He thought he was fast, but Ari was even faster and he knew every inch of the town. They ducked into another side street, then crossed a wider road to another alley, emerging into a secluded courtyard where Ari finally came to a stop. Max bent over, hands on knees, and panted for breath.

'Is safe here,' Ari said.

'Thank you,' Max gasped. He straightened up, still breathing heavily. His face and back were dripping with sweat. He wiped his forehead with his hand.

Ari grinned at him. 'Running from policemens is fun, no?' He said it as if he'd done it many times himself. 'Why they chase you?'

'I don't know,' Max replied.

He wondered about it now for the first time. Why *had* the police stopped them, told them they were under arrest? Was Penhall behind it, or Julius Clark? They'd done nothing wrong, committed no offence, as far as Max was aware. His decision to flee had been instinctive, but he knew it had been the right thing to do. He didn't trust the authorities – not back home in England, and particularly not here in Borneo. No one was going to lock him up again. Not if he could help it.

'What you do now?' Ari asked.

Max had to think about that. Chris and Consuela were in custody, he didn't know for how long. He was on his own: he had to make a decision. Did he wait for them to be released – if they *were* going to be released – or did he carry on with the task they'd come to Borneo to carry out? It didn't take him long to make up his mind.

'Mrs Anwar told us that Rescomin has a big oil-palm plantation and processing plant upriver from here. Can you take me there?'

'Is long way,' Ari said doubtfully. 'Two days by boat.'

'Is there not a road, or a bus or something?'

'No road, no bus. Is rainforest. River is only way through.'

'Can we get a boat then?'

'I can fix, yes. But it will cost money. I get *ces* for us.'

'*Ces?*'

'Is canoe with motor.'

Max checked his pockets. He had only a small amount of rupiahs, the local currency. The rest of his money he'd left in his hotel room. 'I have to go back to my hotel first.'

'I come with you. Which hotel?'

Max gave him the name.

'I know it,' Ari said. 'We go this way. Is not far.'

They headed for Max's hotel, walking now, not running – they didn't want to draw attention to themselves. Max kept a sharp eye out for the police, but didn't see any sign of them. They were a couple of kilometres from the street market, in a quieter residential area. With any luck, the officers would still be scouring the town centre.

Ten minutes later they were standing behind a tree fifty metres from the hotel, on the opposite side of the road. Max studied the building. Did the police know where he was staying? Would they come here? He knew there was a good chance they would, but he had to risk it – he needed his money.

'I keep watch for you. Whistle if police come, OK?' Ari said, reading Max's mind.

Max nodded. They crossed the road together and walked rapidly towards the hotel.

'Where your room?' Ari asked.

'Upstairs – that one at the end,' Max replied, pointing up at the first-floor balcony.

He went into the hotel warily, preparing to run if there was a welcome party waiting for him, but the entrance hall was deserted. The manager came out from his office when he heard the footsteps. Max got his key and went up to his room. His money was locked in his suitcase under the bed. He retrieved it quickly – a wad of rupiahs and some US dollars – and grabbed his passport as well.

He was pushing the case back under the bed when he heard a sharp whistle from the rear of the hotel. He stepped over to the window and looked out. Ari was in the yard, waving to him urgently. Max waved back and hurried across the room. He opened his door and peeped out cautiously. A police officer was just coming up the stairs onto the balcony. Max closed and locked his door, then ran to the window and pushed it open. He clambered over the sill, hung by his arms and dropped to the ground. Ari caught him, helping to break his fall, then they ran across the yard, scrambled over a fence and sprinted away from the hotel.

After four hundred metres they slowed to a fast walk, Max glancing back every few seconds to make sure the police weren't on their tail. They headed out of town along a dusty road, then skirted round the back of some houses to the river. The Sungai Arot was broad and slow-moving, its waters a cloudy brown colour, as if saturated with mud and silt. The banks were fringed with luxuriant tropical vegetation – long grasses, shrubs, and a dozen or more varieties of palm tree.

Jutting out from the near bank was a short wooden jetty from which a gang of boys about Ari and Max's age were jumping into the river amid much boisterous shouting and laughing. They were wearing nothing but skimpy shorts, their nut-brown bodies gleaming wet.

Seeing Ari arrive, the lads broke off from their games and crowded round, staring and smiling at Max, asking questions in their own language. Ari must have told them that Max was English, for two of the boys suddenly threw out a couple of phrases they had no doubt picked up from visiting tourists – 'Good morning, how do you do?' 'What time is it? Is it time for tea?' – then fell about in convulsions of laughter.

'Boys will look after you,' Ari said. 'No one find you here. I go into town and hire *ces*.'

Max gave him some money and watched him walk away along the riverbank. The boys had resumed their sport, racing out along the jetty and hurling themselves into the water. One of them came up to Max and gestured towards the river.

'You want swim with us?'

Max was tempted. It was baking hot in the fierce morning sun and the thought of a cool dip was very appealing. But he didn't like the look of the Sungai Arot. It was very murky and you couldn't tell what dangers lurked beneath the surface. He knew there were water snakes in Borneo, and crocodiles. The boys didn't seem to be worried, but maybe they were used to the risks.

'What about crocodiles?' Max asked.

'Crocodile?' The boy shook his head. 'Not here. That way, and that way, yes.' He pointed up and then down the river. 'Here, too many peoples, too many boat. Crocodile no like.'

Why shouldn't I join in? Max thought. It looked like fun. For a moment he thought about Consuela and Chris, wondering whether he should go back into town and try to find out what had happened to them. But he knew that would be dangerous. He was likely to be caught too, and then their trip to Borneo would have been for nothing. So he stripped down to his boxer shorts, ran out along the jetty and leaped into the river. The water was tepid, like a warm bath, but it was still cooler than the searing air on the bank. The other boys grabbed hold of him and pushed him under playfully. Max fought back, and soon the whole gang was tussling in the water, ducking and diving, then scrambling out and jumping back in again.

Max lost track of time, but it must have been at least an hour later that Ari returned, coming upstream from Pangkalan Bun in a motorized canoe – maybe five metres long with a pointed bow and low sides. Ari sat in the stern, nursing the outboard motor with a look of unconcealed joy on his face – like a western teenager with a sports car. He pulled in alongside the jetty and the gang swarmed down into the canoe, all clamouring to be allowed a go with the motor, but Ari pushed them away, clinging fiercely to his position as skipper.

Max gathered up his clothes and joined them all in the *ces*. Ari revved the outboard motor to show off, then engaged the gears. The canoe shot forward like a bullet, the force knocking two of the boys backwards off their seats. Everyone yelled and screamed with delight. They raced up the river for a hundred metres, then Ari throttled back and shouted something at his mates, jabbing his thumb towards the bank. Max guessed he was telling them the ride was over – he and his important English friend had business to transact and they weren't taking this rabble with them. The boys went over the side reluctantly, then rocked the canoe up and down gleefully to try to capsize it until Ari bawled at them to get out of the way, and opened up the throttle again. His mates splashed to the shore and made catcalls and rude gestures from the bank as the *ces* surged away up the river.

Ari slowed to a more manageable pace once his friends were out of sight. Max sat on the wooden plank at the front of the canoe and enjoyed the ride, the water creaming past beneath the bow, the cooling breeze blowing over his bare torso, moderating the clammy, burning heat of the sun.

The forests on both sides of the river had been cleared to make paddy fields for growing rice, but as the canoe got further upstream the jungle returned – a wall of dense green vegetation, massive trees clinging to the banks, their branches overhanging the water. Max saw a monkey swinging down from a branch and splashing across the river directly in front of the *ces*. Ari throttled back to avoid hitting it.

'What's it doing?' Max asked.

'Canoe motor frighten crocodile away,' Ari replied. 'Is safe place to cross river. Monkey do it all the time.'

'What kind of monkey is that?'

'Proboscis. *Monyet belanda*, we say. You see its long nose? Lots of proboscis monkey here.'

'What other animals do you get?'

'Sun bears, wild boars, gibbons, pythons, sambar deer. But you no see by the river now. They very shy, stay hidden in deep forest.'

'What about orang-utans?'

Ari shook his head. 'Not many orang-utan left. You go to Tanjung Puting National Park, you see orang-utan, and also in sanctuary Jaya look after. But here, orang-utan all gone. Man kill them, drive them away. Is very sad.'

They weren't the only people on the river. Other

motorized canoes came past carrying passengers and goods, some of them so overloaded that their sides were only a few centimetres above the water. Larger vessels also floated by: houseboats that Ari called *klotok*, with cabins for sleeping in, and huge commercial barges stacked with tree trunks that had been logged upriver and were being transported to the coast. Several times Ari had to pull over to the bank to let convoys of barges past. Max was stunned by how many trees had been felled. But it wasn't just logs the barges were carrying. Many were laden with dozens of big metal containers, which had a logo and the name RESCOMIN painted on their sides.

'What are those?' Max asked.

'Palm oil,' Ari replied. 'From the plantations. They process palm nuts to make oil, then put in big tanks like that and send to port on coast. It go all over the world.'

'How far away are the plantations now?'

'Long way. We get there day after tomorrow.'

Max realized that he hadn't given much thought to this trip. He had relied on Ari to make all the arrangements. 'What about tonight?' he wondered. 'Where will we spend the night? Are there villages – somewhere we can sleep?'

'We sleep by river,' Ari told him.

In the early evening he steered the canoe in to the bank and cut the outboard motor. The two of them jumped into the shallow water and dragged the boat up onto a small shingle beach. They collected bits of wood from the shore and the edge of the rainforest and Ari made a fire. He'd bought supplies in Pangkalan Bun when he'd hired the *ces* – rice, vegetables, spoons, two billy cans, bottles of water and a heavy iron cooking pot. He gave Max the task of chopping onions and chillies while he sharpened a long, sturdy stick into a spear. Then he waded out into the river and waited patiently, still as a rock, his eyes fixed on the water, the spear poised in his hand. Max watched silently from the shore. Suddenly Ari's spear lanced down into the river. When he pulled it out, there was a silvery fish wriggling on the point. He waded back out and killed the creature by hitting its head on a stone, then returned to the water and resumed his motionless position. Ten minutes and a couple of misses later, he'd caught a second fish. He gutted both with his knife and laid them out on a flat stone that he'd earlier placed in the fire to heat. The cooking pot containing rice and vegetables was put on the fire beside the stone and fifteen minutes later their meal was ready.

Max tucked in greedily. He hadn't eaten anything since breakfast and was ravenous. The rice and vegetables were hot and spicy, the chillies burning his throat, but the fish was tasteless and full of bones. It was like eating a barbecued hairbrush.

'What sort of fish are these?' he asked Ari.

'Sebarau.'

'You were really good at spearing them. That must take a lot of practice.'

Ari shrugged modestly. 'I do it since I was little.'

'You said you grew up in the forest. Was it near here?'

'Not near. Is over that way.' He waved a hand vaguely in the air.

'A village?' Max asked.

'*Rumah betang*. You call it longhouse. It gone now.'

'Longhouse?'

'Big house where lots of peoples live.'

'What happened to it?'

Ari pulled a clump of fish bones from his mouth and threw them into the fire. Max thought he wasn't going to answer the question, but he was just taking his time, thinking about it. 'It burn,' he said eventually.

'Burn?'

'Land around longhouse was forest. Rescomin take land and chop down trees. Then they burn ground to clear for oil palms. Fire very big. Wind catch it and fire spread to longhouse. Many peoples die.'

Max stared at him, aghast. 'And your family?' he

asked, though he already suspected what the answer would be.

'They die,' Ari replied calmly. 'My mother, my father, my sisters. I was not there. I was at river. I get away from fire in boat.'

Max didn't know what to say. So this was what Rita Anwar had meant when she said Ari's parents had been murdered by Rescomin militias. They hadn't been killed deliberately, but the militias' reckless actions had led to their deaths.

'I'm very sorry,' Max said. It sounded feeble, but it came from the heart. 'When was this?'

'Three year ago.'

'And has anyone been punished for it? Has Rescomin paid compensation?'

'No, nothing happen. Mr Anwar, he try to help us, the ones who survive the fire, but he get nowhere. Rescomin too powerful. They have important high-up friends. Mr and Mrs Anwar, they very good to me. They give me home, if I need. They find me jobs, bits of work.'

'Will Mrs Anwar worry if you're not there tonight?'

'I telephone her when I go to get *ces*. Tell her I take you upriver. She no worry. I come and go all time.'

Ari threw the remains of his fish onto the fire and stood up. He obviously didn't want to talk any more. Max washed the cooking pot in the river and helped Ari gather more wood. Then they settled down by the fire as darkness fell.

Max had thought that the rainforest at night would be absolutely still and quiet and was surprised by how noisy it was. There seemed to be sounds coming from the jungle all the time: hoots and low howls and strange, unsettling cries. They disturbed him at first, but he soon got used to them. He felt safe by the fire, with Ari curled up next to him.

He thought about what the Dayak boy had told him – about the fire, his parents dying. How did you get over something as horrific as that? How did you get on with your life when you were only fourteen and your family had been burned to death? Max admired the way Ari seemed to be coping with his loss. But was he really coping? Or was he being eaten up by grief underneath that calm exterior?

Max couldn't imagine what it must be like to be an orphan. He had gone through a traumatic couple of years since his dad had disappeared and his mum had been imprisoned, but at least his parents were still alive. He saw his mum every week and had a powerful feeling that he would soon find his dad. *You're not far away, I can sense it, Dad*, he thought. *But where?*

* * *

They were up at first light. The rainforest animals were

already out foraging for food. Birds with dazzling red, green and yellow plumage flitted to and fro across the river – kingfishers, Ari said – and in the trees above them proboscis monkeys were swinging from branch to branch, calling loudly to one another.

Max heard a whooshing sound and turned to see two huge birds swooping down over the water and landing in the top of a tree on the far side. They were the size of swans, with long trailing tail plumes, orange necks and red and yellow beaks.

'Hornbills,' Ari said. 'They good birds. They bring luck.'

'Really?' Max replied. 'I hope so.'

Ari put the cooking pot on the fire and they had more boiled rice and vegetables for breakfast, then they kicked out the embers, loaded up the canoe and were on their way. All day they headed upriver, forking off left at one point up a smaller tributary, where they encountered convoy after convoy of palm-oil barges travelling downstream.

Towards evening the rainforest on the left bank began to peter out, the land cleared to make paddy fields. Then, beyond the fields, Max saw a huge wooden building on stilts.

'Longhouse,' Ari said. 'We stay there tonight.'

They tied the canoe to a wooden jetty and

disembarked. A couple of local Dayak boys, who were fishing off the end of the jetty, hitched up their lines, ran over to Ari and chattered away at him excitedly. Then they turned and raced ahead of them along a well-trodden path through the paddy fields. By the time Max and Ari reached the longhouse, there was a crowd of young boys and girls waiting to greet them. They were escorted up a ladder made from a notched tree trunk onto the veranda of the longhouse, which must have been nearly a hundred metres long. A palm-thatched roof overhung the veranda to provide shelter from the weather.

Adults appeared in doorways, staring inquisitively at the visitors as they were taken to a communal space at one end of the building and presented to the long-house chief – a broad, muscular middle-aged man who had a face like crumpled leather and tattoos on almost every bit of his exposed skin. Ari conversed politely with the chief in their own language, then the man said a few words to Max.

'He says you are welcome,' Ari translated. 'We can sleep here and eat with them.'

Max smiled at the chief. 'Thank you.'

Ari had brought a canvas sack with him from the canoe, which he now opened to reveal an assortment of gifts.

'I use your money to buy,' he whispered to Max as he gave the chief some rolls of fishing line, packets of spices, honey and other provisions that, Max guessed, were luxuries in this remote part of Kalimantan.

The chief thanked them graciously, then withdrew into his apartment, leaving them to the care of the longhouse children, who gathered round, peering shyly at Max and talking animatedly to Ari.

'Do they all live in this one building?' Max asked Ari.

'Yes. Longhouse is traditional Dayak way. Everyone together. All families have own space inside longhouse, but share open areas. I get them to show you.'

Ari spoke to their hosts, who responded enthusiastically, taking them along the veranda and showing them the apartments where they all lived. In one room an elderly man was carving sculptures out of wood – beautifully crafted monkeys and lemurs and other rainforest animals.

'They're really good,' Max said.

'He make to sell to tourist in Pangkalan Bun,' Ari explained. 'Tourist like wooden animal.'

Later that evening they ate with one of the longhouse families, a simple meal of rice and grilled turtle. The turtle was smoky and as tough as an old car tyre.

'If we adults,' Ari said, 'they give us *tuak* – rice wine – and get us drunk, then make us dance and sing song. But we childrens so we OK. We no have to sing and dance.'

'Thank goodness for that,' Max said.

They spent the night in a corner of the communal hall, sleeping on mats woven out of leaves, with a blanket wrapped around them. Then, in the morning, after a breakfast of rice and fruit, they continued upstream in the canoe.

The paddy fields around the longhouse soon gave way to oil-palm plantations. The rows of trees came almost to the river – only a narrow strip along the bank remained uncultivated – and they went on for mile after mile.

'Was all this once rainforest?' Max asked.

Ari nodded. 'Yes; now Rescomin have it all. Very big area, many square kilometres.'

'And their processing plant?'

'Is just up here. I show you. But we must be careful. There is guards with guns. They drive around plantations.'

Ari steered the canoe in to the bank and cut the motor, letting the vessel glide the last few metres. Max jumped out and tied the bow rope to a tree stump, then they walked along the bank. After two hundred metres they rounded a bend and came across a long line of barges moored at the side of the river, each one stacked with metal containers.

Ari slowed and looked around warily. 'Processing

plant not far now. These empty containers. They wait here, then go to plant to get palm oil.'

They walked past the barges. None of them had their own engines or wheelhouses: they were just floating cargo decks that had to be towed by a tug. As they neared the front of the line, Ari suddenly dropped to the ground, signalling to Max to do the same. Max flung himself down into the grass.

'Guards,' Ari whispered.

Max heard the noise of a vehicle, then saw a black jeep coming towards them along the plantation's perimeter track, which ran parallel to the river. There were two men in uniform in the front, the passenger holding a semi-automatic rifle across his chest. Max wondered for a moment whether they'd been spotted, then realized that this was just a routine patrol. The jeep rattled past, leaving a cloud of dust in its wake.

Ari scrambled to his feet and continued walking along the bank for another hundred metres before lying down again in the shelter of a bush. Max crawled up next to him. Ari pointed ahead and Max saw a high chain-link fence topped with razor wire blocking the riverbank. Beyond the fence was a massive industrial complex with tall chimneys puffing out smoke, a big metal-sided building the size of an aircraft hangar and a cluster of smaller one-storey cabins that looked like offices.

'That the processing plant,' Ari said.

'Does the fence go all the way round it?'

'Yes. There no way in except gate with guards on it.'

'What about the river?'

'They have big pool next to river – like harbour – for loading barges. There gates across harbour entrance. No way in there either.'

Max studied the plant. Had his father come here? He must have had a reason for returning to Borneo. It wasn't going to be easy to get inside the complex, but Max knew he had to. Somewhere in there was evidence that he could use against Julius Clark.

'Listen!' Ari said suddenly, inclining his head.

His sharp ears must have caught a noise, for he crawled away under the bush, pulling Max in after him. Max heard the faint throb of an engine. Was the jeep returning?

The noise got louder. It was coming from behind them, from the river. A boat? But it didn't sound like a boat. Then Max realized what it was – a helicopter.

Twisting his head round, he saw it scudding low up the river like a huge black insect. It flew past and landed on a patch of open ground just inside the processing-plant fence. The rotor blades clattered to a stop and two men got out. Max didn't have a clear view of one of them, but he recognized the other. Dark suit, pale face, rimless spectacles. It was Julius Clark.

TWENTY

Max watched the two men walk away from the helicopter and disappear behind one of the cabins. So Julius Clark himself was here. Was it a routine visit? Max wondered. Or had he flown in for some specific purpose? More than ever now, Max knew it was essential that he get inside the processing plant.

The metal gates at the entrance to the river harbour swung open and a stubby tug came out towing three barges laden with containers. The convoy chugged slowly away downriver, but then a second tug emerged from the harbour and veered across towards the bank. Max and Ari slithered deeper into the bushes to avoid being seen. The tug manoeuvred round in a circle and reversed up to the line of barges moored at the side of the river. The first of a group of three barges, all linked together, was hitched up to the rear of the tug and towed away into the harbour so the empty containers could be filled with palm oil. Max watched the tug head across to the quayside, then looked at the barges that remained, and an idea began to take shape inside his head.

Peering out carefully to check that he couldn't be seen from the processing plant, Max stood up and scuttled across to the nearest barge, scrambling onto the deck and ducking down behind the containers. They were big rectangular metal vats, about a metre and a half high, two metres wide and three metres long. Max pulled himself up onto one of them and examined the raised hatch on the top. It was a little over thirty centimetres in diameter and capped with a hinged lid held shut by a clamp. Around the edge of the hatch was a line of rivets attaching it to the body of the container.

Max slid back down and returned to Ari in the bushes.

'What you do?' Ari asked. 'Why you look at containers?'

'Can we go back to the longhouse now?' Max said. 'I need to borrow some tools.'

On the trip back downriver, Max explained how he was planning to get inside the Rescomin plant.

Ari stared at him, biting his lip anxiously. 'You crazy,' he said.

'But will it work?' Max asked.

Ari shrugged. 'Maybe it work. But maybe not and you get killed. They bad mens there. They kill many peoples.'

'I'll just have to take that chance,' Max said.

At the longhouse they went to the workshop where the elderly man was carving wooden animals, and Ari negotiated the loan of a hammer and chisel and a thick iron nail, Max paying a few rupiahs as a sort of hire charge for the tools. Then they headed back upstream to the barges.

There were twenty-four of them moored along the riverbank, in eight groups of three. Max chose the last barge in the first group because on the bank next to it was a stand of trees and shrubs that screened it from the processing plant. He climbed on top of one of the containers that had part of the Rescomin name on the side missing – the first and last two letters so it read: SCOM. He unclamped the lid and swung it back on its hinge. Then he peered down into the opening. It was very dark and he could smell the sickly vegetable odour of the palm-oil residue that had been left behind when the container was emptied. He shuddered. The thought of going down into that stinking black hole filled him with dread, but he knew it was the only way he was going to get inside the Rescomin compound.

Ari passed him the hammer and chisel and Max set to work slicing through the rivets that held the hatch in place. One sharp tap was enough to sever each of the soft metal pins, Max spacing out the blows and praying that the noise didn't carry across to the processing plant. The rivets all cut, Max lowered the lid and clamped it shut. It still looked identical to all the other containers, but Max would now be able to remove the whole thing from inside without the clamp being unfastened. He took the thick iron nail and hammered two air holes into the top of the container, then lifted out the hatch and its lid as one unit and climbed down through the opening.

Ari peered in after him. 'You sure you want to do this?' he asked. 'It not too late to stop.'

'I'm sure,' Max replied confidently, though his heart was pumping hard and his stomach was knotted with nerves.

He took his passport and wallet from his pockets and passed them up to Ari. 'Please could you look after these?'

'I wait here for you,' Ari said, handing Max one of the bottles of water they'd brought from the canoe.

'I don't know when I'll be out.'

'Don't matter. I wait.'

'Thanks.'

Ari slid the hatch unit back into the hole and the inside of the container went dark. Glimmers of light trickled in through the two air holes, but they were too feeble to make much difference to the overall blackness. Max felt as if he'd been shut away in a tomb, an image that did nothing to reassure him. He was taking a big risk. If anything went wrong, he knew he might well die inside the container.

'Good luck,' Ari said softly through the lid, then Max heard him climbing down from the container and off the barge.

Max remained underneath the raised hatch, the only place where he could stand up straight. The floor and sides of the container were coated with a greasy film of palm oil and he didn't want to sit in it. He tried to relax – he didn't know how long he was going to be in here – but it wasn't easy. The atmosphere was hot and claustrophobic. Breathing was difficult in the thick, tropical air, the metal walls absorbing the heat of the sun outside and transmitting it into the interior. Max revised his thoughts about this stifling little chamber. He wasn't in a tomb. He was in an oven and he was being slowly roasted to death.

He wished he'd waited until nightfall now, when it would have been cooler. But he didn't know whether the plant operated at night and he was impatient to get inside as soon as possible. How long would it be, he wondered, before his container was taken away to be filled?

His face and neck were streaming with sweat. His clothes were sticking to his skin. Every breath he took felt as if he were inhaling steam. He'd never been in a sauna, but this must be what it felt like. He longed to lift up the hatch and let in a gust of fresh air, but he controlled the urge. He had to wait it out, endure the conditions.

He drank some of his water. He could have emptied the bottle in one go, but restrained himself. It might have to last him a very long time. Then he slowed his breathing, the way he did when he was practising his stage act. He was used to being enclosed in containers – trunks, boxes, cabinets – but none of them had ever been as suffocating as this one. It was un-bearable. He reached out and touched one metal side with his fingers, then pulled back as if he'd been burned – which he had: the sides were almost red-hot. *I'll be cooked to a crisp before I get into the compound*, he thought grimly.

Trying to take his mind off his predicament, he thought again about his father. Why had he come to Pangkalan Bun? Who had he come to see? What had he come to do? And what of Chris and Consuela? Max was worried about them. Were they safe? What had the police done to them? Perhaps he should have stayed with them, but what would that have achieved, all three of them in custody? At least he was still free. He would do what he had to do inside the Rescomin compound, and then find out what had become of them.

He heard a faint noise somewhere in the distance. Was it a tug? He cocked his head to one side, listening intently. The sounds were muffled by the walls of the container, but he could definitely hear the rumble of an engine, then a clank of metal. The floor beneath him suddenly jolted forward a few centimetres. Max flung out his arms to steady himself. The barge was moving. He let out a sigh of relief. Thank God!

Slowly the barge crept forwards. *Twenty metres, thirty* . . . Max pictured it heading up the river, turning in through the harbour gates. Then it stopped. There was a rattle of machinery and he guessed that the crane was starting to unload the containers. It was fifteen or twenty minutes later that he heard a scraping noise on the sides of his own container and felt it rising into the air and swinging round onto the quayside.

He gave it another ten minutes – until he was sure that all the barges had been unloaded – before he risked opening the hatch. He pushed up on the underside of the lid and lifted the whole unit out of its slot, creating a tiny gap through which he could peer. He saw the bottom of the crane gantry and the other containers stacked neatly in rows; then, rotating his head and shoulders, he caught sight of the water in the harbour and the rest of the quayside. He didn't see any people.

It was now or never. Finishing the last of his water, he tossed the empty bottle away and very cautiously lifted the hatch unit clear of the opening and slid it to one side. Then he pulled himself up and poked an eye over the edge of the hole, taking another look around the area. The crane had moved further along the quayside and was busy loading full containers onto some waiting barges. There was a man in overalls supervising the operation, but he had his back turned, looking the other way.

Max hauled himself out of the container, replaced the hatch unit and slipped quickly down to the ground. He paused for a second to get his bearings, shielded by the container. The harbour was to his right, the processing plant to his left. The office blocks, where he wanted to go, were behind him, on the other side of the compound. To reach them, he had to either cross the quay in full view of the crane driver and supervisor, or circle round the processing plant to approach from the opposite direction. It wasn't a difficult choice.

Keeping down low so the containers hid his movements, he ran over to the corner of the processing plant and looked out cautiously. There was a yard at the side of the building that was crowded with more metal containers and a line of parked trucks, presumably used for bringing the harvested palm nuts to the plant. But no people.

Max darted out and sprinted across the yard, sticking close to the wall of the processing plant and using the containers and trucks as cover wherever he could. As he reached the far end, he slowed, then stopped and checked round the corner. There was a vehicle entrance at this end of the plant, and a loading bay inside where the palm nuts were scooped up into large hoppers to be fed into the oil presses. Four trucks with the Rescomin logo on their sides were waiting in line to unload. The drivers had got out of their cabs and were standing together in a group, talking and smoking. Max watched them with dismay. Getting past without being seen was not going to be easy.

'Hands in the air!' a voice barked behind him.

Max froze.

'*Now!*'

Max lifted his arms and turned round slowly. A uniformed guard was standing a metre away, pointing his semi-automatic rifle straight at Max's chest.

It was a small, functional office containing a desk and chairs, a phone and a computer and very little else. But it had the one thing that in this part of the world was essential to any western businessman – air-conditioning.

Max felt the cold draught as soon as he stepped through the door, the armed guard prodding him in the back with the barrel of his rifle, and was almost glad to have been caught. After the hellish heat of the container, the office was a refreshing oasis of coolness. His skin prickled, the hairs standing on end. It might have been the air-conditioning; then again, it might have been the man behind the desk, who radiated an aura of icy intimidation.

'Hello, Max,' Julius Clark said. 'I've been expecting you.'

Expecting me? Max thought. How? Had someone betrayed him? If so, who?

Clark seemed to read his mind, for he went on, 'I have sources here in Borneo. People who keep me informed about anything that might affect my interests in the country. It's a pity the police didn't manage to detain you. But then, I can't say I'm surprised they failed. You have an annoying habit of escaping.'

'What's happened to my friends?' Max demanded.

'They are currently being held in the police cells in Pangkalan Bun.'

'Why?'

Clark gave a harsh laugh. 'Because I asked for them

to be held. The local police are so obliging. A word in the right ear, a few dollars in the right bank account – it's amazing how helpful law-enforcement officers can be.' He waved a hand. 'Don't just stand there, Max. Take a seat.'

The guard jabbed Max forward with his rifle. Max sat down on a metal chair facing the desk and gave Clark a hostile glare. The tycoon seemed calm and relaxed. His greying hair was combed back from his forehead, his face smooth and pale, his eyes behind the rimless spectacles like boreholes in the Arctic icecap. Max remembered the last time he'd seen him – when he'd left Clark trussed and gagged on the floor of his office on Shadow Island. In other circumstances the memory might have made him smile, but not now. Max knew he was in serious trouble.

'I'd like to say it's a pleasure to meet you again,' Clark said. 'Unfortunately, it isn't. You've been a problem for me from the start, since you burned down my fortress on Shadow Island.'

'Shame about that,' Max said sarcastically. 'You'll have to do your brainwashing somewhere else now.'

'So you've worked it out then, have you?'

'I know you've been injecting people with Episuderon – a drug developed by the Nazis – killing many of them in the process.'

'And the ones who survive – and plenty *have* survived – what happens to them?'

'You tell me.'

'You don't know, do you? You've only got half the picture.'

'Then why don't you give me the rest?'

Clark leaned back in his padded swivel chair and linked his hands together across his stomach. 'Do you know what a fifth columnist is, Max?'

'No.'

'You've heard of the Spanish Civil War?'

'Vaguely.'

Clark shook his head and clicked his tongue disapprovingly. 'The modern education system – how it fails our young people.'

'What is this, a history lesson?'

'You should be ashamed of your ignorance, Max. The Spanish Civil War was one of the key events of the twentieth century,' Clark said pompously. 'A brutal three-year conflict between Republicans and Nationalists, which the Nationalists eventually won.'

'And?'

'When the Nationalists were advancing on Madrid, they had four columns of soldiers outside the city. But they had another column – a fifth column – *inside* the city with the Republicans. People who were on *their* side and would work to undermine the Republican defences and aid a Nationalist victory. That's what a fifth columnist is – a friend in the enemy camp.'

'You've been creating fifth columnists – is that what you're saying?'

'That's exactly what we've been doing, and will continue doing. We take people who are opposed to our interests – environmentalists, scientists, troublemakers. We re-educate them with the help of Episuderon, then send them back to their organizations, where they secretly work for us – supplying us with information, obstructing their colleagues, doing their best to make their organizations less effective, less of a problem for me and my businesses. It's so much safer, so much better than simply killing them.'

'You mean you kidnap them, brainwash them with a dangerous drug that kills some and leaves others brain-damaged, then send the ones who are lucky enough to survive back to betray their friends so you can make a few more billion dollars? You're one sick weirdo.'

Clark's cheeks flushed. He opened his mouth to speak, but Max hadn't finished.

'I've seen Redmond Ashworth-Ames,' he continued. 'I've seen what you did to him. You think that was right? To destroy his mind, destroy his life. You think what you're doing here is right too? Stealing people's land, burning their homes, killing them, chopping down the rainforest? You're destroying the world, and you don't care so long as you make money out of it.'

Clark gave a thin smile. 'A fine little speech,' he sneered. 'But don't be so self-righteous. What I do is essential for the welfare of the world's people.'

'*Your* welfare, you mean,' Max fired back.

'Do you have a car back home in London, Max? What are you going to fuel it with when the oil runs out? Do you have electric lights, a television, a computer? How are you going to run them when the coal and gas are gone? We live in a highly advanced consumer society that needs an immense amount of resources – metals, wood, petroleum, minerals. I supply those resources. I supply the resources our world and its population require to survive, so don't lecture me on what's right and what's wrong. Without me, most people in the world would die of starvation and the rest would have to go back to living in caves.'

'That's rubbish!' Max said angrily. 'Let you do what you please or we all starve – those aren't the only choices we have. We can live differently, cut down on all the stuff we use, find alternative sources of energy. We can live well *and* look after the environment at the same time.'

Clark let out a snort of contemptuous laughter.

'What a naïve little idiot you are. Did they teach you that in school, or did you get it from your deluded father and his crazy friends in the Cedar Alliance?'

'They're not crazy – and you know it. That's why you're scared of them. That's why you've done all this kidnapping and brainwashing. Because environmentalists and scientists and all the others are a threat to your money-making.'

'Think what you like, Max. It doesn't matter now. Neither you nor your father will trouble me further.'

Max felt his guts turn to ice. 'What are you talking about?' he asked hoarsely.

Clark nodded at the guard by the door. 'Bring him in now.'

Max twisted round in his chair. Was his father here? But it wasn't his dad who was escorted into the office by the guard – it was Jaya, from the orang-utan sanctuary. A wave of disappointment washed over Max.

'You're surprised, I see,' Clark said. 'You've met Jaya already, I know that. But what you didn't know is that he is one of my fifth columnists – one of the people who went to Shadow Island and returned as my faithful servant. Ostensibly working to save those cute little orange apes, but really working for me. Making a few eco-friendly noises for the press and gullible tourists, but doing absolutely nothing concrete to stand in the way of my oil-palm plantations. There are hundreds more like him all around the world, and many more to follow in the years ahead, until all serious opposition to my global businesses has been eliminated.'

'Where's my dad?' Max demanded. 'What's happened to him?'

'Tell him,' Clark ordered Jaya.

Jaya didn't look at Max. His eyes – glazed over a little, as if he were in a semi-trance – were fixed on the tycoon. 'Your father is dead,' he said expressionlessly.

'*No!*' Max cried. 'No, he can't be. When? Where?'

'Two days ago in Pangkalan Bun,' Jaya replied.

'You're lying.'

'I saw his body in the hospital, spoke to the doctor who treated him. I watched him being put in a coffin and buried.'

'What did he die of?'

'Heart failure.'

Max stared at him bleakly. Was Jaya telling the truth? Max had a terrible conviction that he was. A great sorrow passed through him, then a surge of blind fury.

'Episuderon, that's what killed him,' he yelled. 'You killed him.'

He launched himself up from his chair and over the desk, his hands trying to grasp Clark around the neck, throttle him. But the guard stepped in and knocked Max to the floor.

Clark adjusted his tie and dusted off his jacket. Then he smiled icily at Max. 'Your protector is dead, the thorn in my side is dead. I left you alive because I thought you might lead me to your father, might lead me to the top of the Cedar Alliance. But he's gone now, Max. And you have outlived your usefulness.'

Max staggered to his feet, rubbing his head where the guard had hit him. 'What're you saying?'

'You're an irritation, like a fly buzzing around an elephant,' Clark said. 'Sooner or later the elephant gets tired and treads on the fly.'

'You're going to kill me? You can't get away with that. People know I'm here.'

'Consuela Navarra and Chris Moncrieffe? They too will disappear.'

Clark got up from his chair and looked at the guard. 'Take him outside. You made a fool of me on Shadow Island, Max. But you won't do it twice. This time I'm going to make sure the job's done properly.'

TWENTY-ONE

There was a second armed guard waiting outside the building. He was holding a length of rope.

'Hands behind your back, Max,' Clark commanded.

'Get stuffed,' Max retorted defiantly.

Clark nodded at the guards. One of them seized hold of Max, restraining him, while the other forced his hands round behind his back and bound them with the rope. Max tensed his muscles as the knots were being tied, making his wrists expand so that there'd be a bit of slack in the bonds. It was a thick rope – that was good. It was harder to tie tight knots in thick rope, and easier to undo them. Max was in a frightening situation, but he was still thinking clearly, still calculating how he might get out of it.

'Search him,' Clark instructed the guards.

They frisked him thoroughly, checking beneath his clothes, in his pockets, in his socks and shoes.

'Nothing, sir,' one of them said.

'What are you going to do with me?' Max asked.

'You'll see.'

The guards took hold of Max's arms and marched him across to the quay and down a flight of concrete steps to a small dinghy with an outboard motor. Max was made to sit on the middle seat while the guards tied his ankles together, then fastened a heavy iron weight around his waist.

'You're going to drown me?' Max said to Clark, who had taken the seat in the bow just a metre away from him.

Clark smiled ghoulishly. 'If you're lucky.'

'What do you mean?'

Clark gave a signal to a man on the other side of the harbour, who activated a switch on the wall behind him. The wide metal gates between the harbour and the river started to swing open.

'You see over there?' Clark said, pointing across the river. 'On the bank?'

Max turned his head to look and his heart almost stopped. On the far side of the river, basking on a patch of mud, was an enormous crocodile, at least four metres long from snout to tail.

'My men call him Raja, which means prince or ruler,' Clark said. 'He's quite a size, isn't he? And he has such an appetite.'

'You're feeding me to him?' Max said, feeling suddenly faint with terror.

'You're not the first. Raja has helped out with a few other difficult individuals. He's so good at removing all the evidence. I'd like to tell you it will be a painless death, Max, but I fear it won't.'

The guard in the stern started the outboard motor and steered the dinghy out across the harbour. When they reached the middle, he cut the motor and let the dinghy drift. Max glanced over the side. The water was cloudy and opaque. It was impossible to tell how deep it was.

'It's time to go now, Max,' Clark said. 'Time to join your father. You didn't find him in life, but maybe you'll be reunited in death.'

The guards grabbed Max by the arms. He made no attempt to resist. He was bound and weighted, a boy against three men. There was no point in struggling or fighting – that would only tire him out needlessly. He had to concentrate on his breathing, on taking in enough air to allow him to stay underwater for the longest possible time.

He went limp as the guards lifted him off the seat and swung him out over the side of the boat, then sucked in as much air as he could, filling every crevice of his lungs before he hit the water.

He sank like a stone, the iron weight around his waist carrying him five metres straight down to the river bed. Max looked up. He couldn't see the dinghy above him, not even a vague outline of its hull. That gave him a glimmer of hope. If he couldn't see the boat, that meant Clark and the guards couldn't see him; couldn't see where he was or what he was doing. He'd been working discreetly on his bonds from the moment they'd been tied, trying to loosen the knots. Now he had to get his hands round in front of him to finish the job. This was something he'd practised countless times for his stage show. He'd even done it underwater a few times, though never with a hungry crocodile in the vicinity. Where was Raja? He might have slid into the water by now and be swimming out in search of his dinner. Max had to get his hands free before the creature reached him. If he didn't, he was dead.

He bent his legs and brought his knees up to his chest, then hooked his bound hands down underneath his bottom and around his feet. Thank goodness they'd attached the weight to his waist, not his ankles.

Max lifted his hands to his face and gnawed at the knots with his teeth, exhaling a little to stop his mouth flooding with water. How long had he been under? Half a minute, no more. He was still feeling comfortable, still had plenty of air in his lungs.

One strand of rope came undone. Max tugged on the loop, stretching the rope with both his teeth and wrists, twisting and turning his hands until one of them came free – only just in time, for out of the murky depths there suddenly erupted a long, shadowy shape. Max caught a glimpse of a gleaming snout, a jaw snapping open, a row of pointed teeth, and threw himself sideways.

The crocodile swept past, only inches away from Max's face. His swinging tail lashed out, catching Max on the shoulder and knocking him flying. Max twisted round, his upper arm stinging from the blow. There was no sign of Raja. He had disappeared into the gloom. But he'd be back. Back soon.

Max looked down at his body. Should he untie his ankles next, so he could swim away from the crocodile, or tackle the weight around his waist? He made a split-second decision to go for the weight. He knew he'd never out-swim Raja – he'd be stupid to even try – but the weight might just be a useful weapon.

He clawed at the rope – a big single knot that was getting tighter as the strands absorbed water. He could feel the pressure on his lungs now. He was using up oxygen at a dangerous rate and didn't know how much longer he could stay down. The knot started to come apart. Max glanced up briefly. Where was Raja? He couldn't be far away. The first strand came undone, then the next. Max tore the weight from his waist. It was about the size of a house brick, but much heavier. Max held it in both hands. Raja should have been back by now. Where *was* he? Max peered through the inky water, then felt a vibration behind him. He spun round. The crocodile had come in a full circle to approach from the opposite direction. He was two metres away, shooting towards Max like a missile. Max ducked and flung up his arms. The iron weight smashed into Raja's snout and Max felt the jawbone fracture. The creature streaked past, the water churning and bubbling behind him. Then he was gone.

Max did a three-hundred-and-sixty-degree scan, watching for the crocodile coming back. Had he driven Raja away with that crushing blow, or had he simply antagonized him, made him even angrier? Max's chest was in agony now. He'd been under for more than two minutes and using a lot of energy, a lot of oxygen, for his muscles. He couldn't stay down any longer.

Reluctantly, but knowing he had no choice, he let go of the weight and bent over to untie the rope around his ankles. Then he kicked upwards, feeling utterly vulnerable. If Raja came back now, he had no way of defending himself. He saw the hull of the dinghy emerging through the foggy water and changed course to come up directly underneath it. Where would Clark and his men be looking? Max couldn't be certain. He couldn't afford to give them even the tiniest suspicion that he was still alive. They had to think he was down there being devoured by the crocodile.

Max examined the hull of the boat. His chest was ready to explode, his vision blurring. He had to have oxygen, but if he surfaced, there was a good chance he would be spotted. Then he noticed that the stern of the dinghy dipped in just below the outboard motor housing, leaving a small cavity that couldn't be seen from above. Max turned onto his back and pushed his face up into the cavity. His mouth broke the surface and he took a few gulps of air, trying to make no noise.

'You see anything?' he heard Clark say.

'No, sir,' one of the guards replied.

'How long has he been under?'

'Nearly four minutes. He must be dead now, sir. No one can stay down that long, especially a kid.'

'He's no ordinary kid,' Clark said. 'Give it another couple of minutes. What about Raja?'

'He's down there, sir. I saw his tail. He's probably chewing on the boy right now.'

'Let's hope so.'

Max floated quietly beneath the dinghy. His chest and legs were touching the underside of the hull, his face directly behind the drive shaft of the outboard motor.

'OK, that's long enough,' Clark said. 'Six minutes. He's gone for sure.'

Max filled his lungs again and ducked back down, making sure he stayed out of sight below the boat. Then he felt a pulse through the water, like a mini shock wave, and rolled over to see the crocodile hurtling towards him, jaws parted. There was no time to get out of the way, and he had no weapons except his bare hands and feet. He clenched his fists, getting ready to lash out, even though he knew he had no chance. The creature's snout loomed up only a few metres away. Max could see the glint in Raja's eyes, malevolent and triumphant, and braced himself for the impact – an impact he knew would be the last thing he ever felt.

Then the water by his face suddenly exploded into a foaming maelstrom of bubbles – and something else that looked like tiny pieces of flesh and droplets of blood. Max recoiled, realizing what had happened. The outboard motor had started up at the exact moment Raja was passing beneath it, and the spinning propeller had cut into his snout, slicing through the skin and muscle. The creature veered away in agony and fright and vanished into the bowels of the river.

The dinghy was on the move now. Max swam along beneath it at the same pace and remained under the hull when the boat docked against the harbour steps.

Only when he was certain that Clark and the two guards had left the boat and climbed up onto the quay did he let himself bob up by the outboard motor and start breathing again.

He was completely exhausted. His lungs were burning, his head aching. Clinging to the side of the dinghy, gasping for breath, he looked around the harbour and across the river, trying to catch sight of Raja. Was he still lurking close by, waiting for the opportunity to strike back, or had he retired to some hollow along the riverbank to nurse his wounds? Max couldn't be sure, but he knew he shouldn't stay in the water. Regardless of the crocodile, he was too exposed if anyone happened to look down from the quayside. He had to find somewhere to hole up for the rest of the day, and wait for darkness to cover his next move. But where?

Climbing the steps onto the quay was out of the question – someone would spot him for certain. The barges? There were several tied up, waiting to be loaded with containers, but they probably wouldn't be there for long. Once their cargoes were on board they'd be towed away downstream and Max didn't want to leave the compound just yet. He still had business to take care of.

Then he noticed another barge tucked away in a corner of the harbour. It appeared older, shabbier than the other. Its sides were caked with rust and its deck cluttered with crates, ropes, boxes and dented oil drums. It looked like some kind of floating store, a dumping area for discarded junk – and maybe a perfect place to hide.

Max scanned the water again. It was smooth and calm, no obvious sign of Raja. He just had to take a chance and hope the crocodile had gone. Inhaling deeply, he ducked down beneath the dinghy and struck out underwater towards the barge. It was the longest fifty-metre swim of his life. His heart was beating like a jackhammer, his eyes turning from side to side, expecting any second to see the furious creature bursting out of the cloudy water.

But nothing happened. Max reached the barge safely and surfaced by the stern. He hauled himself up onto the deck and crouched down behind some boxes. A dirty tarpaulin was piled in a crumpled heap next to the boxes. Max lifted one end of it and slipped underneath, covering his whole body but leaving a small opening by his head so he could breathe. He stretched out, closed his eyes and waited for nightfall.

Max poked his head cautiously out from the tarpaulin and listened for a moment. The sky was dark, a few stars glinting over the horizon. He'd been undercover for several hours, a hot, uncomfortable period during which he'd dwelt at length on his father's death, hearing Jaya's words over and over again in his mind. *I saw his body in the hospital, spoke to the doctor who treated him. I watched him being put in a coffin and buried.*

I was so close, Max thought bitterly, shedding a few quiet tears. *I nearly found you, Dad. And now you've been taken from me.*

Whatever the apparent cause of death, Max knew it was Julius Clark who'd killed his father. And he wasn't going to let him get away with it.

He crawled out from under the tarpaulin, crouched in the shelter of a box and looked around. It was late evening, but the processing plant was still operating. There was a floodlight illuminating the quayside where the containers were stacked, and from behind the metal walls of the building came the hum of machinery.

Max rummaged around in the debris on the deck and found a short piece of thick wire. Then he crept to the side of the barge and climbed up the steel ladder that was bolted to the concrete wall of the harbour. At the top he paused and spied out the land. The high rear doors of the plant were open, and the gantry crane was sliding in and out carrying containers. Max could see the driver in his glass-walled cab and a couple of other workers on the ground inside the doors. Even if they looked his way, Max knew they wouldn't see him. The lighting was very localized and the quayside nearby was in shadow.

He waited a few more seconds, then scrambled up off the ladder and flitted across to the first of the single-storey office blocks. He pressed himself against the wall and stole round the back of the building. Thirty metres away, on the open ground by the perimeter fence, was the helicopter that had flown Julius Clark in earlier.

Max counted off the blocks, working out which one contained Clark's office, then darted across to it. The light was on, spilling out through the window. Max crouched down, then slowly straightened up and peeped over the windowsill. Clark was seated at his desk. He was half turned away from the window, work-ing at his computer. Max had a clear view of the screen and keyboard.

The screen was displaying some kind of financial information – long lines of numbers that Max thought were probably accounts. Clark scrolled down through the figures, then reached sideways into one of the desk drawers and took out a slim memory stick. He inserted the stick into the USB port on the front of the computer system unit and saved the file to it. Then he removed the stick and tucked it away in his jacket pocket.

He closed the file on the screen and clicked the mouse to open a new folder. A password box appeared.

Clark hit a series of keys. Max watched intently, noting exactly where the man's fingers went. A folder icon popped up and Clark opened a file within it. More figures and some text came up on the screen, too small for Max to read from the window. Clark added a few numbers, as if he were updating records, then closed the file and shut down the system.

He stood up, stretching his shoulders and back, and headed for the door. Max ducked down out of sight, in case Clark turned round, and stayed crouching against the wall for a few minutes, giving him plenty of time to leave the building. Max was about to get up when a couple of floodlights near the perimeter fence suddenly blazed into life, bathing the side of the compound in bright white light. Max threw himself flat on the ground, convinced that a guard must have spotted him. He waited for a shout of alarm, or worse, gunfire, but no sound came until he heard a couple of faint voices somewhere in the distance. Two figures emerged from behind the first office block and walked across to the helicopter. Max realized that the lights were on simply to illuminate the helipad. He recognized one of the men – it was Jaya. The other, he guessed, was the pilot. The men climbed into the helicopter. The engine turned over and the rotor blades began to spin, sending out a draught so powerful that Max could feel it on his face.

A third man came out into the open and ran in a crouch over to the helicopter, one hand across his chest to stop his jacket and tie blowing around. It was Julius Clark. He clambered into the rear of the helicopter, which took off immediately, lifting slowly into the air, then turning through one hundred and eighty degrees and flying off south along the river.

A few minutes later, the helipad lights went out. Max waited a while to let his eyes readjust to the darkness, then crept round to the front of the office block. The main door was locked, but Max took the piece of wire from his pocket and had it open in seconds. Clark's office door was no more of a problem. Max slipped inside and locked the door behind him – he didn't want any unexpected interruptions. Going across to the desk, he lowered the blind over the window, sat down and switched on the computer. While the machine booted up, he picked the locks on the desk drawers and rummaged through the contents. In the second drawer down he found what he was looking for – a new, unused 8GB memory stick, enough to store a few thousand pages of files.

The computer screen lit up, glowing softly in the dark. Max clicked on the 'Shortcut to Documents' icon and a list of folders appeared. He tried to access the one Julius Clark had opened and got a 'Password Required' box. He stared hard at the keyboard, trying to remember exactly which letters and numbers Clark had entered. There had been seven elements – six letters followed by one number. Max had seen Clark's fingers hit the keys, but he'd been too low down to note the actual letters on the keys. All he had was a pattern of movements, of spacings between keys. But could he recall that pattern?

Where had Clark begun? The bottom row of the keyboard, somewhere near the middle. The letter B. Then he'd jumped up two rows, moving to the right. Max studied the letters. It had to have been an O. Then he'd gone back to the bottom row, to the letter immediately to the left of B – V. Next was another letter on the top row – a Y, followed by another on the same row – P. The final letter had also been on the top row, but towards the left. An R or a T. Max closed his eyes, picturing Clark's hands on the keyboard. It was a T. Then the number to end. It had been over to the left of the row . . . 2. It had been a 2. BOVYPT2. It was an odd password, but then many passwords were. Random collections of letters and numbers were often more secure than proper words. Max typed it in. 'Password Invalid' flashed up on the screen.

Max paused to reconsider, annoyed with himself. Which bit had he got wrong? The pattern of letters was definitely correct. Maybe it was the number that was an error. Perhaps Clark had typed 1, not 2. Max gave it a go. BOVYPT1. 'Password Invalid' came up again.

What now? How many failed attempts did the computer allow before it decided that enough was enough? Max didn't know for sure. Three? Three attempts was normal on many systems – after which the computer would close down, or sometimes activate an alarm. Would Clark's system be alarmed? Probably. He was a careful man, with a lot of secrets to protect. That meant Max had only one more go. Get it wrong again and the office would be swarming with security men.

He studied the letters, aware of his pounding heart. This was important. If he could access Clark's computer records, he could discover exactly what he'd been doing: maybe find evidence of his illegal activities – what his companies had been up to, whom he'd paid off, whom he'd kidnapped and brainwashed into becoming his 'fifth columnists'. Max had one more attempt. *Don't blow it*, he said to himself.

He adjusted his hands a fraction. What if he'd got the pattern right, but the starting point wrong? What if the first letter hadn't been a B, but the letter next to it – a V? He spelled out the new sequence, moving one space to the left each time, and got VICTOR1. That made more sense. It fitted Clark's supreme arrogance, his belief that he couldn't lose. *Go for it. You know it feels right.*

Max typed in the sequence and almost didn't dare look. 'Password Accepted' flashed up. He collapsed back in his chair, smiling with relief and delight, and watched the folder open. He glanced at a few of the files. Some he could read, others appeared to be encrypted. There was no time to read them now. He inserted the memory stick into the USB port and saved all the files. Then he saved all the other folders he could, removed the memory stick, wrapped it in a plastic bag he found in a drawer and stowed it safely away in his pocket.

He shut down the computer and opened the blind before unlocking the office door and going out, locking both that door and then the main door behind him. He'd done what he'd come for. Now he had to find a way out of the compound.

One of the barges? he wondered. That was how he'd come in, after all. But he'd hidden inside an empty container then. The containers leaving the compound would all be full of palm oil, which ruled them out as a method of escape. What about waiting for a convoy to leave and swimming out underwater while the harbour gates were open? Max rejected the idea immediately. He wasn't going back into the harbour while Raja was still about. One encounter with the crocodile was all he could take. So that left the perimeter fence. It was high and topped with razor wire. He couldn't climb over it, but maybe he could find something with which to cut the metal strands – a hacksaw or some bolt cutters. This was an industrial plant: there had to be a tool store somewhere. But where?

Max decided to try inside the processing plant first. That was where the machinery was. Maybe the tools would be there too. He looked across the yard that separated the plant from the office blocks. Light from the quayside was seeping out across one end, but the middle of the yard was in darkness. Max dashed across and flattened himself against the wall next to a side door into the building. He eased the door open and peered through the gap. Inside, he saw a vast, high-roofed shed illuminated by fluorescent tubes on the metal rafters. At one end, near the loading bay he had seen earlier, were two huge hoppers the size of houses in which the palm nuts were stored; then came a row of heavy machines which, Max guessed, were the presses for squeezing the oil from the nuts. Running under the presses was a horseshoe-shaped conveyor belt lined with metal containers – empties coming in at one side, the full ones going out at the other. Max could hear the steady throb of machinery, feel the vibrations through his feet, although the conveyor belt wasn't moving. Maybe it had shut down for the night.

Pushing the door wider, he slipped inside and paused, feeling very exposed. There was no cover at all here, just the high metal wall of the building, then a four-metre-wide open space next to the production line. Max looked around for something that might be a tool store and caught a glimpse of two men coming out from behind a network of pipes near the pressing machines. He reacted instantly, knowing he would be caught if he remained where he was. Darting across the open space, he scrambled up onto the conveyor belt and was starting to crouch down between two containers when he realized that he could be seen from the side if the men came past. He had to find somewhere better to hide.

He looked along the production line and saw a container four ahead of him that looked familiar. Climbing swiftly up onto the container next to him, he ran along the line, jumping from one to the next until he reached his target. This was the one – he recognized the shortened logo, SCOM, the two air holes he'd made in the top. The lid was already open. Max dropped down inside the container. Had he been seen? He didn't think so.

He waited in the semi-darkness, a circle of light coming in through the hatch. Then he heard the squeak of a cog and felt the container suddenly jerk forward. With a jolt of alarm, he realized that the conveyor belt had started up. He had to get out – get out immediately.

He poked his head up through the hatch and risked a quick look out, then ducked back down rapidly. The two men, both wearing overalls and yellow hard hats, were standing right beside his container, having a discussion. He was trapped.

What should he do? Climb out now and be caught, or stay where he was for a moment and hope the two men moved away. He went for the second option – that, at least, gave him some hope of avoiding detection. The container was still moving. Max waited ten more seconds, then decided to chance another look out of the hatch.

He glanced up and saw the end of a pipe just above the container. Before he could move, the pipe dropped into the opening of the hatch and a gush of liquid knocked him off his feet. It was like being hit by a tidal wave. He was turned upside down and hurled against the side of the container. The liquid was all around him, a viscous, swirling mass of palm oil. It was in his hair and in his eyes. Fortunately he'd had the presence of mind to hold his breath. He picked himself slowly up from the floor, blinded by the sticky oil, and fumbled upwards, trying to find the way out. But the lid had been clamped shut. He tried to push up the hatch unit that he'd cut free earlier, but he couldn't budge it. Something heavy was pressing down on it from the outside.

Max's alarm turned to panic. He was shut in. He was going to drown in palm oil. This was it – the end. Then he remembered the air holes. He reached up desperately, feeling around the roof of the container, and found a tiny hole. Tilting his head back, he put his lips around the hole and exhaled, encountering no resistance as the stale air in his lungs blew out. Then he inhaled and was relieved to feel fresh air rushing between his lips. He could breathe.

His eyes closed, his hands pressed against the walls of the container to hold himself in position, he took another few breaths, telling himself to relax. He was in control. He was submerged in palm oil, but he was still alive.

He was aware of the container moving along the conveyor belt. Then he heard a clang on the sides and felt the container rising into the air and then going back down again. It was being loaded onto a barge in the harbour.

For twenty minutes, maybe half an hour, he stayed there, taking shallow breaths, the palm oil oozing around him, saturating his clothes and seeping into his skin. Then he felt movement again – the barge being towed away from the harbour. He counted the seconds, estimating how long it would be before they were clear of the gates. *Two . . . three minutes.* He detached his mouth from the air hole and felt his way across to the hatch. It was like swimming through honey. He pushed up on the hatch and felt it give. The weight above had gone. He pushed harder, lifting the hatch out of the hole.

He stuck his head through the aperture, opened his eyes, wiping away the palm oil with his fingers, and took a long, deep breath of warm night air. They were on the river, heading downstream. Max waited until the Rescomin plant was out of sight, then hauled himself out of the container. He lay flat on the top for a moment, making sure the tug pilot wasn't looking back, then slid down to the deck of the barge and dropped over the side.

It was only a few metres to the riverbank. Max swam with long, slow strokes, trying not to create too many ripples. If there were crocodiles nearby, he didn't want them to know he was there. As he reached the bank, he sensed a movement above him and glanced up in alarm.

'Is me,' said Ari, grabbing Max's hand and pulling him up out of the water. 'I said I wait for you.'

TWENTY-TWO

They went downriver in the *ces* and moored at the jetty by the Dayak longhouse where they'd spent the night. Ari left Max in the canoe while he ran across to the longhouse with some of Max's rupiahs, returning twenty minutes later with soap and a fresh set of clothes which he'd bought from one of the local boys.

Max stripped off his palm-oil-saturated garments and waded out into the shallows, scrubbing his body and hair until he'd got rid of all the sticky goo. Then he put on the new shorts and T-shirt, transferring the memory stick to the pocket. It was still wrapped in its plastic bag and seemed undamaged by the palm oil.

Ari took the rudder and they continued on down the river. Max was tired. He lay down in the bottom of the canoe and dozed restlessly, preoccupied by anxieties about Consuela and Chris, wondering whether he would be in time to save them. Were they still in custody in Pangkalan Bun, or had Julius Clark carried out his threat to make them 'disappear'?

At daybreak, when Ari's skill was no longer so

essential to navigate them through the darkness, Max took a spell at the outboard motor to allow Ari to sleep.

They kept going throughout the day, taking it in turns to steer while the other rested. There were still provisions on board – rice and vegetables and water – but they didn't stop to eat. Making a fire and cooking the food would have used up valuable time – time they didn't have. Max wanted to be back in Pangkalan Bun as soon as possible.

It was dark when they reached the town. They tied the *ces* up by a jetty and climbed out. Ari took some money and vanished for ten minutes, coming back with a *roti* and a bottle of lime juice each, which they wolfed down greedily as they walked to the police station on the outskirts of Pangkalan Bun.

The station was a one-storey concrete building, set in its own fenced compound. They studied it from a distance, half hidden by some bushes across the road.

'You know anything about it?' Max asked.

'I been in there one time,' Ari replied.

'You have? For what?'

'I get in fight in town. Police arrest me, put me in cells for one night.'

'What's it like inside? Where are the cells?'

'At back.'

'How secure are they?'

'I don't know. There is one big room like cage and some smaller cells too.'

'Are there guards outside the cells?'

'No, cells are locked. There no need for guards.'

'What about CCTV cameras?'

'What that?' Ari asked with a puzzled frown.

'Never mind.' Max reminded himself where they were – a small provincial town in Borneo. The police station was a very basic facility – offices and a few cells. There was no need, and no money, for sophisticated security measures like CCTV cameras. Nor were there any floodlights in the compound, or razor wire on top of the perimeter fence.

'How can I find out whether my friends are still there?' Max said. 'Do the cells have windows?'

'Small ones. With bars on them.'

'Can we get round the back?'

Ari nodded. 'Is easy.'

They crossed the road and followed the fence round to the rear of the police station.

'Give me a leg up,' said Max.

'Is not safe,' Ari said. 'What if policemens catch you?'

'They won't.'

Ari looked at him doubtfully for a moment, then shrugged and cupped his hands together in front of him, making a stirrup for Max's foot. He heaved upwards and Max scrambled over the fence. He flitted across the compound to the back of the building. High up on the wall were five small windows with steel bars over them, but no glass. Max stood beneath the first window, then jumped up and grabbed hold of the bars, pulling himself up so that he could peer through the opening.

He saw a man inside, lying on a low wooden platform, apparently asleep. It wasn't Chris. Max moved on along the line of windows, checking each cell. In the fourth he found Consuela. She was lying on another wooden platform, but she sat up quickly when Max called out softly to her.

'Consuela, it's me.'

'Max?' She got up from the bed and came to the window. 'Max, thank goodness. Are you all right? Can you get us out of here?'

'I'm going to try. Where's Chris?'

'In the next cell. Max, there are policemen around. Be careful.'

'I will. I'll be back soon.'

Max dropped down to the ground, ran back across the compound and clambered over the fence to rejoin Ari.

'The time you were arrested – who were you fighting?' Max asked.

'Other boys,' Ari replied. 'Was not really fight. We just playing around, making lots of noises. Police didn't like.'

'And you just spent a night in the cells? Nothing worse?'

'No. We not bad criminals. We get one night and then they let us go.'

'You know your friends – the ones I went swimming with? Can you round them all up for me, as many as you can?'

'Yes, is possible. Why?'

'We're going to have a party.'

There were ten of them in total – Max and Ari and eight of Ari's friends – each clutching a large bottle of fizzy cola that Ari had bought using Max's money. They walked into the centre of Pangkalan Bun, where the streets were busy, the restaurant terraces crowded with diners; then, on a prearranged signal from Ari, they all suddenly went berserk – chasing each other in circles, yelling and screaming, shaking their bottles of cola and then uncapping them to spray one another with frothy liquid.

Max had borrowed a cap from one of the boys to hide his blond hair and smeared dirt over his face to darken his skin, so he looked little different from the others. They charged around the pavement, jeering and laughing, dodging in and out of the restaurant tables, creating as much disturbance as they could. A shower of cola landed on one of the diners, who leaped angrily to his feet and tried to catch the boys. But they were too quick for him, darting agilely out of the way and haring off across the road to annoy the customers at another restaurant.

The noise was deafening – ten teenage boys whooping and bawling – the disruption infuriating, and it wasn't long before the police arrived. They rounded up the gang without difficulty. Max had told the boys to allow themselves to be caught, and paid each of them 50,000 rupiahs – about three pounds – for their trouble. They were tossed roughly into the back of a van and driven to the police station. As Max had expected from Ari's information, there were no formalities. No one filled out any forms, took fingerprints or even asked for names or looked closely at the boys. They were simply given a cuff around the ear and thrown into a large holding pen – a steel cage the size of a sitting room with a bare concrete floor and wooden benches around the edges. An officer locked them in, then went back through the door into the front part of the police station.

Max thanked the boys for helping him. They grinned

and shrugged, none of them remotely worried about being locked up. Many of them had been here before and they knew they'd be out in the morning.

Max went to the front of the holding pen and peered through the mesh at the row of five steel doors to his left, working out which cells contained Consuela and Chris. He reached into his sock and pulled out the piece of wire he'd used at the processing plant. Then he knelt down and picked the lock on the holding pen door, the other boys gathering round to watch him at work. It wasn't a hard job. Half a minute of probing through the keyhole and the door was open. Max and Ari slipped out and Max locked the door behind them.

'Sorry to leave you, guys,' he said to the boys, Ari translating for him. 'Thanks again for your help.'

He went to the door of Consuela's cell, inserted the wire into the lock and clicked back the tumblers one by one. When he opened the door, Consuela threw her arms around him.

'Oh, Max, I'm so glad you're OK,' she whispered.

'What about you?' Max said.

'I'm fine.'

Max went to the adjoining door and picked the lock. Chris stepped out and gave him a big bear hug and a slap on the back.

'What the hell took you so long?' he asked with a grin.

There was another door beyond the row of cells that had a tiny barred glass window in the centre. Max squinted through the pane and saw the yard at the rear of the police station. The door was locked, but Max had no trouble getting it open. They dashed across the yard and scrambled over the fence, then carried on running, only slowing to a walk when they'd gone five hundred metres.

'You know something, Max?' Chris said. 'You're a useful guy to have around in a tricky situation.'

'Do the police check the cells during the night?' Max asked.

'They haven't so far,' Consuela replied.

'So they won't know you've gone until morning?'

'Probably not. Where've you been, Max? I was so worried about you.'

'I'll tell you later.'

'Why not now?'

'We have things to do,' Max said. 'And we haven't got much time.'

The first thing they did was find a public telephone. Max took Sammy Lin's business card out of his wallet and rang him in Kuching. It was very late, but Sammy had said to call any time, day or night, if he was needed. Max asked him to fly to Pangkalan Bun to collect them, promising him a big bonus if he could be there by dawn.

Then Ari guided them to the local hospital, a small building near the river with a single ambulance parked outside. Max showed the nurse at the reception desk his passport and said he'd come about his father.

The nurse, a young Indonesian woman in a white uniform, looked surprised, then uncomfortable. 'Alexander Cassidy?' she said awkwardly. 'You are his son?'

'Yes.'

'We do not know he have family, or we try to contact you. I am very sorry.'

'What happened to him?' Max asked.

'He come in with bad fever,' the nurse replied. 'High temperature, aching limbs. He is hallucinating, his speech is rambling. Dr Halstead do his best, but we are not big city hospital. Your father's body, his heart, are not strong enough.'

'Could I speak to Dr Halstead? Is he on duty tonight?'

'Dr Halstead go back to America. He leave yesterday.'

'He's American? How long will he be away?'

'He go for good. He is on a three-year contract here which come to end. He has new post at hospital in San Francisco, I think.'

'And my father's body?' Max said.

The nurse looked uncomfortable again. 'He is buried in local cemetery. Dr Halstead take care of all arrangements. It seem best thing to do. We don't know how contagious his illness is and in our climate . . . well, we bury our dead quick. Of course, if we know he has son . . . How you find out?'

'Jaya told me – the man who runs the orang-utan sanctuary.'

'Ah, yes, Jaya. He was at funeral, I believe. With Dr Halstead.'

'Just the two of them?'

'I think so.'

'Is the cemetery far away?'

'On edge of town, maybe three kilometres.'

'Is there anywhere round here we can get a taxi?'

'I call one for you.'

The nurse picked up the telephone and rang for a cab. 'It come in two minutes. I am very sorry about your father. We do everything we can for him.'

'I'm sure you did,' Max said.

No one spoke on the short journey to the cemetery. Max was deep in thought, thinking about what the nurse had told them. His dad's fever – had that been caused by Episuderon, or by something else – a tropical virus, maybe? He felt numb. Not only was his father dead, but he was buried as well. This Dr Halstead sounded like a good man – treating Alex first and then kindly taking care of the funeral. Max made a mental note to try to trace the doctor when he got home to thank him for everything he'd done.

The cemetery was some way from the nearest houses, a patch of open ground with lush rainforest encroaching on its boundaries. Max gazed out across the rows of tombs and headstones and wondered how he was going to find his father's grave in the dark.

Ari must have been thinking the same thing, for he suddenly said, 'We need torch. I go to taxi.'

They'd asked the cab to wait for them outside the cemetery gates. The driver gave Ari the torch he kept in his glove compartment and they headed for the far side of the cemetery, where the graves were newest. Alexander Cassidy's was the last in a row: just a mound of bare earth, with a simple rectangular headstone engraved with his name and the date of his death.

Max stood at the end of the grave with his head bowed, saying a silent prayer for his father. Consuela stood beside him, her arm around his shoulders, tears rolling down her cheeks. Chris and Ari waited behind them, watching respectfully from a distance.

Max stared down at the mound of earth, his vision blurring, his heart breaking. He remembered how he'd grieved for his father two years earlier; then his dad had come back from the dead. He wouldn't come back again. This time it was all over. *Why did this have to happen?* he thought. *Why didn't you come home? Goodbye, Dad. I love you.*

It wasn't much of a final resting place. A tiny strip of a cemetery in an obscure corner of Borneo. No proper headstone, no memorial service, no family present, no obituaries in the papers. Just a cold burial with only a couple of strangers looking on. That wasn't a fitting end for a man like Alexander Cassidy – a loving father and husband, but also a world-famous escapologist. He deserved better.

Then a tiny niggle of doubt began to creep into Max's mind. Why had Jaya – one of Julius Clark's fifth columnists – been there at the burial? He had barely known his father. How had he heard of his death? Presumably Dr Halstead or someone else at the hospital had told him. But why? Why tell Jaya?

I wonder . . . Max thought. *Is there more to this than meets the eye?*

He looked back across the cemetery. By the entrance was a tiny wooden hut. Max strode across to it. The door was held closed with a padlock. Max used his piece of wire to pick the lock and went inside. There were a couple of bamboo chairs and a table at one end, and tools stacked against the walls: machetes and shears and hoes for keeping the cemetery neat and tidy, and – this being the gravediggers' hut – three spades. Max grabbed the spades and went back to his father's grave.

'Max, what are you doing?' Consuela said, staring in horror at the tools. 'You're not going to—'

'I have to know,' Max replied. 'I have to know for certain.'

He started to dig away the mound of earth. Consuela reached out to restrain him, then changed her mind and stepped back. Chris took a spade and began digging at the other end of the grave. Ari watched uncertainly for a few minutes, then put aside his qualms, picked up the third spade and joined in.

They dug down steadily, throwing the soft earth to one side. The hole got deeper; then, two metres down, Max's spade hit wood. They shovelled away the last soil to reveal a coffin. Max gazed at the wooden box, feeling suddenly nervous, terrified to go on.

'Let me do this bit,' Chris said gently.

He straddled the coffin, wedged the spade under the lid and levered it off. Max averted his eyes: he couldn't look.

'Max . . .' Consuela was shining the torch into the hole. 'Max . . .'

Max looked down.

The coffin was empty.

'How did you know?' Chris asked in amazement.

'I didn't know. I just guessed.'

Max stared at the box, feeling an uplifting surge of joy. His father wasn't dead. His illness, his heart failure, his burial – it had all been a trick – just like the buried-alive trick he had performed so many times during his career. But why? Why had he done it?

To fool his enemies. To fool Julius Clark into believing he was gone so that the hunt would be called off. That was the only answer. Now it became clear why Jaya had been at the burial. Alex must somehow have suspected that he was one of Clark's men and had made sure he was present in order to convince Clark that he was dead. That meant that Dr Halstead had to have been a party to the deception. Who was he, this mysterious American doctor? Max knew he had to track him down. If he found Halstead, maybe he would also find his dad.

'You seen enough?' Chris said.

Max nodded. Chris replaced the coffin lid and climbed out of the hole, then they shovelled the earth back in. Max took a last look at the fake headstone and glanced up at the sky. Dawn was breaking. It was time they were on their way.

The taxi took them to the hotel to pick up their luggage and Chris and Consuela's passports. Max waited anxiously outside while the two of them went into the building. What if the police had discovered their escape from custody? What if they were inside, lying in wait for them?

But five minutes later, Max was relieved to see Chris and Consuela coming back out with their cases. The taxi turned round and headed out to the airport. It was getting lighter by the minute. What time did the police check the cells? Max wondered. They could be checking them right now, raising the alarm. And the first place they'd notify would be the airport. Max asked the taxi driver to put his foot down.

They sped through the gates of the airport, and as they turned into the car park outside the terminal building, a small Cessna was just coming in to land.

Max took out the last of his rupiahs and some dollars and handed them to Ari. 'Thanks for your help,' he said with a smile. 'I couldn't have done it without you.'

Ari glanced at the money. 'Is too much,' he said.

'Take it,' Max insisted. 'You deserve it. Buy your mates some bottles of cola.'

Ari grinned. 'Was fun,' he said. 'You find your father, you let me know, OK? Send message to Mrs Anwar.'

'I will.'

They shook hands.

'Goodbye,' Max said.

'*Selamat jalan* – goodbye,' Ari replied.

They hurried through into the departure area, Max glancing around nervously looking for any signs of the police. But no one tried to stop them. Sammy Lin was waiting for them on the apron beside his Cessna. They climbed on board and the plane took off immediately. Max looked down out of the window as they cleared the runway and began to turn north, and saw Ari waving from the car park. He waved back, though he knew Ari probably couldn't see him.

The plane began to climb. Max sagged back in his seat, drained by everything that had happened over the past few days. He was physically tired, but his emotions were also in shreds. For the second time his father had come back from the dead. That made him happy, but underneath he was also angry with his dad for putting him through such a traumatic ordeal. *You're playing games with us all*, he thought. *Except this isn't a game – it's a matter of life and death.*

Julius Clark had tried to kill him, just as the men in Stockholm had tried to kill him. Max knew he was a target. He knew he had to fight back. This wasn't just a question of finding his father, it was a question of personal survival.

He felt the slight bulge of the memory stick in his pocket. *I'm closing in on you, Julius Clark. And I'm going to nail you. Provided I live that long.*

Max turned to look out of the window. He saw oil-palm plantations and isolated patches of rainforest below. Then the plane soared into low cloud and everything disappeared in a swirling white mist.

A MAX CASSIDY ADVENTURE

MAX'S MISSION IS NOT OVER YET . . .

attack
at dead man's bay

COMING SOON

Max Cassidy now knows for sure that his mother did not kill his father, and his father is not even dead . . . But there are still people very determined to prevent Max from discovering the truth – people who want him dead.

In this, the final instalment of the thrilling Max Cassidy series, Max travels across the world; from London to San Francisco to Russia in his dangerous quest to be reunited with his family.

Escapology is dangerous, but not nearly as dangerous as real life . . .